Legacy & Lace

Rebecka Cole

Rocky Coast Publishing

Legacy & Lace
Copyright © 2026 Rebecka Cole

All rights reserved.

No part of this book may be reproduced, distributed, or transmitted in any form or by any means, including photocopying, recording, or other electronic or mechanical methods, without the prior written permission of the publisher, except in the case of brief quotations embodied in reviews and certain other noncommercial uses permitted by copyright law.

This is a work of fiction. Names, characters, places, businesses, events, and incidents are either the product of the author's imagination or used fictitiously. Any resemblance to actual persons, living or dead, or real events is purely coincidental.

Published by Rocky Coast Publishing

ISBN: 979-8-9946861-0-2

Cover design by Rebecka Cole

First Edition

Printed in the United States of America

Contents

Dedication 1

Prologue 3

1. Chapter 1 9
2. Chapter 2 22
3. Chapter 3 43
4. Chapter 4 54
5. Chapter 5 63
6. Chapter 6 69
7. Chapter 7 83
8. Chapter 8 93
9. Chapter 9 102
10. Chapter 10 112
11. Chapter 11 121
12. Chapter 12 132
13. Chapter 13 143
14. Chapter 14 152

15.	Chapter 15	163
16.	Chapter 16	173
17.	Chapter 17	182
18.	Chapter 18	192
19.	Chapter 19	203
20.	Chapter 20	212
21.	Chapter 21	222
22.	Chapter 22	234
23.	Chapter 23	242
24.	Chapter 24	253
25.	Chapter 25	268
26.	Chapter 26	279
27.	Chapter 27	286
28.	Chapter 28	298
29.	Chapter 29	306
30.	Chapter 30	318
31.	Chapter 31	329
32.	Chapter 32	342
33.	Chapter 33	357
34.	Chapter 34	366
35.	Chapter 35	374
36.	Chapter 36	386

37. Chapter 37	403
Epilogue	416
Call To Action	425
Sneak Peak	426
Also by Rebecka Cole	428
Rebecka's Reading group	429
Acknowledgements	430
About the author	432

For the ones who leave.
And the ones who stay anyway.

Prologue: Hazel - Five years ago

I wake up before dawn and know immediately that I need to leave.

The house is too quiet.

The wrong kind of quiet.

The kind that makes your chest tight and your thoughts too loud.

He's still asleep beside me. I can tell from the steady rhythm of his breathing, the warmth of him taking up space in a bed that's supposed to be just mine.

Has always been just mine.

Until last night.

I stare at the ceiling and try not to think about it.

About the way he'd looked at me when he finally said it. When he finally put words to the thing we'd been dancing around since we were teenagers.

I love you, Haze. I've always loved you.

Three months after my father's funeral.

Three months of me barely holding it together, and he chose last night to crack us both wide open.

My body still remembers his hands. The weight of him. The way I'd pulled him closer even though some part of me—some quiet, reasonable part—knew it was the wrong time.

Wrong timing.

Wrong everything.

But grief makes you reckless. Makes you reach for anything that feels like relief, even when you know you'll pay for it later.

I'm paying for it now.

I turn my head just enough to look at him.

His face is unguarded in sleep. Peaceful in a way it never is when he's awake. One arm thrown out across the pillow, relaxed. His hat's on the bedside table, brim curved the way he likes it.

I used to steal that hat when we were kids.

Used to wear it while we trained horses together, while we competed, while we pretended the thing between us didn't exist.

If I stay, I'll have to talk about this.

Explain something I don't even understand myself.

Pretend I'm okay when every part of me is screaming that I'm not.

I can't do that.

Won't do that to him.

I slip out of bed as carefully as I can. The floor's cold under my bare feet. The boards creak—they always creak in this old house—but he doesn't stir.

I grab my clothes from the chair. Jeans. Sweater. Boots I can pull on fast.

My hands shake while I'm getting dressed.

I press them flat against my thighs until they stop.

My phone's on the dresser, screen dark. The email notification is still there when I wake it up. The one I've been staring at for three days, trying to decide if I'm brave enough.

Job offer. Junior analyst position. Denver. Start date: two weeks.

I'd applied last month.

Back when the ranch felt like it was suffocating me. When every corner reminded me that Dad was gone and wasn't coming back. When Mae kept looking at me like I might break, and Eli kept hovering like he could fix me if he just stayed close enough.

Denver is roughly 10 hours away.

Far enough that maybe I can breathe again.

Far enough that I won't have to see the look on everyone's faces when they realize what I've done.

I pull my duffel from the closet and start packing. Not everything. Just enough. Clothes. Laptop. Toothbrush. The essentials.

I move quickly. Hands busy. Brain quiet.

Don't think. Just pack.

There's a photo on the dresser.

Dad at last year's Fourth of July. Mid-laugh. Sunburned and happy and alive.

Looking at it makes my throat close up.

Three months.

He's been gone three months, and I still expect to hear his voice in the kitchen. Still expect to see his truck in the drive when I come home from town.

Still expect him to walk through the door and tell me I'm worrying about nothing.

But he's not coming back.

And I can't stay here drowning in his absence.

I zip the bag. Sling it over my shoulder.

The hallway's dim. Morning light just starting to show through the windows at the far end of the house. I move quietly through the kitchen—it still smells like yesterday's coffee, like Mae's biscuits, like home.

The front door is right there.

Ten steps.

Maybe less.

All I have to do is open it.

I stop with my hand on the knob.

Behind me, down the hall, the bedroom door is still closed. He's still asleep. Still trusting that when he wakes up, I'll be there.

If I go back now—if I wake him up and try to explain—he'll ask me to stay.

And the problem is I might say yes.

I can't afford that.

Can't afford to let him see how broken I actually am. Can't afford to let him think he can fix this. Fix *me*.

Some things can't be fixed.

I turn the knob.

Step outside.

The air hits me like a slap—cold and sharp after the warmth of the house. The sky's just starting to lighten. That pale gray before sunrise. The barn's a dark shape against the horizon. Everything smells like dirt and hay and five generations of Clarks who knew exactly who they were.

I'm not one of them anymore.

I don't know what I am.

I make myself keep walking.

My truck's where I left it yesterday. I throw the bag in back and climb into the driver's seat. The steering wheel is freezing under my hands. I grip it tight, waiting for my heart to slow down.

It doesn't slow down.

I start the engine anyway.

It's too loud in the quiet morning. Too final.

Like the sound of something ending.

I put the truck in drive, and pull away slowly.

In the rearview mirror, I watch the house get smaller. Watch the porch light. Watch the bedroom window where he's still asleep, still believing I'll be there when he wakes up.

I watch until the curve of the driveway swallows it all.

Then there's just road.

Empty road stretching out ahead of me.

The sky's lighter now. Pink creeping in at the edges. It's going to be a clear day. A good day for ranch work. For riding. For all the things I'm walking away from.

My phone buzzes.

I don't look at it.

Can't look at it.

I turn the radio up instead and keep driving.

Chapter One

Hazel

Montana doesn't do subtle.

The sky is ridiculous out here—massive and blue, stacked on more blue, clouds piled along the horizon like they're waiting for something interesting to happen. My hands tighten on the steering wheel and I realize how small my truck feels.

Nothing out here apologizes for taking up space.

In the city, quiet costs money. Apps. Headphones. Sealed windows. There's always a hum underneath, some reminder that you're never really alone. This quiet is different. It doesn't hum or buzz or rush. It just exists.

Wind hits my truck as I crest another rise, and somewhere in the distance, cattle low. The sound carries, slow and familiar, settling into my chest before I can stop it. I roll my shoulders and take a breath deeper than any I've managed in the last twelve hours.

It's the drive. That's all. Twelve hours of highway and gas stations that blur together and bad coffee sitting heavy in my stomach. Anyone would feel off-kilter coming back to a place like this after so long.

The road curves the way it always has, and I follow it without thinking. Fence posts cut across the land in uneven lines—some standing straight, others leaning like they've earned the right. Grass bends low in the breeze, dry and sun-warmed. I crack the window and air slips through, carrying dust and hay and something sharper underneath. Leather, maybe. Iron. Or just animals and earth and work layered together.

It smells like home.

My shoulders go rigid, but I don't slow down.

I glance at the rearview mirror and the woman staring back doesn't belong here anymore. Hair pulled back because it's practical, not because it looks good. Dark circles I haven't bothered to hide. There are always meetings to get to, deadlines to hit, presentations to clients who think "operational efficiency" means magic instead of hard work.

Five years in Denver doing strategy consulting. Long hours, good money, a title that impresses people at cocktail parties—people who've never seen me barefoot in the dirt or sunburned from a full day of ranch work. I'm good at it. The data analysis, the presentations, the careful language that makes hard truths sound like opportunities.

My phone buzzes in the cupholder—a Slack notification from my boss, another from a colleague asking about deliverables. I silence it and keep driving.

My phone rings just as the town sign comes into view.

I answer without looking. "Hey, Shae."

"Oh my god." Shaelynn's voice fills the car, loud and bright and impossible to ignore. "You're actually doing it. You're actually coming back."

"I'm literally five minutes out."

"Holy shit. This is real. You're really here."

I can hear the grin in her voice, the disbelief threading through every word.

"Don't make it a thing," I say.

"Too late. It's already a thing. Do you have any idea how fast word's gonna spread?"

My stomach tightens. "Great."

"I'm serious, Hazel. People are gonna lose their minds."

"That's what I'm afraid of."

She laughs. "Good. You deserve to squirm a little."

I huff. "Thanks for the support."

"Always." A pause, and her voice softens. "How are you feeling? Really?"

I watch the town sign pass—*Welcome to Ashford Ridge*, paint chipped and sun-faded but still standing.

"I don't know yet," I say honestly.

"Fair enough. Well, I'm glad you're back. Even if it's temporary."

"It is temporary."

"Sure it is." Her tone says she doesn't believe me for a second. "Call me when you're settled. I want to hear everything."

"There's nothing to tell."

"Liar. Call me."

She hangs up before I can argue, and I set the phone down, tightening my grip on the wheel.

Main Street appears in pieces the way it always has.

The café comes first—squat and familiar, its windows catching the afternoon light. For a moment I can almost smell pancakes and burnt coffee, hear the clatter of plates behind the counter. I remember sitting in those booths after school, boots kicked up on the vinyl, telling myself I'd never be the kind of person who leaves.

So much for that.

The general store sits across the way, its porch cluttered with crates and a faded bench worn smooth by decades of use. A man steps out carrying a box, moving without hurry, like there's nowhere else he needs to be. I look away before he can glance up.

Faces flicker at the edges of my vision. A woman stepping off the sidewalk with a grocery bag balanced on her hip. A couple leaning into each other beside a truck I don't recognize. People who might know me, people who might not. I feel that uneasy sense of being noticed without being acknowledged yet, like the town is clocking my presence before deciding what to do with it.

I left, but Ashford Ridge never changed.

There are newer trucks along the street, fresh paint on buildings I remember peeling. And still, beneath it all, the same shape. The same rhythm. The same quiet certainty that life here goes on whether I take part in it or not.

I try not to think about running down this street years ago, but it comes anyway—boots slapping pavement, laughter too loud. My dad calling after me, telling me to slow down before I crack my head open. I force it away, jaw tightening as I fix my gaze ahead.

Five years since the funeral. Five years I stayed away.

The asphalt thins beyond town, giving way to dirt and gravel. The gravel snaps under my tires like it knows me, the sound traveling through the steering wheel, up my arms, into my chest—sharp and familiar. Dust lifts behind me in a pale cloud, catching the late-day sun instead of settling right away.

I'd forgotten how loud gravel is. How it announces you. In the city, arrival is quiet—garages swallow cars whole, elevators carry you upward without ceremony. Out here, arrival is acknowledged. No apology. No disguise.

My pulse steadies and my grip loosens by a fraction.

The ranch gate comes into view. *Clark Ranch.* The wooden sign hangs crooked now, one chain lower than the other, swinging slightly in the breeze.

I pull over and cut the engine. The sudden quiet rings in my ears. I sit there longer than I mean to, hands resting in my lap, staring through the windshield.

How did I stay away this long?

I push open the door and climb out slowly, like the ground might feel different than I remember. My shoes hit the dirt with a solid thud that sends a steadying jolt up my legs. The air fills my lungs at once—dry and warm, carrying animals and earth and old wood layered together. It feels thicker somehow, heavier, like breathing asks for more intention.

I close my eyes and just listen.

The ranch sounds are there—hooves shifting in distant paddocks, the low call of cattle, a gate creaking somewhere down the line. I remember summer mornings when this place hummed with activity. Horses whinnying from full stalls. Truck engines starting before dawn as hands headed to the pastures. My dad's voice carrying across the yard, directing work that always seemed to get done before the heat hit.

Trailers lined the drive back then. Boarders arriving with horses to train, their owners trusting Dad with animals worth more than most people's cars. I'd watch him work the round pen for hours—patient, methodical, reading every flick of an ear or shift of weight like it was a language only he understood.

I used to think this place would always be like that. Constant. Full.

I open my eyes and make myself move.

The fence line runs alongside the drive, and I follow it without thinking, my body settling into an old cadence before my mind can catch up. My hand trails along the top rail—sun-warmed wood, familiar grain beneath my palm.

The barn sits farther back, its red paint dulled by sun and years but still standing solid. I slow a few yards short of it, my heart ticking faster than it needs to.

I haven't been inside in five years.

The realization presses against my chest, heavy and unwelcome. I swallow and make myself keep moving, angling back toward the house instead.

The porch boards creak under my weight, that familiar sound settling something in my chest. I pause at the bottom step, fingers brushing the railing, tracing a groove worn smooth by years of use. My father's hands have rested here. I can see them easily—broad and steady, leaning out over the yard.

I climb the steps and lift my fist to knock, but the door opens before I can.

"There you are."

Aunt Mae stands in the doorway, relief softening her features. She doesn't wait for me to speak. She steps forward and pulls me into a hug that smells like coffee and laundry soap and something faintly medicinal. I laugh softly into her shoulder, the sound catching halfway out.

"You made it," Mae says, easing back to look at me. "I was starting to think you'd hit traffic."

I smile. "Not much traffic out here."

Mae waves it off with a huff. "You never know."

My gaze drops to Mae's leg immediately. It's braced against the doorframe, her weight shifted just slightly to one side. The movement is practiced, learned.

"How's your leg?" I ask.

Mae scoffs. "Nothing worth fussing over. Just a twist. I'm fine."

Fine has never meant fine in this house.

I nod anyway. I knew about the injury before I ever packed the car. Mae mentioned it weeks ago, tucked into a phone call the way she tucks anything that threatens to become inconvenient. A misstep fixing a fence. A sharp pain walked off. Nothing that requires company or concern.

I believed her. Or tried to.

It wasn't until Shae called—voice lowered, careful—and said folks around Ashford Ridge were starting to worry that Mae was struggling to keep up with things.

Five years is a long time to stay gone. Long enough to convince yourself absence is normal. Long enough to pretend you aren't choosing it.

I ended the call, stared at my calendar, and knew there wasn't another excuse left that would sit right in my chest.

I called my boss that afternoon. Family emergency, I needed flexibility for a few weeks. She agreed to let me work remotely as long as I stayed available. Temporary. Flexible. Under control—or at least that's what I told her.

I step inside, and the familiar coolness of the house settles around me. It smells the same as it always has—old wood, dust, coffee brewed too strong. Sunlight slants through the windows, catching on worn furniture and scuffed floors.

The house feels smaller than I remember. Or maybe I've grown used to spaces that echo.

"You didn't have to come rushing back," Mae says, closing the door. "I was managing."

"Shae called."

Mae's mouth curves into a small, knowing smile. "Of course she did. This town's never been very good at minding its own."

I huff quietly.

We move into the kitchen together. Mae busies herself at the counter, fussing with nothing, and I lean against the doorway, watching her. Noticing the things I know better than to name. The way she avoids putting too much weight on her leg. The tightness around her mouth when she reaches for the kettle.

Coffee mugs appear between us. I wrap my hands around mine, letting the heat seep into my palms.

The kitchen looks the same in all the ways that matter. The worn edge of the counter where I slipped once and split my lip open. My mother at the sink, steady and brisk, telling me to hold still, this would sting, don't be dramatic.

My gaze drifts to my forearm. The scar is still there—faint now, pale against my skin, but unmistakable. I press my thumb to it once, then drop my hand back to the mug before I let myself think about it too long.

"I won't be here long," I say, because I need to say it. "Just until you're back on your feet."

Mae doesn't answer right away. She stirs her coffee longer than necessary, eyes on the slow swirl.

"I've had help," Mae says finally. "Someone keeping things running while I've been laid up."

I wait for her to elaborate, but she just takes another sip of coffee.

"Well," she adds, casual as anything. "I appreciate you being here."

Silence settles between us. Not uncomfortable. Just full.

"You can take your things to your room," Mae says. "It's the same as you left it."

I carry my bag down the hallway, my steps echoing softly. My bedroom door sticks for a moment before giving way, and the room feels smaller than I remember. Or maybe I've just outgrown it.

My old quilt lies folded at the foot of the bed, colors faded but intact. Riding ribbons hang crooked on the wall—dusty blues and reds from junior rodeo, a few regional buckles catching the afternoon light. The whole town used to show up to watch me compete. Friday nights under the arena lights, bleachers packed with people who knew my name, who cheered when I cleared the barrels clean.

I don't look at them long. That's not me anymore.

My eyes catch on the stand beside my bed. A cowboy hat sits there—faded black, the brim curved and broken in just the way he liked it. The front dipped low, the back kicked up slightly. A thin leather band wraps the crown, worn smooth in places from years of hands adjusting it.

I used to steal that hat.

It's too big for me. Always was.

My chest tightens.

I don't touch it. I don't even let myself look at it twice.

I turn away and set my bag on the bed.

I sit on the edge of the mattress and it dips the same way it always has. For a moment, a flash—sitting here with someone else. Late nights, low voices, laughter that came easy. The kind of closeness that didn't need explaining.

I stand up fast.

Not going there either.

I unpack without thinking. Clothes in the dresser. Toiletries in the bathroom down the hall. Laptop on the desk. When I'm done, I just stand there in the middle of the room.

Who I was here feels close enough to reach. Who I am now hovers at the edges, waiting to be invited in.

By evening, I'm restless enough that I step onto the porch. The sky burns orange and gold near the horizon, clouds darkening farther out. Wind moves across the land, carrying the promise of a storm. I lean against the railing, letting the cool wood press into my palms.

The ranch shifts around me—cattle moving in the distance, a gate creaking somewhere. I focus on the way the land seems to watch me. Not accusing. Not welcoming. Just present.

This place doesn't ask anything of me yet. It just waits to see what I'll do.

Movement catches my eye near the barn. I freeze. There's someone down there—tall, moving with purpose toward the open doors. Too far to see clearly in the fading light, just a silhouette against the barn's dark frame.

One of the hands Mae mentioned, probably. She said she had help keeping things running.

My heart kicks hard against my ribs anyway.

I should go down there. Introduce myself. Ask what needs doing tomorrow, what the schedule looks like, how I can actually be useful instead of just taking up space.

I don't move.

The figure disappears inside the barn, swallowed by shadows, and I stand there a moment longer before turning away. The porch boards creak under my feet as I head back inside, closing the door behind me with more care than necessary. Like if I'm quiet enough, I can slip back into the house unnoticed. Postpone all of it—the questions, the explanations, the inevitable conversations about how long I'm staying and what I'm planning to do.

Tomorrow. I'll deal with all of it tomorrow.

I make my way down the hall to my room, exhaustion settling into my bones. The day feels longer than it should, twelve hours of driving catching up with me all at once. I sit on the edge of the bed and pull off my shoes, letting them drop to the floor one at a time.

My phone buzzes against the mattress.

Shae: You're officially HOME!!!

I smile despite myself.

Me: It's temporary, remember. Don't get excited.

I've said *temporary* more times than I can count now. Like if I repeat it enough, it'll stay true.

Shae: Temporary my ass. Bar tonight. Six o'clock.

I close my eyes.

Me: I'm tired.

Shae: No excuses. We're not letting you hide.

I stare at the screen. Shae won't let this go, and part of me doesn't want her to. I just need one more night before I face everyone. Before the questions start.

Me: Fine. Tomorrow night then. One drink.

Shae: We both know that's a lie.

I laugh softly and set the phone aside.

Tomorrow. One drink.

What could possibly go wrong?

Chapter Two

Hazel

I wake before dawn.

The room is still dark, the house quiet around me. Too quiet. Five years of city noise trained me to sleep through sirens and traffic, but this silence—this deep, heavy silence—won't let me rest.

I lie there for a while, staring at the ceiling, trying to convince myself to go back to sleep.

It doesn't work.

Finally, I give up and get dressed. Jeans. Boots. One of my old flannels pulled from the back of the closet, smelling faintly of dust and cedar.

I slip out before Mae wakes.

The sky is starting to lighten at the edges, pale gray bleeding into the dark. Stars still visible overhead, fading. The air smells like dew and grass and earth turned over by recent rain.

My feet carry me without deciding. Past the barn. Past the equipment shed. Out toward the fence line where the land rises slightly, cresting a low hill.

The family cemetery.

Generations of Clarks are buried here, tucked under the cottonwoods on the north edge of the property. My great-great-grandfather chose this spot—high enough to see the whole ranch spread out below, sheltered enough that the wind doesn't cut too hard in winter.

I haven't been here in five years.

Not since the funeral. Not since I stood in a black dress I bought the day before, numb and hollow, while the whole town gathered on this hill and watched me cry.

The wrought-iron gate creaks when I push it open.

I move slowly, weaving between headstones I've known my whole life. Names I learned before I could read. My great-grandparents. My grandparents.

I find his grave near the back, under the big cottonwood.

The headstone is simple. Gray granite. His name. The dates.

John Michael Clark
Beloved Brother, Father, Friend

No flowers. The grass is trimmed neat—Mae's doing, probably—but there's nothing decorative. Nothing soft.

That feels right somehow. He wouldn't have wanted fuss.

I stop a few feet away, hands shoved deep in my pockets.

My throat is already tight.

"Hey, Daddy," I say quietly.

The words feel strange in my mouth. Too small. Too normal for how long it's been.

The cottonwood shifts overhead, leaves rustling in the breeze. Somewhere in the distance, cattle low. The sun creeps higher, painting the sky in shades of pink and gold.

I take a step closer.

"I'm sorry," I say, and my voice cracks. "I'm sorry I stayed away so long."

The apology sits there between us—me and a piece of stone—but I can't take it back now.

I sink down onto the grass, knees pulled up, arms wrapped around them.

"I couldn't—" I stop. Start again. "I couldn't be here without you."

The words come easier now, tumbling out before I can stop them.

"Mae hurt her leg. She needs my help, even if she won't admit it."

I swallow hard.

"I should have come back sooner. I know that. But I kept telling myself she was fine. That the ranch was fine. That I could stay away a little longer."

My throat tightens.

"I was scared. Scared it wouldn't be the same. Scared it would be exactly the same and I still wouldn't be able to handle it."

"I didn't know what else to do," I whisper. "You were gone and I just—I couldn't breathe here anymore."

My vision blurs.

I press the heels of my palms against my eyes, but the tears come anyway.

"I thought if I left, it would hurt less. That I could start over somewhere new and just... forget how much it hurt to lose you."

I laugh, bitter and wet.

"Didn't work."

The sun breaks fully over the horizon now, spilling gold across the hillside. Light catches on the dew, turning everything bright and sharp.

I drop my hands and look at the headstone.

"I'm here now," I say. "I don't know for how long. I keep telling everyone it's temporary and maybe it is."

I pause.

"But I'm here."

The breeze picks up, cooler now, carrying the smell of the ranch—hay and horses and dust. I close my eyes and let it wash over me.

I'm twelve, maybe thirteen. Sitting on the top rail of the round pen, boots hooked on the middle rung. Dad's in the center with a young mare—skittish, green, fresh off the trailer from some ranch in Wyoming.

"Watch her ears," he says without looking at me. "She'll tell you everything you need to know before she does it."

I watch. The mare's ears flick back. Forward. Back again.

"She's deciding," I say.

"That's right." He shifts his weight slightly, angling away, giving her space. "Let her make the choice. She'll come around."

And she does. Takes three steps toward him. Stops. Another two steps. Finally close enough to blow air at his outstretched hand.

He doesn't move. Just waits.

When she finally nuzzles his palm, he smiles.

"See? Patience, Hazelnut. That's all it takes."

I open my eyes.

"I don't have your patience," I tell the headstone. "I never did."

The wind rustles through the cottonwood, and for just a second, I swear I can hear his voice.

You've got more than you think, Hazelnut. You just gotta give yourself room to use it.

I push to my feet, brushing grass and dew from my jeans.

For a long moment, I just stand there, looking down at his name carved into stone.

Then I look past it, down the hill toward the ranch.

The barn sits dark in the early light. The house with its porch light still burning. The pastures stretching out beyond, cattle already moving toward the feed. The whole place spread out like he would have seen it every morning when he came up here.

It's still standing.

It's still his.

"I don't know what I'm supposed to do here," I say quietly. "But I'll figure it out."

The sun climbs higher, warming my face.

I reach out and rest my hand on top of the headstone. The granite is cold and smooth beneath my palm.

"I miss you," I whisper.

Then I turn and walk back down the hill.

By the time I reach the house, Mae's already up. I can see her silhouette moving past the kitchen window.

I take a breath, wipe my face one more time, and head inside.

She looks up when I come through the door, coffee mug halfway to her mouth.

"You're up early," she says.

"Couldn't sleep."

Her eyes track over my face—the red rims, the wet streaks I probably didn't get all the way. She doesn't comment. Just nods and turns back to the counter.

"Coffee's fresh," she says.

I pour myself a cup and wrap my hands around it, letting the heat seep into my palms.

We stand there in the quiet kitchen, both of us pretending this is normal.

And maybe, for now, that's enough.

I spend the rest of the morning working the ranch—checking fence lines, hauling feed, cleaning the tack room. My body remembers the rhythm before my mind catches up, even if the place itself feels different. Quieter. Growing up, this place hummed with activity—a full crew living in the bunkhouse, cowboys rotating through shifts, voices carrying across the yard at dawn. Now the bunkhouse windows sit dark and the yard is still except for the cattle and me.

I don't see anyone else all morning. No ranch hands, no trucks on the drive. Whoever I saw at the barn last night is nowhere to be found today.

By afternoon, my muscles ache in ways I'd forgotten, and sweat has soaked through my shirt.

It feels good. Grounding.

Then my phone buzzes.

Shae: Bar tonight. Six o'clock. Don't forget.

Dread blooms low and steady.

Me: I don't know—

Shae: Too late. Everyone knows you're back.

I stare at the screen longer than necessary. Shae Barker and I became inseparable junior year—two girls testing every limit this town had to offer. She's the only one who drove hours to see me in the city, who never made me explain why I couldn't come back, who kept showing up even when I didn't deserve it.

Which is exactly why I can't say no now.

I set the phone down and head for the shower.

The hot water helps. I take my time, let the steam ease the tension, then dry off and face the mirror.

My hair falls in loose waves past my shoulders, blonde and still damp at the ends. I let it air-dry, the natural wave taking over.

Dark jeans that fit the way expensive jeans should. A soft blouse that brings out the green in my eyes.

Heels instead of boots.

I catch my reflection. Polished. Put-together. The version of myself I built in Denver.

My gaze flicks to the cowboy boots shoved to the back of the closet. Worn leather, scuffed from years of work and arena dirt. Next to them, barely visible in the shadows, are my old riding gloves and a coil of lead rope I haven't touched in five years.

The whole town used to show up on Friday nights to watch me run barrels. Now they'll show up to see if I'll talk about why I stopped. I close the closet door.

Not tonight.

Outside, the sky leans toward evening. I grab my keys and pause at the door, hand resting on the knob longer than necessary.

This is just a bar. Just people I grew up with. Just one night.

I square my shoulders and step out.

***

The bar is louder than I remember.

Sound hits me the moment I walk in—country music pushed too loud through tired speakers, boots scuffing across the floor, chairs scraping back. Conversations overlap and collide and laugh right over one another.

In the city, bars are designed to feel temporary—neutral lighting, seasonal menus, music meant to blend. Here, nothing has been updated on purpose. The same men sit on the same stools they claimed years ago. Names don't need repeating.

The air smells like beer soaked into wood, fried food clinging to the walls, old cigarette smoke no coat of paint ever managed to hide.

I step inside and let the door swing shut behind me.

For a moment, no one notices. I'm just another body in the dim light. I could turn around. Leave. Pretend I tried.

Then someone at the bar glances over.

Their gaze catches. Holds.

I watch recognition flicker across their face before they lean toward the person beside them, mouth moving. That person looks up. Then another.

The awareness spreads like a ripple.

Conversations don't stop exactly. They just... shift. Lower. My name surfaces in fragments I'm not supposed to hear.

"Is that—"

"She's back?"

"I heard she was in town, but I didn't think—"

Heat crawls up my neck. I force myself to keep moving, weaving between tables toward the bar like I have a destination, like I belong here.

A woman I vaguely recognize—someone's older sister, maybe—steps into my path and pulls me into a hug before I can react.

"Look at you," she says, pulling back to study my face. "I heard you were back."

I manage a smile. "Word travels fast."

"Always does." She squeezes my arm. "How long are you staying?"

"Just visiting. Helping Mae out for a bit."

"Well, it's good to see you."

She drifts away, and immediately someone else appears. Then another. Hands on my shoulders. Questions I don't have answers for.

"You still in Denver?"

"What brought you back?"

"Are you staying?"

I nod. Smile. Deflect with practiced ease, the same way I handle clients who ask too many questions in meetings.

When I finally reach the bar, I order without looking at the menu. The bartender—older now, grayer, but the same—slides the drink toward me without comment.

Like I never left.

I take the first sip too fast. It burns going down, but I welcome it.

"There she is!"

I turn and Shae is already there—all red curls and bright energy that cuts through the noise of the bar like she brings her own light source. She pulls me into a hug that smells like her perfume, something floral and sweet, exactly like her.

Relief loosens something in my chest.

"I can't believe you're actually here," she says, stepping back to look at me with those sharp green eyes that miss nothing. "Thought you'd bail."

"You didn't give me much choice."

She grins, wide and unapologetic. "Damn right I didn't."

We fall into it easier than I expected — voices overlapping, catching up in fragments. Shae's halfway through her vet tech program and has opinions about everything she's learning. But it's different being here instead of Denver. Here, we can't avoid the elephant in the room: everyone I left. Everything I ran from. The life I walked away from.

Shae squeezes my hand once. She knows.

"You look good," she says, then grins. "Exhausted, but good."

"Gee, thanks."

"What? I'm being honest." She nudges my shoulder. "How's Mae really doing?"

"Not great. She's been downplaying it."

"Sounds about right." Shae rolls her eyes. "Stubborn runs in your family."

Before I can think about it too hard, I hear it—a laugh near the door. Loud, easy, unmistakable.

I look up and shake my head, but I'm smiling.

"Of course," I mutter.

Chace Walker.

He stands just inside the doorway like he owns the place, one hand already reaching for a beer, the other lifted in greeting. His grin is pure trouble—crooked and confident.

His eyes land on me and light up.

"Well I'll be damned," he says, already heading our way. "City girl actually came back."

I barely set my glass down before he's there, wrapping me up in a hug that lifts me clean off the floor.

"Put me down, Chace Walker," I say, swatting his shoulder as he spins me once.

"Nope. This is happening."

When he finally sets me down, he ruffles my hair like I'm twelve.

I swat him away. "Don't."

"You love it."

He steps back, looking me over with exaggerated appreciation. "Well damn. Look at you, all sexy and sophisticated. I could eat you up!"

"You say that to every woman who walks through that door."

"Most of them," he admits, grinning. "But you're the only one I've known since braces and bad bangs."

I laugh despite myself. "Shut up."

It's easy with Chace. Always has been. All charm, no spark—exactly how I like it with him.

Shae elbows him. "Leave her alone for five seconds."

"Can't. Missed her too much." He takes a pull from his beer, then gestures around the bar. "Besides, someone's gotta show you around. Place has changed. New jukebox and everything."

"Wow. Revolutionary."

"Hey, don't mock small-town progress." He grins. "We also got a strip club last year."

Shae throws a napkin at him. "We did not!"

Chace dodges it with the reflexes of someone who's had a lot of things thrown at him. "See, this is why I have trust issues."

The three of us fall into conversation—Chace filling the space with stories about who stayed, who left, who came back when life didn't go the way they planned. Shae adds color, correcting his exaggerations, laughing at the right moments.

I listen more than I speak. The edge of my nerves softens as the alcohol warms me, but something still feels off. Like I'm watching them instead of being with them.

Like I don't quite fit anymore.

A woman walks past and Chace's attention follows automatically, grin already forming.

Shae snaps her fingers in front of his face. "Focus."

"I'm multitasking."

"You're a disaster."

"That too."

I laugh, and for a second it almost feels like before.

Almost.

The door opens.

And before my mind can catch up, my body knows.

Eli Dawson doesn't announce himself. He never has. He steps inside and the room adjusts—not dramatically, just a subtle shift, like the air remembers him.

Recognition hits low and sharp, stealing my breath.

Five years.

Time has been good to him. Unfairly so.

He's broader now—shoulders that claim space, arms roped with muscle earned from years of ranch work. His forearms are sun-darkened and marked with ink I don't remember, dark lines wrapped around tanned skin. His hair is darker than I remember, almost black, cut shorter but still long enough to curl slightly at his neck. Rough shadow lines his jaw, the kind that suggests he hasn't shaved in days and doesn't care.

Faded jeans sit low on his hips. Scuffed boots. Plain black T-shirt stretched across his chest, sleeves pushed high enough to bare those tattooed forearms.

He looks like a man who knows exactly where he stands.

Heat flickers low in my stomach despite everything I tell myself.

No. Not going there.

"Well, shit," Chace says, grin widening. "Look who finally decided to show up."

He moves toward Eli immediately, clapping him on the shoulder. Eli returns it, familiar and solid. Best friends. Still.

Chace pulls him toward us. "Been a minute since we've had the whole crew together, huh?"

The whole crew. The words point at the empty space where I used to stand.

Eli's gaze sweeps the room once—a habit I remember—before landing on me. Something flickers. Something hard.

His jaw tightens and he looks away first, like I'm not worth the effort.

It stings more than it should.

"Hazel." His voice is low and even. Not welcoming. Not cruel. Just there.

"Eli." I'm surprised my voice doesn't shake.

He steps closer and I catch his scent—soap and sun and something woodsy I'd recognize anywhere. The familiarity physically hurts.

I step back and cross my arms.

My body doesn't get a vote here.

"How long you staying?" Eli asks, but he's not really asking—he's confirming I'll leave again.

I tighten my grip on my glass. "Just until Mae's back on her feet."

"Good." There's an edge to it now, sharp enough to cut. "Wouldn't want you to get too comfortable."

The words land like a slap.

Chace laughs nervously. "Come on, man—"

"I'm getting another beer," Eli says, already turning away.

And just like that, he's done with me.

***

We fall into an awkward cluster after that—the four of us trying to pretend this is normal. Chace fills the silence the way he always has, talking about fence repairs and last spring's storm.

Shae adds details, keeps things moving with sheer determination.

They're trying so hard to make this feel like before.

But Eli's jaw stays tight and I can't stop gripping my glass like it's the only thing keeping me grounded. Chace and Shae notice—I see it in the way their eyes flick between us.

They know this isn't working.

Eli listens more than he speaks. When he does contribute, it's clipped. He doesn't ask me questions. Doesn't offer anything personal. He's here but not present.

I notice him anyway.

The flex of his forearms when he lifts his beer. A faint scar along his knuckle I don't remember. The way he stands like the floor belongs to him, weight balanced, completely at ease in his own skin.

He's grown into himself. Become exactly who he was always meant to be.

And I wasn't here to see any of it.

My gaze drifts to his hands wrapped around the bottle and something in my chest cracks. I remember those hands—calloused and careful, teaching me how to gentle a spooked horse. Steadying me in the saddle. The last time they touched me, five years ago in the dark.

I turn to Shae fast and laugh at something she hasn't even finished saying.

It isn't subtle, the way Eli avoids me. His attention slides past whenever I speak, his answers neutral when forced to respond.

The space between us is charged with everything we're not saying.

It shouldn't irritate me this much. I'm the one who left.

It irritates me anyway.

I catch the flex of his hands around the bottle and I'm back in the round pen—the two of us working a nervous colt together. Moving in perfect sync without needing words.

I shut it down hard, but the ache lingers.

There was nothing to end—that's the worst part. There was no blowup. No line drawn. I just let the space stretch. Let weeks turn into months. Let silence do the work I didn't have the courage to do.

And now here we are. Strangers who know each other too well.

"I'm heading out," Shae says eventually, shrugging into her jacket. "Early start tomorrow."

She hugs me, whispers: "You okay?"

I nod. "Yeah. Fine."

She doesn't look convinced. Her eyes flick to Eli, then back. "Call me tomorrow."

"I will."

"I mean it."

She squeezes my hand once, then disappears into the crowd.

I order another drink. The alcohol slides easier this time, smoothing the sharp edges. The tight coil in my chest loosens and laughter comes without effort.

Chace talks about the rodeo circuit, about watching from the sidelines this year instead of competing. A woman calls his name from the pool tables, and his grin returns immediately, the heaviness gone. The conversation dies before it can go deeper.

"Duty calls," he says, grinning. He glances at the empty space where Eli was standing a moment ago, then back at me. "Try not to drink too much while I'm gone."

"No promises."

He laughs and heads toward the pool tables, and I'm suddenly acutely aware of how empty our little corner has become.

Shae left. Chace is across the bar. And Eli—

I glance around, searching. He's nowhere. I can't even remember when he slipped away, just that one moment he was there and the next he wasn't.

The not knowing needles at me more than it should.

I take another sip.

Chace reappears near the pool table, laughing with a group I half-recognize. He catches my eye and lifts his beer in a silent question—*you good?*

I nod. Wave him off.

I take another drink. Whatever.

When I turn back toward the bar, Eli is there—close enough to make me startle. His hand closes around my elbow, firm and steady.

"Time to go," he says quietly.

I pull back. "You left."

"And I came back." His voice is even. "Let's go, Hazel."

"You don't get to decide when I leave."

His mouth sets in a hard line. "You're done."

"Five years, Eli." The words come out before I can stop them. "Five years and you never came to see me. Not once."

Something flickers across his face—there and gone so fast I almost miss it. Pain, maybe. Or guilt.

He goes very still.

I know I'm the one who left. I know I have no right to be angry about this. But the alcohol loosens something in my chest that's been sitting there since the moment he walked through that door tonight.

"Hazel—"

"You couldn't even pick up the phone."

His hand drops from my elbow. "We're not doing this here."

"When, then?"

"Not now." He reaches past me for my jacket and won't meet my eyes. "Let's go."

The room tilts when I shift my weight. His grip returns automatically, steadying me.

"Let's go," he says, quieter now but no less final.

***

The ride home spins. I watch gravel blur beneath the headlights, the rhythm tugging loose memories I don't want. Too many nights riding shotgun in this truck. Mud on the tires. Music low. Silence that never needed filling.

Comforting. Disorienting. Both at once.

When he turns into the drive, my throat tightens.

"Eli," I say softly. "I'm sorry." We both know I'm not apologizing just for tonight.

He doesn't look at me as he cuts the engine. His hands grip the steering wheel, knuckles white.

"Don't." His voice is flat. "You're drunk."

The words hit like a door slamming shut.

The porch light is already on. Aunt Mae stands in its glow. Eli opens my door and lifts me without comment, the motion smooth and practiced.

Mae's gaze flicks between us. "Eli," she says quietly.

He nods once, stepping through the doorway with me still in his arms. Mae holds the door open but doesn't say anything more.

Eli doesn't answer.

He carries me inside, moving through the house with the ease of someone who knows it as well as his own. He finds my room without hesitation and sets me down gently, hands lingering only long enough to be sure I'm steady.

I curl into the familiar shape of the bed, exhaustion pulling me under before I can fight it.

Somewhere between waking and sleep, a thought surfaces: I spent five years not needing anyone.

And the first night back, I needed him.

My body is still warm where he held me steady. I notice that. I hate that I notice that.

Sleep takes me before I can figure out why.

Chapter Three

Hazel

The hangover hits before I even open my eyes.

I groan and roll onto my side, pressing my face into the pillow. My head pounds in time with my pulse, mouth dry, stomach rolling. Light leaks through the gap between curtain and window—too bright, too insistent.

The bar comes back in fragments—music, Chace's laugh, Shae's concern. Then Eli's hand on my elbow, his truck, his voice cutting through the haze: *You're done.* My breath catches at the memory.

I force myself upright, pausing when the room tilts. I breathe through it until the world steadies, then swing my legs over the side of the bed and sit there longer than necessary, elbows on my knees, head in my hands.

Eli Dawson.

We'd spent our whole lives in each other's barns. Learned to ride together, showed horses together. Our fathers traded labor during busy seasons.

Best friends our whole lives.

Until I left.

The smell of coffee pulls me to the kitchen.

Aunt Mae stands at the stove, bacon sizzling in the pan.

"Well," she says without turning. "You survived."

I slide into a chair. "Barely."

She glances over her shoulder, amused. "How many times have I told you to pace yourself?."

"My whole life."

"And you never listen." She sets a plate in front of me and slides over water. "Drink that first."

I obey.

Mae leans against the counter, watching me with that knowing look she's perfected over the years. "Eli dropped you off late."

I freeze for half a second, then pick up my fork. "Yeah."

"Didn't stay long. Just made sure you were inside."

I nod. "That sounds like him."

She studies me a moment longer. "You should check on Blaze today. He's been restless, pacing the fence line like he's waiting for something."

My grip tightens on the fork. "He probably knows I'm back."

Mae's voice softens. "He's missed you."

So has everything else I left behind.

The barn is cooler inside, layered with familiar scents—hay and leather and dust. Wood creaks softly as the structure settles around me.

I walk slowly, letting my eyes adjust to the dimmer light.

Then I notice what's missing. Empty stalls line the far wall, doors latched open to nothing. Feed bins sit unused against the wall, clean and waiting for horses to fill them. The barn feels too big, too quiet—like something vital has been hollowed out.

These stalls used to hold horses people drove in from three states away to board and train with us. My dad's reputation meant something back then.

Now they're empty.

I keep walking until I reach the third stall on the left. Blaze stands with one hip cocked, grayer now around the muzzle, but his eyes are still bright and knowing. When he turns his head toward me, recognition flickers instantly. He steps closer, breath warm against my shoulder, a low nicker rumbling out like a greeting he's been holding onto.

I swallow hard.

I got Blaze when I was sixteen. We won a lot of ribbons together before I left him behind.

I step into the stall and rest my forehead against his neck, feeling the solid warmth of him. "I'm sorry, boy. I know I've been gone too long."

He huffs softly, like he's considering whether to forgive me.

My dad died five years ago—sudden heart attack in the back field. After that, every fence post felt like his hands, every horse like his voice, every success like something I no longer deserved. I couldn't stay.

My mom left when I was five. Dad and Aunt Mae raised me after that, and this ranch became everything—until it wasn't anymore.

I pull back and wipe at my eyes. "Still handsome. Even if you're retired."

He bumps my shoulder gently, like he's arguing the point.

Movement catches my attention—a colt in the stall opposite Blaze. Three years old, maybe, just coming into himself. There's something in his build that makes me pause. Good bone structure, clean lines, intelligent eyes watching me with curiosity instead of fear.

This isn't just any colt.

"Well," I say softly, stepping toward him. "You look like trouble."

He tosses his head, clearly unimpressed by the assessment.

I smile despite myself and reach for the halter. "Let's see what you know."

***

The sun climbs quickly once I'm in the round pen. By the time I wipe my forearm across my brow, sweat clings to the back of my neck and my shirt sticks where fabric meets skin.

The colt tests me at first—crowding my space, tossing his head, all nervous energy and instinct. I stay calm, steady my breathing the way I always have. I ask for small things. A step back. A turn. A pause.

Pressure on. Pressure off.

The language comes back like muscle memory—the timing, the patience, the quiet insistence that doesn't need to be loud to be heard. The things my daddy taught me.

The colt circles the pen, but his ears pin back when I step toward his shoulder. White shows around his eyes. His stride shortens, head high, looking for an exit. I've seen this before—a horse that learned handlers mean pain.

I hold my ground but soften my posture. Wait.

He bolts left, testing me. I don't chase. Just keep the pressure light and steady, asking without demanding. His ears flick back and forth, weighing whether I'm a threat. It takes three more circles before his head drops an inch. Four before his stride lengthens.

Patience, Hazelnut. That's all it takes.

I adjust my position, read his body language, give space when he needs it and step in when he pushes too far. He snorts once, tosses his head like he's shaking off old memories, then settles—just a fraction, but enough to matter.

I slow him to a stop and approach carefully, palm open. He tenses, but holds. I rest a hand against his neck, feeling the heat of him, the tremble beneath his skin that's finally starting to ease.

Underneath the fear, he moves with a natural grace that makes my chest tighten. Responsive when he trusts. Smart enough to learn fast. The kind of horse my dad would've been excited about. The kind worth fighting for.

"Good," I murmur. "That's good."

"Well shit."

I turn, startled, then can't help but laugh.

Chace leans against the fence, hat tipped back, grin wide and familiar. "Look at you, city girl. Guess you haven't forgotten how to be a cowgirl yet."

I wipe my hands on my jeans. "Careful. I might start charging for lessons."

Up close, I catch the subtle hitch in his movement—the way he favors his left shoulder when he shifts his weight. Shae told me last year about the accident, her voice quiet over the phone. Bad ride. His career stalled. Chace back in Ashford Ridge pretending he'd chosen it.

I never called him. The guilt sits heavy, but I don't know how to name it now.

The colt tosses his head and I adjust my position without thinking, reading his body language, giving pressure then releasing it. He settles, ears flicking back toward me.

"Damn," Chace says quietly. "You really haven't lost it."

I glance at him. "What?"

"That." He nods toward the pen. "The timing. Most people would've yanked the rope by now."

"He's just nervous."

"Yeah, and you're reading him like a book." Chace grins, genuine warmth in it. "Forgot how good you were at this."

The compliment warms me more than it should.

"So," Chace says, and his tone shifts just slightly. "Does Eli know you're in here working the colt?"

I frown. "Why would Eli need to—"

"Get out of that pen, Hazel. Now."

The voice cuts across the yard like a whip.

I turn as Eli storms toward us, long strides eating up the distance between the barn and the round pen. His jaw is set hard, eyes locked on the colt before snapping to me with something that looks an awful lot like fury.

"He's not ready," Eli says, already climbing the fence. "Get out."

My temper flares hot and immediate. "Excuse me?"

"You heard me." He's moving between me and the colt now, deliberately placing himself in the space. "Get. Out."

I plant my feet. "I was handling him just fine."

"You don't know what you're handling." His voice drops, dangerous and controlled. "You've been gone five years. You don't get to walk back in here and pretend you know how things work."

The hit lands sharp and precise.

"That colt's been through hell and he spooks at everything," Eli continues, eyes hard. "He doesn't trust handlers yet. One wrong move and he could hurt himself. Or you."

"I know what I'm—"

"We're liable for that horse. Owner pulls him if something happens, and right now we need every bit of income we can get."

Eli's voice is flat, matter-of-fact, which somehow makes it worse. "So no. You don't get to risk our boarding contract because you feel like playing cowgirl again."

The words sink in, spreading through my chest like ice water.

"Okay, okay," Chace says, hopping off the fence and stepping between us with his hands up. "How about we all take a breath here before—"

"Stay out of it, Chace," Eli snaps without even looking at him.

"Can't do that." Chace's tone is light but his eyes are sharp, tracking between us. "You're about to say something you'll regret."

"I regret plenty already." The words point straight at me like an arrow.

Pain flares, quick and sharp. I shove it down.

I look between them, voice harder than intended. "Why do you—" I gesture at Eli, at the pen, at his commanding presence here. "What gives you the right to—"

"I'm foreman," Eli cuts in, flat and matter-of-fact. "Have been for years now."

The words hit like cold water.

Foreman. Of my family's ranch. For years.

"Mae didn't..." I trail off, looking at Chace for confirmation.

Chace grimaces slightly. "Yeah. He runs the place, Haze."

I turn back to Eli, still trying to process. "You're—you run Clark Ranch?"

"Someone had to." His voice is cold. "Your aunt's holding it together with duct tape and stubbornness. Money's tight. Hands are few. That colt isn't a hobby—he's a necessity."

My stomach drops. "She didn't tell me things were this bad—"

"Why would she?" He's in my space now, close enough that I have to tilt my head back to meet his eyes. "You talked to her every week and never once asked how things really were. You didn't want to know, so you didn't ask."

The accusation lands hard because it's true.

"Five years, Hazel." His voice drops lower. "You asked just enough to feel like you cared. Never the hard questions. Never how bad things really were."

My chest tightens. "That's not—"

"Your aunt was struggling and you didn't see it because you didn't want to see it."

He stops himself, jaw working like he's physically biting back the rest of the sentence.

"How bad is it?" I press, needing to know. "What aren't you saying?"

"Ask her yourself." His eyes are cold, distant in a way that hurts more than anger. "Since you're so good at showing up when it's convenient."

"That's not fair—"

"Fair?" Something breaks in his voice, just for a second. "You walked away clean while the rest of us stayed and dealt with the fallout. Don't talk to me about fair."

My throat closes around whatever response I might have had.

"Okay, timeout," Chace tries again, stepping forward with exaggerated calm. "Before someone says something they can't take back, how about Hazel grabs some water, you take a walk, and we all reconvene when we're feeling less flammable?"

"I talk to Mae every week," I say, needing him to understand. "She never told me any of this."

"Yeah, well." His jaw works. "She's good at that."

His shoulders tense, but he takes a step back. "Just stay out of the pen unless you clear it with me first."

Something flickers across his face—confirmation and resentment and bone-deep exhaustion all at once.

"Yeah." His voice is flat, empty. "Funny how things fall to the people who stick around."

The words hit exactly where he meant them to, precise as a knife between ribs.

He turns and walks away, boots biting into dirt with each step, leaving nothing but dust and silence behind him.

I stand there with my hands curling into fists at my sides, the sun hot on my back and shame burning hotter in my chest.

Chace exhales slowly and turns to me. "So that could've gone better."

I don't laugh.

"In my defense, I tried." He attempts his usual grin but it doesn't quite land. He watches Eli's retreating figure, concern flickering across his face before he masks it. "He's been wound pretty tight lately."

I stare at the dirt where Eli stood, his words still ringing in my ears. *Money's tight. Hands are few. That colt's a necessity.*

"How bad is it really?" I ask quietly. "The ranch."

Chace's expression shifts—careful now. "Bad enough that every decision matters. Every dollar. Every risk."

My stomach drops. "And Mae just... didn't say anything."

"She didn't want you worrying. Didn't want to pull you back here out of guilt." He pauses. "But yeah. It's been rough. For a while now."

"I should've known." The words scrape out. "I should've asked the right questions. Should've—"

"Yeah," Chace says quietly, and the honesty stings. "Maybe you should've."

I swallow hard. He doesn't offer comfort or an easy out. Just the truth sitting heavy between us.

"Yeah." He squeezes my shoulder once, the gesture meant to comfort me. "Look, just... check in before working the horses. For now. Ok?"

The fact that Chace—easy-going, rule-bending Chace—is asking me this tells me everything.

I watch Eli disappear beyond the barn, a new understanding settling heavy and unwelcome in my chest.

The ranch is in trouble. Real trouble. Eli's been carrying all of it—the weight of keeping this place running, keeping Mae safe, keeping everything from falling apart—while I've been gone.

Nothing here is as simple as I hoped.

And I have a feeling it's about to get worse.

Chapter Four

Hazel

We work through the afternoon—fence lines, feed bins, the endless small repairs that keep a ranch running. Chace moves alongside me with easy commentary, never pushing when I go quiet.

It comes back faster than I expect, my body remembering rhythms my mind had tried to forget.

The south fence line is worse up close. Posts lean at tired angles, their bases chewed away by weather and time. Boards have been patched and re-patched, newer wood bolted onto older grain in a way that holds for now but won't forever. I kneel in the dirt and run my hand along a cracked rail, feel where it bows under pressure.

"I knew it was rough," I say quietly. "I just didn't realize how much."

Chace shrugs, driving a post deeper with a practiced swing. "Hard to keep up when it's just one person trying to do everything."

He doesn't need to say my dad's name.

We work in companionable silence, replacing what we can, reinforcing the rest. Not enough to fix the problem, but enough to keep it from getting worse.

I watch Chace lift another post, the way he shifts his grip to favor his good shoulder.

"I should've called," I say. "After your accident. Shae told me and I just... didn't."

He pauses, then shrugs. "You were busy being a fancy city girl. Couldn't risk associating with a washed-up cowboy."

"Chace—"

"I'm kidding." He grins, eyes mischievous. "Water under the bridge, Haze."

"Still. I'm sorry."

"Yeah, well." He drives the post deeper with a decisive hit. "You're here now. That counts for something."

The moment settles between us, and just like that, we're good.

"Boarders used to be full, right?" I ask.

Chace leans against the rail, wiping sweat from the back of his neck. "Back when your dad was training full-time. Folks want someone active, someone competing." His mouth tips into a rueful smile. "Hard to keep business without it."

The weight of it settles then—how much has been slipping away while I've been gone, how much has been held together with nothing but grit and stubbornness.

I don't see Eli again all afternoon. The absence gnaws at me more than I want to admit.

By the time the sun begins to dip, we're loading tools back into the barn when the sound reaches us—the rhythmic thud of hooves from the east, growing louder as dust kicks up along the road.

Chace shades his eyes, squinting. "That'll be Addie."

The horse pulls up beside the barn in a cloud of dust, moving fast enough to make a point. Addie swings down in one smooth motion, boots hitting the ground with purpose. No greeting, no wave. Just a sharp sweep of the yard that lands on me and sticks for a beat too long.

"Have you seen my brother?" she asks, and her voice is different than I remember—lower, more assured, like she's used to being listened to.

The last time I saw Addie Dawson, she was fresh out of high school, all sharp edges and big opinions. Now she's grown into someone else entirely—hair dark and loose down her back, chin up, shoulders back. She moves like she's used to being the best rider in any arena and knows it. Beautiful, but in a way that dares you to say something about it.

She barely glances at me, but I catch the assessment. Quick, thorough, dismissive.

Fair enough. I left.

"Have you seen Eli?" she asks again, this time directed at both of us.

Chace grins wide. "Wow. Not even a 'hey Chace, you're looking sexy as fuck today.'"

She doesn't even look at him. "Have you seen Eli?"

"I'm great, thanks for asking," Chace continues, unbothered. "Had a real productive day. Fixed some fence, hauled some feed—"

"Chace." Her voice is flat, but there's a warning in it.

Addie finally turns to face him fully, and I catch the exact moment her patience snaps. "Do you ever stop talking? Like, genuinely. Is it a choice, or is it some kind of medical condition?"

"Little of both," Chace says cheerfully.

I bite back a smile, watching them. The tension is obvious—the way he needles her just to get a rise, the way she bristles even as she stays put. She's fighting not to crack, and he knows it.

"Haven't seen Eli since this morning," Chace supplies. "Man's been making himself scarce."

Addie mutters something under her breath that sounds distinctly uncomplimentary.

Chace's grin widens. "What was that?"

"Nothing you need to hear."

"Come on, you can tell me." He takes a step closer. "We're friends, right?"

"We're absolutely not friends."

"Ouch." He clutches his chest. "You're really doing a number on my self-esteem today."

"Your self-esteem could survive a nuclear blast," Addie shoots back, but there's something in her voice now—not quite amusement, but close.

Chace catches it too. "Was that almost a joke, Addie? Are we bonding?"

"No."

"Pretty sure we are."

She opens her mouth—probably to say something cutting—but the sound of hooves interrupts. Both of them turn, and I catch the brief flicker of relief on Addie's face before she schools it back to neutral.

Eli rides in from the low pasture without any sense of urgency, dust rising in his wake as he slows near the barn. He swings down in one fluid motion, reins loose in one hand, and his eyes lift immediately to his sister.

"Looking for me?" he asks.

"You're still helping me load up tonight, right?" She doesn't wait for an answer before her gaze shifts to me. "You should come. To the rodeo."

I blink. "Tonight?"

"Yeah." Something in her expression softens slightly. "Plus everyone's going to be there anyway."

"She's not going." Eli snaps.

The words drop like a stone.

I turn slowly. Eli's jaw is set, eyes fixed somewhere past my shoulder.

"Excuse me?" I keep my voice level.

"Long day. You've been working since morning." He still won't look at me. "You should rest."

"I'm fine."

"You don't know these people anymore." His voice is flat. "Things have changed."

Heat flares in my chest. "You don't get to decide where I go."

Silence drops hard between us.

Chace shifts his weight, trying not to grin. Addie watches us with open interest, head tilted like she's enjoying this.

Eli's jaw is so tight I'm surprised his teeth don't crack.

"I'd love to come," I say firmly, eyes never leaving Eli's face. "Thank you for the invite."

"Good," Addie says, warmth threading through her earlier suspicion. "Chace'll swing by at eight to get you." She offers for him.

"Perfect." I smile at her, then turn that smile on Eli—bright and sharp. "See you there."

He doesn't respond. Just watches me with those dark eyes that used to know every thought in my head.

I turn and head for the house, boots striking dirt with more force than necessary.

Behind me, Chace's laughter carries. "This is gonna be fun!"

I don't give Eli the satisfaction of looking back. I push through the back door and let it swing shut behind me.

The house greets me with familiar sounds—the low hum of the fridge, the creak of floorboards, the faint clatter of something on the stove.

Mae stands at the counter, sleeves rolled up, stirring a pot. She glances over when I come in.

"Going to the rodeo tonight," I say, grabbing a glass from the cabinet.

"With Eli and Chace?"

"Yeah."

Mae nods once. "Good. You should go."

I fill the glass with water, down half of it. Something in my chest loosens.

"Eli tried to tell me I couldn't," I add, unable to keep the edge out of my voice.

Mae's stirring doesn't pause. "He's got a lot on his plate. Give him time."

"I know." I set the glass down. "But he doesn't get to tell me what to do."

"No," Mae agrees. "He doesn't." She glances over. "But try not to poke the bear just because you can."

Despite myself, I almost smile. "No promises."

"Didn't think so." She turns back to the stove. "Have fun tonight."

I head down the hall, feeling steadier than I did two minutes ago.

I make it to my room and shut the door behind me, leaning against it with eyes closed.

He has every right to be angry. Doesn't mean I have to let him control me while he works through it.

I push off the door and strip out of my clothes, irritation buzzing under my skin.

I reach for the jeans folded on the bed—dark denim, the kind that hug every curve like a second skin. I know exactly what I'm doing when I button them. Know exactly how they fit.

The blouse comes next. White, soft, dipping just enough at the neckline to be intentional. I roll the sleeves to my elbows, exposing sun-browned forearms.

Then my boots. The good ones.

I pull them on and stand, turning toward the mirror.

There. Not the girl who left. Not the corporate consultant who learned to smooth her edges.

Montana Hazel doesn't apologize.

Outside, a truck engine idles.

I grab my jacket, leave it open, and step out into the warm evening air. Chace leans against his truck, hat tipped back, grin already waiting.

"Damn, Hazel," he says. "Guess the ranch hasn't dulled your edge."

I smile brightly. "You ready?"

"Born ready."

I climb into the passenger seat and buckle in as Chace pulls away from the house. The ranch disappears behind us, darkness settling over the road ahead.

I stare out, jaw tight.

There was a time Eli would've been the first person I called about going to a rodeo. Would've met me at the truck with that half-smile he saved for when it was just us, would've bought me a beer and stood close enough that I felt his presence all night.

Now he's the person trying to stop me from going at all.

I don't know which version hurts more—the one I lost, or the one I'm stuck with now.

The truck slows as we reach the fairgrounds. Dust and noise and laughter, the smell of fried food and sweat hitting me all at once.

I step down from the truck and square my shoulders, boots hitting the ground with purpose.

If Eli wants to act like I'm a problem, I'll meet him exactly as I am—unapologetic, uncontained, and very much my own person.

Let him be angry.

I'm done asking permission.

Chapter Five

Eli

I stand near the edge of the fairgrounds with my hands hooked in my back pockets, boots planted in dirt I've known my whole life.

The rodeo is already alive around me—music spilling from tinny speakers, laughter rising and falling, the smell of fried food and dust hanging thick in the warm evening air. Familiar sounds, familiar chaos.

I barely notice any of it.

Because Hazel Clark has just stepped through the gates, and my eyes find her before I can stop them. Before I even realize I'm looking.

Damn it.

She walks in like she belongs here, like she never left. Jeans that hug every curve, boots worn smooth from real use, white blouse catching the breeze just enough to remind me of skin I'm not supposed to think about. Her hair pulled back just enough to expose the line of her neck - the same spot I kissed that night, right below her ear where she gasped.

Heat rushes through me—want and fury tangled so tight I can't separate them.

I drag my gaze away, jaw tightening.

This is the problem. Five years and she still gets under my skin like this. Five years of telling myself I'm over it, that I've moved on, that what happened between us was just one night born out of grief and bad timing.

Five years of lying to myself. She walked back through those gates and undid all of it in about ten seconds.

Because the truth is, I wanted her then. I want her now. And I'm a damn fool for it.

I let out a quiet breath through my nose and stare toward the pens, anywhere but at her. My chest feels tight, irritated, familiar in a way I don't appreciate.

When I saw her the other night at the bar, my eyes found her across the room and the air left my lungs like I'd been hit.

My Hazel. But different.

Older, sharper around the edges, less open. More contained. Not mine.

The thought makes me laugh under my breath, short and bitter. She was mine, once. For one night. In the dark, when her decision to leave made us reckless and desperate and honest in ways we'd never been before. I laid myself bare that night. Thought it would matter. She left anyway.

So no. Not mine. Not anymore. Maybe never was in a way that mattered anyway.

And that's part of what makes the anger sit so heavy in my gut. It isn't just that she left—it's how she left. How she ran without looking back, not just on me, but on everyone. On our friends, on the life we'd built in quiet pieces, on her aunt, on the ranch she loved like it was part of her own blood.

I understood at first. God, I did. Her dad's death ripped something out of all of us, but it hollowed Hazel. I watched her go quiet, watched the light dim, watched her carry grief like a weight she refused to set down.

So I gave her space. Days turned into weeks. Weeks into months.

I told myself she needed time, that she'd call when she could breathe again.

And Mae—stubborn as hell—tried to hold it together alone. I watched fences sag, watched the boarding operation dry up, watched her work herself to the bone and refuse to tell Hazel how bad things had gotten.

Mae called her every week and lied through her teeth about everything being fine.

I wanted to call Hazel myself a hundred times, tell her the truth Mae wouldn't say. I told myself I was respecting Mae's choice. But maybe I was just as much of a coward as Hazel, afraid of what calling her would mean.

So I kept my mouth shut and worked harder. And resented Hazel a little more with every fence I fixed that she should've been here to see falling apart.

Not long after she left, I offered to come on full-time. Mae resisted at first—said she didn't want charity. I told her it wasn't charity. I'd grown up on this land as much as my own, learned half of what I knew about ranching from her brother. The place mattered.

So I stayed.

Now I'm stretched between two places. Clark Ranch during the day—every day. My family's ranch whenever I can squeeze it in. Dad runs it mostly, but he's getting older, needs help I can't always give.

Long nights. Short sleep. Never enough hours for either place.

That's why I brought Chace in. After the accident, he needed something solid, somewhere he could work without the pressure of proving anything. And Clark Ranch made sense—he'd worked there for Hazel's dad before the circuit, knew the land, knew the rhythm. I guess technically he worked for my dad's ranch, but the extra hands at Clark Ranch help.

It helped both of us. I needed reliable help. He needed purpose.

Or it did help. Until Hazel came back and everything got complicated.

I shift my weight and finally let myself look at her again.

She's laughing now, head tipped back, the sound carrying just enough to hit me square in the chest. I remember that laugh—summer nights after long days, the four of us sprawled in the bed of someone's truck, talking about nothing and everything. Her laugh was the best sound, uninhibited and genuine, the kind that made everyone else start laughing too.

I haven't heard it in five years. Now Chace gets it. Gets her ease, her warmth, her presence.

And I get her walls.

She doesn't get to slide into the rhythm we all bled to maintain and act like the past is something we can politely ignore. And she sure as hell doesn't get to pretend there wasn't something between us.

I shouldn't have yelled at her about the colt. The danger was real, but so was the anger I've been carrying for five years. Watching her step in like she belonged there—it cracked something open.

I scrub a hand over my jaw, guilt creeping in despite my best efforts. I shouldn't have yelled at her like that, shouldn't have dressed her down in front of Chace, shouldn't have made her feel small on her own family's land. Mae would've been disappointed in me. Hazel's dad would've been too.

But damn it, she makes it hard to be fair.

And then the rodeo. I shouldn't have told her she couldn't come. The second the words left my mouth, I knew it was a mistake, knew how she'd take it, knew exactly what fire I was lighting.

But I couldn't help it. The thought of her here—at our rodeo, with our people, slipping back into the life she abandoned like she'd earned the right—made something snap inside me.

She doesn't get to just show up and reclaim everything. Not without acknowledging what she left behind.

Not without acknowledging me.

The music swells, the announcer's voice cutting through the air as the next event is called. Around me, people cheer and shift, moving toward the stands.

Across the grounds, Hazel lifts her chin and scans the crowd. For half a second—just long enough to feel dangerous—her eyes land on me.

Something flickers there—heat, challenge, something I recognize too well.

Then she turns away, dismissing me like I'm nothing.

I exhale slowly, heat crawling up the back of my neck—longing mixed with fury, tangled so tight I can't separate them.

Fine. If she wants to pretend she didn't blow my world apart five years ago, I can play that game too.

I'm not done being angry. Not yet.

Not until she understands what it cost to keep this place standing while she was gone.

Not until she sees what she walked away from.

Chapter Six

Hazel

The rodeo hits me all at once.

I hadn't realized how much I'd missed it until I'm standing in the middle of it, surrounded by sound and movement and the low, vibrating hum of something that lives in my bones. The announcer's voice crackles over the speakers. Boots scuff dirt. Laughter rises and falls in loose waves, and somewhere nearby a horse snorts, impatient and familiar.

The air smells like dust and sweat and fried food, like leather and hay and summer heat. My chest tightens, then loosens, like something inside me has finally recognized where it is.

I take a slow breath and let myself stand there for a moment, just feeling it. The noise. The lights. The way my pulse seems to match the rhythm of it all. I feel awake in a way I haven't in years—not the sharp alertness of a city street or the constant hum of being on, but something deeper and older. My body remembers this place even if my life wandered far from it.

I watch the first event unfold, eyes tracking instinctively, muscles in my own body responding as if I'm still the one riding. The tension in the chute. The split second of stillness before release. The crowd roaring as rider and horse burst into motion. My mouth curves into a smile before I can stop it.

God, I missed this.

Memory brushes against me, light but present. Sitting on the rail with my friends, legs swinging, sunburned and loud and invincible. My dad leaning against the fence nearby, hat low over his eyes, pretending not to watch me while never missing a thing. The sound of his wince when someone wiped out in the dirt. The way he always smelled faintly of leather and coffee and the land itself.

The familiar ache comes, but softer than it used to be. Still there. Still real. Just not sharp enough to take me out at the knees. I let it sit, let it pass. Tonight isn't about what I lost—it's about what still lives in me.

A ripple of excitement rolls through the crowd, pulling my attention back to the arena. I lean forward slightly as the next group prepares, and that's when it hits me.

Addie.

I blink, scanning the lineup again to make sure I'm not imagining it. There she is, helmet tucked under her arm, posture focused and ready in a way that stops me cold. Addie is competing.

Not just tagging along, not just helping out—competing. The kind that takes time and training and commitment.

My chest tightens. I didn't know she'd gotten this serious.

The announcer calls Addie's name.

She mounts with confident ease, settling into the saddle like she belongs there, and something in my chest both swells and aches at once. Whatever else I missed, I'm here for this moment. That has to count for something.

The gate opens. Addie and her horse explode into motion, fast and clean, and the crowd roars.

I find myself holding my breath, body tense, watching every stride like I'm the one riding. My hands grip the rail and muscle memory floods through me—the lean into the turn, the calculated risk, the thunder of hooves beneath you.

I miss this. The energy, the electricity, being part of something that lives in your bones.

But I don't miss being out there. Don't miss the spotlight, the nerves before every run, the way my stomach would twist waiting at the gate. Don't miss competing against myself as much as the clock, trying to prove something I could never quite name.

This—watching, cheering, feeling the rush without my heart in my throat—this I can handle.

The third barrel is where riders lose time, where nerves make you pull too early or lean too late. But Addie reads it perfect, her body already angled before the turn begins, and her horse responds like they're one creature.

When she crosses the line, applause thunders through the arena.

Second place. Pride blooms bright and clean in my chest. She earned that. Every second of it.

My dad's face surfaces, uninvited. The way he took Addie under his wing years ago, patient and encouraging, giving lessons that were equal parts instruction and belief. He was always good with kids who needed someone steady, someone who saw potential and treated it like fact. I can almost see them in the round pen together, his hand on her shoulder as he adjusted her grip, his quiet voice saying, "That's it. You've got it."

My throat tightens. I would've known about this. Should've known. If I'd been here. If I'd stayed.

The guilt sinks its teeth in sharp, but I shove it down before it can take hold. Not now. I won't survive every moment here if I let regret lead the way.

My gaze drifts without permission, searching the crowd until it lands on him.

Eli stands near the far rail, profile sharp against the lights, hat low enough to shadow his eyes but not enough to hide the line of his jaw. He's watching Addie too, shoulders loose in a way they never are around me now. There's something almost soft in his posture, something proud and protective that makes my stomach twist.

He would've been here for every practice. Every competition. Every moment I missed.

I force myself to look away before he catches me staring, but it's too late. The awareness settles under my skin, warm and unwelcome. I know without checking that if I look back, I'll find him watching me. I felt it the moment I walked through the gates earlier too—that pull, that attention, the same way I always used to.

My eyes searched for him first tonight. Old habit. Stupid habit.

"Beer?"

The voice cuts into my thoughts, close and familiar. I turn to find Shae grinning at me, one eyebrow arched, a cold bottle already pressed into my hand.

"Figured you'd need this," she says. "You've got that look."

I huff a laugh and take it. "What look?"

"The one that says you're feeling about fifteen things at once and trying real hard to feel none of them." She leans her hip against the rail, eyes still on the arena as she tips her beer back. "Welcome home."

I lift the bottle, the cool glass grounding me as I take a long sip. The alcohol hits smooth and familiar, loosening something in my chest that's been wound tight since I got here.

Shae turns then, studying me with that look that's always made me feel both seen and gently called out. "So," she says lightly, like she's not about to poke a bruise. "How bad is it? With the ranch, I mean."

I snort. "Well, the stalls are empty, the fences are held together with spite and baling wire, and Eli's being a controlling ass. So, you know. Living the dream."

Her mouth twitches. "I figured as much." She pauses, something softer crossing her face. "He's not usually like this, you know. He's still a good man, Hazel."

"Could've fooled me."

"Hazel—"

"Don't," I say, but without heat. "I know what you're going to say. That he's been holding everything together. That I left. That I don't get to be mad." I take another sip of beer. "Trust me, I'm very aware."

Shae opens her mouth to respond, but an arm slings itself around my shoulders before she can.

"Well hell," Chace says cheerfully, pulling me against his side like we've been doing it our whole lives. "If you keep staring across the fairgrounds like that, people are gonna start thinking you're picturing me naked."

I choke on my beer. "Chace!"

"What?" He grins down at me, all innocence and mischief. "I'm just saying. That's a very specific kind of look."

I smack his chest without any real force, laughing despite myself. "You're disgusting."

"Only on weekends," he shoots back. "And since you cleaned up real nice tonight, I figured I'd shoot my shot. You know, for old times' sake."

Shae barks a laugh. "You're going to get yourself killed."

"Been threatened with worse," Chace says easily, but there's something grounding in the way he keeps his arm around me. Familiar. Safe. The same way it's always been between us—uncomplicated.

I let myself lean into it for a moment, into the ease of someone who doesn't expect me to explain myself.

Then I feel it.

That shift in the air. The weight of someone's attention.

I glance up, and sure enough, Eli's looking right at us. Not casually. Not accidentally. His eyes are locked on Chace's arm around my shoulders, and the expression on his face is dark enough to make my pulse stutter. It's gone in a blink, replaced by that unreadable mask he's so good at now, but I saw it.

Heat flashes through me—frustration and something more dangerous underneath.

I look away first, hating myself for it.

Chace drops his arm, oblivious, already craning his neck to see something in the arena. I exhale slowly and take another sip of beer, willing my heart rate to settle.

"See?" Shae murmurs, quiet enough that only I can hear. "That's what I'm talking about."

I open my mouth to tell her she's wrong, that whatever she thinks she's seeing isn't there, when another voice slides in smooth and sharp.

"Well if it isn't the prodigal daughter returned."

I turn slowly.

Cole Maddox stands there, hat tipped back just enough to show the sharp angles of his face, that familiar smile playing at his lips. The kind of smile that says he knows exactly what he's doing and enjoys every second of it. His gaze sweeps over me with the lazy confidence of someone who's never been told no in a way that mattered.

Chace's easy posture vanishes. His shoulders go rigid, the playfulness draining from his face in an instant. Beside me, Shae shifts closer, her body angled like she's bracing for impact.

Across the way, Eli turns and he starts walking toward us with long, deliberate strides, and I can feel the intent radiating off him even from here.

I wondered how long it would take for this to happen.

The Maddoxs and my family weren't friends. Never pretended to be. Two ranches with neighboring properties and competing interests—my dad building a reputation as one of the best horse trainers in the state, Cole's father running a bigger operation that always seemed to want more. More land. More clients. More of everything. The rivalry was quiet but constant, the kind that simmered under polite nods at the feed store.

And now Cole's taken over. Expanded. Looking to keep growing.

"Cole," I say, voice flat. Nothing warm. Nothing inviting. "How's the ranch?"

"Pretty damn good," he says easily, like we're old friends catching up. "Been busy lately, actually." His gaze slides past me, deliberate and calculating. "A lot of your previous boarders have moved their horses to our stables. Seems folks prefer a place that can promise consistency."

My nails dig into my palms.

He shrugs, all casual indifference. "Too bad about your daddy's place. Hate to see good land struggle like that." He pauses, lets the words settle. "Course, I've made Mae a fair offer. More than fair, really. But she won't even discuss it."

Something hot and sharp flares behind my ribs.

An offer. He's been trying to buy us out?

I'm vaguely aware of Chace stepping in closer on my right, Shae on my left, both of them silent but solid. Eli closes the distance and stops just behind my shoulder, close enough that I can feel the heat coming off him, close enough that Cole's eyes flick to him with something like amusement.

"Well I'll be damned," Cole says, that humorless smile widening. "Looks like you've still got your guard dogs, Hazel."

Eli's hand curls into a fist at his side. I can feel the tension radiating off him, tightly leashed but dangerous. Cole notices too. Of course he does.

Cole lifts both hands in mock surrender. "Easy now. I'm going." But he leans in slightly as he says it, just enough to make the moment feel intimate. Threatening. His voice drops. "But that land's going to be mine eventually. One way or another."

The words land heavy, a promise and a threat wrapped together.

Then Cole tips his hat to me, turns on his heel, and walks away like he hasn't just confirmed what I suspected—he's been circling, waiting for us to fail so he can swoop in and buy the place out from under us.

The noise of the rodeo rushes back in all at once—music and laughter and the announcer's voice crackling over the speakers. But it feels distant, muted, like I'm hearing it through water.

I exhale slowly and look at Eli.

That look on his face—I've seen it before. Years ago, when Cole's father tried to poach one of our trainers. When someone at the feed store made a crack about my dad's methods. Eli's always been protective of this place, of us. I'd just forgotten how much.

Chace shifts beside me, breaking the silence. "Man, don't let him get to you. Cole's all talk."

"No, he's not," Eli says quietly. Dangerously.

The moment stretches. Thick. Uncomfortable.

Before I can say anything, Addie comes barreling through the tension like sunlight cutting through storm clouds.

"Did you see?" she says breathlessly, flushed and bright-eyed, ribbon clutched in her hand like she can't quite believe it's real. "I placed! Second!"

The shift in energy she brings is so abrupt it almost gives me whiplash. I turn toward her, and the smile that comes is genuine, cutting through everything else. "Addie, that was incredible. You rode it clean."

She laughs, bouncing slightly on the balls of her feet. "I know! I thought I screwed up that second turn, but—" She stops, finally noticing the tension still hovering around us like smoke. Her smile fades. "What happened? What did I miss?"

I don't answer. I'm looking at Eli again, and the question is out before I can stop it.

"What did he mean?" My voice comes out steadier than I feel. "What offer?"

Eli turns on me so fast it makes me flinch.

"Don't worry about it," he snaps. "You won't be around long enough for it to matter."

The words hit like a physical blow. *Won't be around long enough.*

I blink. Once. Twice. "Excuse me?"

"Eli, don't," Addie says, voice strained. "Come on. Not here."

But he's not looking at her. He's looking at me, and there's something raw in his expression now, something that's been building for days finally cracking through.

"You've been a complete ass since I got home," I say, heat flaring fast and sharp in my chest. "Snapping at me. Shutting me out. Acting like I'm some stranger who wandered onto the property—"

"You are," Eli cuts in.

The words drop between us like a stone into still water.

I step closer, pulse pounding hard enough I can hear it in my ears. "This is my family's ranch, Eli. I have every right to know what the hell is going on."

His laugh is sharp and humorless. "Your family's ranch." He shakes his head. "You want to know what's going on, Hazel? Really?"

"Yes," I fire back. "I do."

"Then talk to your aunt." His voice is hard. Final.

"Don't put this on Mae—"

"I'm not putting anything on anyone," he says, and there's something in his tone now that makes my stomach twist. Something like hurt underneath the anger. "This has been going on for years. You just weren't here to see it."

The truth of it lands hard because I know he's right. The boarders leaving. Cole circling like a vulture, making offers. All of it happening while I was gone, while I was pretending I could just walk away and nothing would change here.

Addie moves forward, voice pleading. "Eli, stop. You're being unfair—"

"No," he says, still not looking at her. His eyes are locked on mine. "I'm done pretending."

"Pretending what?" My voice comes out hoarse.

For a moment, he doesn't answer. Just looks at me with something that might be disappointment, might be grief, might be fury—I can't tell anymore. When he finally speaks, his voice is rough and too real.

"That you give a damn about any of this."

I freeze. "That's not fair—"

"Funny how things fall to people who stick around," he says, and the words cut deeper than any of the others. "Five years,

Hazel. Not a call. Not a text. You walked away from everything—from everyone—and now you show up expecting what? A parade? Answers? Forgiveness?"

"I didn't expect anything," I say, but my voice wavers.

"You ran," Eli says flatly. "And you don't get to come back and act shocked that the world kept turning without you."

The rodeo noise crashes around us—cheers and music and laughter that feels obscene against the moment unfolding between us.

"I came back to help," I manage.

"Then help," Eli says, eyes hard and hurting in a way that makes my chest ache. "But stop acting like you're owed something. Stop acting like you didn't leave us all to pick up the pieces."

"You think I don't know I left?" My voice shakes but I don't look away. "You think I don't live with that every single day? You want me to apologize for surviving? For choosing myself when staying here was killing me?"

For a second—just a second—something flickers in his expression. Then it hardens again.

Chace steps forward, jaw tight. "Eli, that's enough—"

"Stay out of it, Chace," Eli snaps, rounding on him. "You and Shae, acting like she didn't ghost all of us. Like it's fine that she just gets to walk back in—"

"That's not what we're doing," Chace says, voice low and careful.

"Isn't it?" Eli's laugh is bitter. "She left. And now I'm the asshole for being the only one who won't pretend it didn't happen."

Shae's hand tightens on her beer bottle, but she stays quiet.

Eli looks back at me, and something in his expression shifts—closes off, like a door slamming shut.

"Talk to your aunt," he says again, quieter this time but no less final. "Ask her about Cole's offers. Ask her how many times he's come around trying to buy the place. Ask her why she's been lying to you every week for five years." He pauses, jaw working. "If you're still here long enough to care."

Then he turns and walks away, shoulders rigid, disappearing into the crowd without looking back.

I stand there, heart hammering, chest tight like I've taken a blow I never saw coming.

Addie stares after him, stricken. "Hazel, I'm so sorry. He didn't mean—"

"Yes, he did," I say softly.

And the worst part is, he's right.

Because for the first time since I came home, the truth settles in—heavy and undeniable and impossible to ignore.

This isn't just about me leaving. It's about what I left behind. And what someone else has been waiting to take.

Chapter Seven

Hazel

I'm already mucking stalls when the sun finally clears the ridge.

The barn smells like damp earth and hay and animals that don't care what kind of night I had. Steam rises faintly from the bedding as I work, pitchfork scraping, boots sinking into packed dirt that remembers every step taken before mine. My shoulders ache in a way that feels earned, not alarming.

Familiar. Good.

I spent too many mornings in the city waking to silence that wasn't real—walls too clean, nothing that needed me. This is different. This is honest work with immediate results. I lift another forkful and toss it into the wheelbarrow, muscles protesting but obeying. My body knows this even if my head is still catching up.

Mae was asleep when I came in from the rodeo. Fully out, door cracked, lamp off. I stood there a moment longer than necessary, watching her chest rise and fall, listening to the quiet of the house settle back into place. I didn't wake her. Whatever conversation we need to have could wait until morning.

Except this morning, she's already gone.

I noticed when I padded into the kitchen earlier. The coffeepot cold. Mae's mug missing from its hook. A note on the counter in her looping handwriting.

Town. Back later.

So much for talking to her about Cole right away.

I adjust my grip and shove the wheelbarrow forward, jaw tightening as the weight shifts. My throat feels dry no matter how much water I drink. Dust clings to my skin, settling into the creases of my hands, the line of my wrist. My body carries a low, persistent soreness—not sharp, just there. Like a reminder.

I welcome it. It's easier to focus on physical aches than everything else.

My phone buzzes in my back pocket. I ignore it. It buzzes again. Then a third time. I tip the wheelbarrow at the far end of the aisle and wipe my forearm across my brow. Sunlight filters in through the slats, striping the floor in pale gold. My phone vibrates once more, a longer buzz this time. A call. I pull it out, glance at the screen. Lauren, my boss. I silence it and slip the phone back into my pocket without answering.

I'll deal with Denver when I'm ready. When I figure out what to tell them.

I work through the stalls methodically, falling into the rhythm I grew up with. Clean. Turn. Replace. Move on. It feels good to be useful without explanation, to do something that doesn't ask me to defend my presence or justify my timeline.

I came back to help Mae. That was the plan. Just until her leg healed. But Cole's threat last night shifted something. Mae lied for five years about how bad things are. Eli holding everything together alone. The ranch was bleeding while I built spreadsheets in a glass tower. The problems are bigger than I expected. That's all I know right now.

By the time I finish the last stall, the ache in my arms has settled into something steady. My breath evens out. The tightness in my chest loosens just enough to make room. I lean the pitchfork against the wall and stand there for a moment, hands on my hips, breathing in the barn air.

I'm not hiding. I'm not waiting to be invited.

I'm working.

And for today, that's enough.

***

I'm halfway to the feed shed when my phone buzzes again.

This time I stop and pull it out. Three texts from Lauren. Two from Marcus. A calendar reminder about Monday's presentation. An email notification with "URGENT" in the subject line.

My thumb hovers over the screen. Denver feels distant. Not just in miles, but in relevance. The ranch surrounds me—real and immediate and impossible to ignore. Problems that can't be solved with a pivot table. People who won't wait for me to schedule them into my calendar. But Denver is still my life. My apartment. My job. My carefully constructed routine that makes sense in a way this place hasn't in five years.

I type out a quick response to Lauren: *Family emergency with the ranch. Going to need three more weeks minimum. Will stay in touch on urgent items but need to be offline for most of it.*

It's not a lie. It's also not the whole truth. I hit send before I can overthink it and pocket the phone again.

I push away from the wall and scan the yard, looking for the next task. My eyes catch on the gate down the far fence line—the way it hangs slightly crooked, one hinge sagging.

Good. Work I can fix.

I head toward it, boots crunching over gravel. The gate down the line is crooked, one hinge sagging just enough to throw the alignment off. I crouch to inspect it, fingers testing the loosened bolts, already cataloging what it'll take to fix.

Wrench. New hardware. An hour, maybe two.

I'm about to head back for tools when a shadow crosses the ground beside me.

I don't need to look up to know who it is.

A wrench appears at eye level, held steady.

I pause, then take it. Our fingers brush—just once, a brief and unmistakable contact. Skin against skin. We both go still.

The wrench feels suddenly heavier in my hand. I swallow and focus on the bolt in front of me, forcing my attention downward. I loosen it carefully, metal creaking in protest.

Eli kneels beside me without a word and reaches for the gate. He holds it steady, and I catch the flex of muscle in his forearms as he takes the weight. We work in silence, movements falling into the old rhythm—precise, coordinated, effortless.

I adjust the hinge. Eli shifts his grip.

Our shoulders brush.

My breath hitches, barely audible. I steady it again and tighten the bolt, fingers firm despite the tremor that wants to creep in.

Eli releases the gate slowly, testing the balance. It swings clean this time, settling into place with a soft click. He doesn't look at me. Doesn't acknowledge the moment at all. He stands, dusts his hands off on his jeans, and steps back. For half a second, his eyes meet mine. Something flickers there—not anger, not coldness. Something that looks almost like regret before he shuts it down and turns away. Professional. Controlled. Devastating.

I stand, wrench still in my hand. I turn to the gate once more, confirming the fix, and nod to myself.

When I look up, he's already walking away. No pause. No glance back.

I stand there a second longer than necessary, the quiet ringing in my ears louder than the ranch sounds around me. His silence hurts more than his anger did last night. At least his anger was something—hot and real and directed at me. This distance is worse. It's a door closing. A decision made.

He's already decided I'm leaving. And the worst part is, he's probably right.

I carry the wrench back to the shed and set it where it belongs, aligning it neatly with the others. My phone buzzes again in my pocket. I don't check it.

I check on the colt before heading to the feed shed. He lifts his head when I approach, ears forward instead of pinned. Progress. Small, but real.

I don't go into his stall—Eli made it clear I need permission for that. But I can watch. He's alert when I approach, ears swiveling toward me, but he doesn't pin them back. Doesn't retreat to the far corner. Just watches, wary but not panicked.

I turn away and head toward the far pasture fence, scanning for the next thing that needs fixing.

Chace is already there when I arrive, crouched by a loose board near the corner post. I don't know how long he's been working—long enough to notice me checking on the colt, apparently.

He doesn't ask questions. Doesn't comment. Just works nearby, the way ranch hands do when they're keeping an eye out without making a thing of it.

"Rough night?" There's a hint of amusement in his voice.

I tip the bucket and set it down with a thud. "Yeah."

"Well." He tips his hat back and studies the sky. "You're still here."

The observation lands differently than I expect. Simple. Matter-of-fact. No judgment attached.

"Yeah," I say quietly. "I am."

We work in loose tandem after that. Not assigned, just adjacent. Chace takes on tasks that keep him nearby. Fixing a loose board. Checking another gate. Just two people working the same land, shoulders loose, breathing easier.

The sun climbs. Sweat slicks my spine. Dust clings to my skin, settling into something that feels almost like belonging. With every completed task, a small piece of the noise in my head goes quiet.

By the time I pause for water, my breathing has evened out. The ache in my muscles feels familiar instead of sharp. I lean back against the shed wall for a moment, forearms resting on my knees.

Chace hands me a bottle of water without a word.

I take it, unscrew the cap, and drink deep. Water runs cool and steady down my throat, washing away the dryness I hadn't realized had built up.

"Thanks," I say.

He nods, then glances toward the pasture. "Gonna be a long one today."

I follow his gaze. The ranch stretches out wide and indifferent, work waiting at every turn. Empty stalls where boarders used to be. Fences that need more than patches. A financial crisis I'm only beginning to understand.

That you give a damn about any of this.

Eli's words from last night surface without warning.

Do I?

The question sits heavier than I want it to. Because the truth is, I don't know how to prove I care. Not in a way that makes up for five years of silence. Not in a way that convinces him—or anyone—that I'm not just going through motions until it's time to leave again.

I'm here today. That's all I've got.

Whether it's enough, I don't know.

I drain the last of the water and push to my feet. "Yeah. Let's keep moving."

***

The afternoon stretches long and hot. I work steadily, checking off tasks without fanfare. A loose board replaced. Feed distributed. Troughs scrubbed clean. Small things. Necessary things. The kind that keep a place like this moving forward whether people are ready or not.

I pass the empty stalls more than once. Each time, I slow just slightly, taking in the vacant space. These used to be full. Boarders paying to stable their horses here, clients bringing young prospects for my dad to train. It was my daddy's greatest joy.

I keep walking.

By the time the sun starts its descent, my body has settled into a rhythm that feels almost right. The earlier ache has smoothed into something manageable. The tightness in my chest has loosened—not gone, but no longer sharp enough to stop me.

I pause once, hands on my hips, eyes tracing the line of the pasture fence toward the hills beyond. Somewhere out there is Maddox land. Cole circling, waiting for us to fail so he can swoop in with another offer.

I exhale slowly and turn back to the task in front of me. I pull out my phone and check the message thread with Lauren.

Lauren: Got your message. Three weeks is fine. Keep me posted on anything urgent. Take care of your family.

Relief loosens something in my chest. I didn't realize how much I'd been bracing for pushback until I didn't get it.

Five years of never missing a deadline, of being the one they could count on—it bought me this.

I type back: Thanks. I appreciate it.

Three weeks. I've bought myself three weeks.

I slip the phone away and get back to work.

The sun dips lower, casting long shadows across the yard. I finish the last task on my mental list and stand there for a moment, taking in the quiet. Cows shift in the pasture. A breeze stirs the grass along the fence line. Somewhere, a board creaks as it settles into place.

The ranch doesn't feel like it's opened its arms to me.

But it hasn't shut me out either.

I roll my shoulders and head toward the house, boots crunching over gravel. Mae's truck still isn't back. The conversation we need to have looms somewhere on the horizon—Cole's offers, her lies, what happens next.

But that can wait until tonight.

Three weeks to figure out what this place needs and whether I'm the one who can give it.

That's a question for later.

Right now, there's work waiting for me tomorrow. And I'll be here to do it.

Chapter Eight

Hazel

The porch boards creak softly as I step out and ease myself into the chair beside Mae.

The day is cooling fast, heat bleeding out of the land as the sun slides lower behind the hills. Light stretches across the pasture, catching on fence wire and tall grass before slipping away. The ranch sounds different at this hour—quieter, but not asleep. A gate clangs somewhere down the line. Hooves shift in the distance. The slow exhale of a place winding down.

Mae sits with her elbows on her knees, hands wrapped around a chipped mug. She doesn't look over right away.

I let the moment breathe.

"I fixed the gate on the far pasture today," I say eventually, keeping my voice light. "The hinge was sagging. It swings clean now."

Mae nods once. "Good."

"Restacked feed too. Chace helped." I shift my weight, the wood warm beneath my palms. "Got most of it out of the heat."

"Good," Mae says again, the word worn but genuine.

We sit in silence for a while, watching the light change. This porch has held a thousand evenings just like this—some loud, some quiet, all of them layered with the comfort of routine. It still feels like home. Just thinner somehow, like something vital has been worn away.

"The place looks like it's holding together," I say, my eyes tracing the fence line. "At least on the surface."

Mae's mouth tips up at one corner. Not a smile exactly. "Most days."

The breeze picks up, cool against my skin. I lean back in my chair, listening to it move through the grass, the trees. Waiting.

Mae takes a sip of her coffee and sets the mug down carefully on the railing. The space between us shifts—not sharply, not unkindly—just enough to signal the end of small talk.

I draw a breath.

"Cole Maddox showed up at the rodeo last night."

Mae doesn't startle. She doesn't sigh. She keeps her gaze on the pasture, fingers loosely interlaced.

"Yeah," she says after a moment. "I figured he might."

I nod once. "He said he's made you offers. To buy the place."

Another pause. Longer this time.

Mae exhales slowly through her nose. "He has."

I turn my head then, studying my aunt's profile in the fading light. The lines at the corners of her eyes look deeper than I remember. Not from grief—from effort. From carrying weight she didn't ask for help with.

"How long?" I ask. No edge. Just a question.

Mae doesn't answer right away. She leans back in her chair, eyes lifting to the sky as the last of the sun dips below the ridge.

"First offer came about two years ago," she says finally. "Right after his father passed and he took over."

The words settle heavy but not surprising.

"And since then?" I ask.

"Three more," Mae says. "Each one higher than the last."

I let that sit for a moment, watching the way the light catches in her hair, silver threads I don't remember being there five years ago.

"You said no," I say.

"Every time," Mae confirms. She glances over then, meeting my gaze squarely. There's no defensiveness there. No apology. Just readiness. "This land isn't for sale."

I nod slowly. "What else did he do?"

Mae's hand stills on her mug. "What do you mean?"

"Cole doesn't just make offers and walk away politely when you say no," I say. "So what else?"

Mae is quiet for a long moment, her fingers drumming once against her mug before going still.

"He stopped being a good neighbor," she says finally.

I wait.

"Used to be, if someone's fence went down in a storm, you'd help fix it. If a cow wandered onto your land, you'd call and let them know. Little things." Mae's voice stays even, but there's an edge underneath. "Cole doesn't do that anymore. Hasn't for a while."

"What does he do instead?" I ask.

"Nothing," Mae says. "And that's the problem. Fence goes down on our side near his property line, he doesn't mention it. Stock wanders over, we don't hear about it until we're short a head and have to go looking. Equipment breaks down and we need to borrow something—suddenly everything's in use or getting repaired."

My stomach tightens. "He's making it harder."

"Deliberately," Mae says. "Nothing you could call him on directly. Nothing that looks like sabotage. Just a steady withdrawal of the kind of help ranchers usually give each other."

I picture it easily enough. Small problems becoming bigger ones because the usual safety nets aren't there. Time lost. Money spent on things that used to be solved with a phone call and a handshake.

"And the boarders?" I ask.

Mae's expression shifts, something sadder moving through it. "That started before Cole's offers. Right after your dad died."

My chest tightens, but I don't look away.

"People didn't leave because they wanted to," Mae continues. "They left because we couldn't give them what they needed anymore."

I know what's coming, but I let her say it anyway.

"Your dad was the draw," Mae says simply. "He was the one training their horses, giving lessons, working with their kids. When he died, we lost that." She says.

The guilt lands sharp and familiar, but I force myself to stay present. To not flinch away from it.

"So they went to Cole's place," I say quietly.

Mae nods. "He's been expanding his operation. New facilities. Better rates. And he's got trainers on staff. People who'll be there consistently." She looks at me. "He made it easy for them to leave."

I swallow hard. "How many?"

"We're down to three boarders," Mae says. "Used to have twelve."

I do the math in my head. Twelve boarders at standard rates, plus training fees, lesson income. That's not supplementary money—that's half the ranch's operating budget. The number hits harder than I expected. Twelve down to three. That's not a slow decline—that's hemorrhaging.

"How bad is it?" I ask. "Financially."

Mae takes a long breath before answering. "We've got about a year. Maybe a little more if we're careful and nothing else goes wrong."

"A year until what?"

"Until we can't make it work anymore," Mae says plainly. "Until we have to seriously consider selling. Or losing it some other way."

The words hang there between us, stark and undeniable. A year. Twelve months to turn things around or lose everything my dad built, everything this family has held onto for generations.

"Why didn't you tell me?" The question comes out quieter than I intended. Not accusatory. Just hurt.

Mae looks at me fully then, and something in her expression softens. "Because you were building a life somewhere that didn't hurt to wake up in. I wasn't going to pull you back into all this just because we needed help."

"It's my family's ranch," I say.

"It's mine to manage," Mae counters gently. "You left for a reason. I wasn't going to guilt you into coming back."

I open my mouth to argue, then close it. Because the truth is, I don't know what I would've done if she'd told me two years ago. Would I have come back then? Would I have stayed? Or would I have sent money and told myself that was enough?

"I called you every week," Mae continues, her voice soft. "And every week, you sounded good. Settled. Like you were finally finding your footing." She pauses. "I wasn't going to take that away from you."

"That should've been my choice," I say.

"Maybe," Mae allows. "But I made it mine."

We sit with that for a moment. The light has almost completely faded now, the pasture slipping into shadow. Somewhere in the distance, a horse nickers softly.

"I wasn't trying to lie to you," Mae says after a while. "I was trying to protect you."

I nod slowly. I understand that. I even appreciate it in a twisted way. But it doesn't change the fact that I've been living in a version of reality that wasn't true, making decisions based on information that was incomplete.

"You should've told me," I say again, but there's no heat in it. Just fact.

"Yeah," Mae says quietly. "Probably."

The porch light clicks on with a soft hum, spilling a warm circle across the boards and Mae's worn boots. The pasture beyond is fully dark now, the land holding its shape in shadow.

I lean back in my chair and stare out at the place I grew up. The place I left. The place that kept going without me, struggling in ways I never saw because no one wanted me to.

"So what now?" I ask.

Mae shifts, joints cracking quietly. "Now we figure it out. One day at a time."

"That's not a plan," I say.

"No," Mae agrees. "But it's what we've got."

I want to argue. Want to demand a strategy, a timeline, a clear path forward. But the truth is, I don't have those things either. I came back to help Mae with her leg. Temporary. Manageable. A week or two at most.

This is bigger than that.

This is a year of slow bleeding that I didn't know was happening. A neighbor circling like a vulture. A family legacy that's one bad season away from disappearing.

And I don't know if I'm the person who can fix it.

I don't even know if I'm staying long enough to try.

Mae stands and stretches, the movement slow and tired. "It's been a long day. We can talk more tomorrow."

I stand too, my body heavy with more than just physical exhaustion. "Yeah."

We move toward the door together, the night air cool and settled around us. Mae pauses with her hand on the screen door, looking back at me.

"I'm glad you're here, Hazel," she says quietly. "Even if it's just for a little while."

The words sit in my chest, warm and painful at the same time.

I nod, not trusting my voice.

Mae heads inside, and I linger on the porch a moment longer. The ranch looks the same as it did this morning. Gates closed. Fences standing. Animals quiet in the dark.

Nothing has shifted on the surface.

But I feel it anyway—the difference, subtle and undeniable.

A year. That's what Mae has. What *we* have.

One year to turn around five years of slow bleeding.

I turn and follow Mae inside, the screen door clicking softly shut behind me. The weight of it settles over my shoulders—not crushing, just there. Present. Real.

Tomorrow I'll wake up and muck stalls and check fences and do the work that needs doing.

Three weeks from now, I'll have to decide if that's enough.

But tonight, I just need to sit with what I learned.

Chapter Nine

Hazel

Three days pass before I realize I'm counting them.

Not deliberately. Not in any way I can point to or name. It isn't the kind of counting I did when I was younger, when waiting felt sharp and restless and full of expectation. Back then, time dragged because I wanted something to arrive.

This is different. This is quieter—a low, steady awareness that settles in without asking permission. The kind that slips into my thoughts while I'm doing other things. Folding laundry. Washing mugs. Standing at the sink and staring out across the yard longer than necessary.

Eli hasn't been around.

His absence isn't dramatic. There's no single moment where I notice him missing. It reveals itself slowly, in the way days move forward without interruption. In the way no one mentions him until Mae does, casually, over coffee on the third morning.

She says it like it's nothing, like she's talking about the weather.

"He usually comes by a few times a week," Mae says, reaching for the sugar. "Sometimes in the evenings after the sun dips. Sometimes earlier, if there's something that needs checking."

She doesn't look at me when she says it. Just stirs her cup and keeps talking, like the information doesn't carry any weight.

I nod, keep my face neutral, and stare into my mug like the answer might be waiting there.

I tell myself I'm grateful for the space. And that's true, at least in part. My body has unclenched a little knowing I won't round a corner and run straight into him. Knowing I can move through the house and the yard without measuring every step, without rehearsing neutral expressions or reminding myself to breathe normally.

The distance gives me room. Gives me time.

And yet there's guilt threaded through it. Not the loud kind that demands attention—the quieter, more persistent kind that sits behind my ribs and hums there, steady and insistent. It whispers his name when I pass the creek where we used to cool the horses after long rides. When I work alone in the barn we used to fill with easy conversation. When I saddle Blaze and remember Eli always checked my cinch without asking, his hands steady and sure, like taking care of me was just part of taking care of the horses.

The absence of him isn't just about distance—it's about losing the person who knew me when I still knew myself.

I thought coming back would mean facing my father's ghost. His voice in the barn. His absence at every turn. But it's Eli haunting me instead—the shape of what we were, outlined in everything we're not anymore.

Then there's the anger. That part is less tidy, less willing to stay quiet. The coldness that's settled between us since I came back. The clipped words when he does speak. The way he looks past me like I'm a problem he's already solved once and doesn't care to revisit.

I can hold gratitude and resentment at the same time. That surprises me—the way both emotions can exist without canceling each other out.

We were close. Closer than most people ever get to someone without naming it.

The Dawson ranch sits just east of ours, a smaller operation but well-run. Our fathers used to trade labor during busy seasons—one family helping the other through haying or branding. That's how Eli and I ended up spending more time together than apart.

I can still see it—summer heat and dust clouds rising behind us as we raced across the back pasture, neck and neck, horses straining beneath us. Neither of us willing to lose. Neither of us cared who won. Just the wind in our faces and his laugh cutting through the thunder of hooves, sharp and alive and so damn easy. The way we'd pulled up at the creek afterward, breathless and grinning, collapsing into the grass like we had all the time in the world.

I exhale and anchor myself in the present. Focus on the dust motes drifting through the kitchen light, on the muted sounds of the ranch settling around me, on anything that doesn't reach backward.

The city feels like another life now.

I can still picture the cubicle if I try. The gray partitions. The hum of fluorescent lights overhead. The way the air never quite moved. The way my eyes burned by mid-afternoon from staring at spreadsheets, optimizing someone else's processes, making someone else's business run smoother.

I'd been good at it. Reliable. Efficient. Invisible, in the way offices quietly reward.

I've been checking emails when I can—early mornings before the ranch wakes up, late evenings after the work is done. Responding to the urgent ones, keeping Lauren minimally satisfied. The work feels distant, like something happening to someone else. Three weeks. That's what I bought myself. It felt like enough when I sent the message.

Now I'm not so sure.

The barn feels like neutral ground. Or maybe that's just wishful thinking. Maybe no place that holds this much history could ever really be neutral.

Still, I go there anyway.

I let my eyes adjust, already cataloging what needs doing. The colt shifts in his stall, restless. Still untouched. Still waiting.

Then I see him.

Eli stands near the far stall, sleeves rolled up, one hand braced against the wood as he is retacking a loose board at the base of the stall. He moves with easy competence, attention fully on the work.

He looks like he belongs there in a way that makes my chest tighten. I let my eyes track over him before I can stop myself — the way his sleeves are rolled to the elbow, the easy competence in his hands, the set of his shoulders. I look away. What's wrong with me?

For a moment, I stay where I am. Just inside the doorway. Long enough for the sight of him to settle.

God, I have missed him, I think.

He looks up.

Our eyes meet.

Something passes between us — not warmth, not anger either. Something older than both. My pulse does something inconvenient that I choose not to examine.

Recognition, maybe. The quiet acknowledgment of shared space. Of shared history. Of the fact that neither of us is a stranger here, even if we feel like strangers to each other now.

He straightens slowly, wiping his hands on his jeans. The movement is unhurried, but I catch the tension in his shoulders. The way his jaw flexes slightly before he speaks.

"Hey," he says.

It isn't unfriendly. It isn't anything.

"Hey," I reply.

The word feels thin, insufficient, but it's all I trust myself to offer.

I should move. Should head to Blaze's stall and go about my business like this is normal. Like we're just two people sharing a barn, nothing more complicated than that.

But I don't.

Instead, I stay where I am, hands curling around the halter I'm holding. The silence stretches between us—dense but not awkward. The kind that comes from history, not absence. From years of working side by side without needing to speak.

It makes my chest ache.

"We can't keep doing this," I say.

Eli's gaze sharpens slightly. "Doing what?"

"Pretending the other doesn't exist."

He doesn't look away. Doesn't soften. "I'm not pretending anything."

The words land heavier than they should. There's no anger in his voice, no edge. Just a flat statement of fact that somehow cuts deeper than if he'd yelled.

I swallow hard. "Eli—"

"You need something?" he asks, nodding toward the halter in my hands. "Or you just here to talk?"

It's not cruel. It's not even dismissive. It's just... controlled. Professional. Like he's already decided how much space to give this conversation and won't let it spill past those boundaries.

I stare at him for a beat longer, searching his face for something—anything—that looks like the person I used to know.

The one who laughed with me in open fields and sat beside me in silence when words were too much.

Something hot pricks behind my eyes. I blink it back before it can become anything more.

He's still in there somewhere. I know he is.

But right now, he's locked down tight, and I don't have the key.

"I'm taking Blaze out," I say finally.

Eli nods once. "Gate's clear."

That's it. No questions. No commentary. No acknowledgment of the tension hanging between us like a held breath.

He turns back to the latch, dismissing me without another word.

I move past him toward Blaze's stall, acutely aware of every inch of space between us. Aware of the way his attention tracks me without being obvious. Aware of how careful he is not to step closer, as if proximity itself might say too much.

My chest feels tight—not from fear, but from the sudden, overwhelming urge to say more. To fill the silence with everything I haven't known how to say. To ask him how he is. To tell him I've missed his friendship more than I allowed myself to admit in years.

But he's made it clear that's not what he wants.

So I don't.

I reach for Blaze's halter, my fingers steady even as my pulse picks up. Blaze snorts softly, bumping my shoulder with his nose like he's reminding me I'm not alone.

"Easy," I murmur, smoothing a hand down his neck.

The horse leans into my touch, solid and warm, grounding me in the present. I focus on him deliberately, on the familiar ritual, on the comfort of something that never left.

Eli doesn't comment on my movements or ask where I'm headed. He just stays where he is, working the board with quiet precision, giving me room in the way he always has.

I lead Blaze out, the sound of his hooves echoing softly against the packed dirt. I saddle him quickly, movements practiced, muscle memory taking over. My body remembers this place even if my heart feels unsure.

When I swing up into the saddle and settle myself, the familiar weight grounding me, I glance back.

He's already turned away, back to his work. But the set of his shoulders is rigid, controlled, like he's holding something in that wants to break loose.

I don't know whether to be relieved or disappointed. What I do know is that my hands aren't quite steady on the reins, and it has nothing to do with the ride ahead.

The land opens up as I ride out, wide and unguarded, the sky stretching endlessly above me. The rhythm of Blaze's gait soothes something restless inside me, each stride pulling me farther from the barn, from the emotions I wasn't prepared to feel all at once.

Out here, I can think.

I let the wind sting my cheeks and tug loose strands of hair from my braid. Let the smell of grass and earth fill my lungs. I loosen my grip on the reins, trusting Blaze to know the path as well as I do.

My mind drifts despite my efforts to keep it anchored.

I remember Eli standing beside me at my father's funeral. Not in front, not hovering. Just there. Close enough that I could feel the heat of him through my black coat when the wind picked up. He didn't speak much. He didn't try to say the right thing.

He just stayed.

When my knees had gone weak at the graveside, he'd shifted closer without a word, his shoulder solid against mine. A quiet brace. A promise of balance. I hadn't leaned on him fully, but I'd known I could.

That had been the kind of closeness we shared. Easy. Unnamed. Deep enough to matter.

The memory settles in my chest as I ride, heavy and warm and painful all at once.

I don't want things to stay like this. The distance. The sharp edges. The way everything unsaid presses between us.

I guide Blaze along the lower fence line, letting the ride ease the anxiousness that's been sitting in my chest for days. By the time I turn back toward the ranch, the sun has started its descent, my thoughts loosened into something manageable. The ride helped. I'd forgotten how good it felt—the simple, physical rightness of it. The way my thoughts quieted the farther I went.

When I step out onto the porch that evening, the anxiousness in my chest has settled. Not disappeared—just eased, like something that had finally been given room to breathe.

The sky has deepened into a soft wash of lavender and blue, the last light stretching thin across the land. The air has cooled, carrying the faint scent of dust and grass. I rest my hands on the porch rail and let myself be still.

Then I notice the light.

It glows warm and steady from the barn, cutting through the dusk.

Eli.

I don't overthink it. The thought comes fully formed and certain: It's now or never.

I'm done pretending time alone will fix what's been broken between us. Done waiting for the tension to dissolve on its own.

I miss my best friend. And I want him back.

Whether he likes it or not.

I push off the porch rail and step down into the yard, boots hitting the dirt with purpose. My heart beats faster, but my resolve holds.

I'm walking toward the silence that's gone on long enough. Toward the person who's known me best for most of my life.

The barn looms ahead, warm light spilling through the open door. I don't slow as I cross the yard.

I square my shoulders and keep moving.

This time, I'm not turning back.

Chapter Ten

Eli

The cattle will need moving at first light, before the heat creeps in. I work through the preparations without rushing, stacking what I'll need, checking straps and gates, laying everything out so the morning moves clean.

I like things ready before they have to be.

The barn settles around me as the light outside thins. Wood shifting. A horse blowing softly. The low hum of insects from the fields.

This is the part of the day that makes sense. My hands know the work. I focus on tomorrow — moving the cattle to fresh pasture. Which section to start with. Where the ground dips near the lower fence line. The rotation we're behind on because there's never enough time, never enough hands.

The colt shifts in his stall, settling for the night. He's coming along—slower than I'd like, but steady. Three months in and he's finally starting to listen. Another project on a long list I never have enough time for.

I stack another coil of rope, jaw tightening as my thoughts drift despite my efforts.

Hazel came into the barn earlier today.

I hadn't expected that to unsettle me. Not like it did.

She paused just inside the doorway, like she was testing whether the space still recognized her. Like she wasn't sure she had the right to step fully inside. I didn't watch her outright. I learned a long time ago how to keep my attention casual.

But I felt it anyway.

The shift in the air. The way my focus fractured the moment she walked in. The way my body went alert without my permission.

She looked steadier than when she arrived. Not fixed. Just present. Like the land had started working its way back into her, piece by piece.

That shouldn't have mattered.

But it did.

I tighten another strap harder than necessary and move on. Distance has rules. Silence has structure. I can live inside both if I'm careful.

But memory doesn't work that way.

I think about how she used to ride when she needed space. How she'd disappear for hours and come back looser, quieter, like she'd left something heavy out in the fields and didn't need to carry it home. I'd wait, pretending I hadn't noticed how long she'd been gone.

At her father's funeral, I stood exactly where I was needed. Not in front. Not behind. Just there. Close enough that she could lean if she had to. I didn't speak then either. I didn't need to. Hazel never required words in moments like that.

Presence had been enough.

That had been easier.

This feels different. Sharper. Like something unfinished pressing against the edges of my control.

I wipe my hands on a rag and lean back against the stall rail, eyes tracking the darkening sky through the open barn door. The last light clings low on the horizon, the fields beyond already settling into shadow.

Tomorrow will come whether I'm ready or not.

The ranch doesn't pause for unresolved history. The cattle don't care about what's been said or left unsaid. They need calm hands and steady movement, and I can give them that.

What I can't give is certainty.

Then I hear it—boots on gravel, moving fast. The barn door swings open before I can turn.

Hazel comes in like she's made a decision—purposeful, carrying the energy of the ride with her. Her hair is loose, wind-tossed, strands catching against her jaw and neck. Dirt on her boots. Color high in her cheeks from the cold air, from motion, from something sharper burning behind her eyes.

She stands a few feet inside, hands on her hips, breathing hard.

I turn. And stop.

My gaze drops before I can stop it. The curve of her waist beneath her jacket. The way her jeans fit her hips like they were made for long days in the saddle. The way she's looking at me—alive in a way that hits me square in the chest.

Heat crawls up my neck. When my eyes lift again, she's watching me—knows exactly where I was looking.

My jaw tightens. My hands curl at my sides.

For a beat, neither of us speaks. The quiet stretches, heavy with everything between us. Years of shared space. Years of unfinished sentences. The weight of wanting something I can't let myself have.

For a second, I think she might lose her nerve. Something flickers across her face—the realization of how much this matters—but then her shoulders square. Resolve settles back into place.

I stay still. Waiting.

"Eli," she says.

My name in her mouth does something to me—always has.

"This needs to stop."

The words don't come with accusation, just certainty.

My jaw tightens, but I don't interrupt.

"I can't fix things here if we're not on the same side," she continues, voice firm.

The barn seems to hold its breath around us. The lantern hums softly. A horse shifts in its stall somewhere behind me.

I watch her, every instinct urging restraint even as something deep in my chest pulls taut, bracing for impact. She stands there, eyes locked on mine, waiting.

And for the first time since she came back, I'm not sure silence will be enough.

I want to let her back in. That's the truth of it—simple and dangerous. The wanting has always been the problem.

"I'm not pushing you away," I say finally. "I'm trying not to make it worse."

Her brows pull together. "By shutting me out?"

"By not pretending this is easy," I snap, then rein it in, breath tight. "You don't just come back and jump into the middle of things like nothing happened."

She takes that in. Really takes it in. Doesn't flinch. Doesn't look away.

"I didn't say nothing happened," she says. "I said I'm here now."

The words land heavier than she probably intends.

Here now. Like that's supposed to be enough.

My jaw locks. I glance past her to the open stalls, the quiet animals, the familiar order of a place that only works if everyone knows their role. If everyone shows up.

"You left," I say, low. Not loud. Not accusing. Just fact. "And I had to figure out how to keep this place standing without you."

Her throat works. "I know."

"No," I say. "You don't."

I step closer before I stop myself. Close enough to crowd her. Close enough that she has to lift her chin to keep eye contact. Close enough to catch her scent—honey and leather and something that's just her.

"I was here when Mae didn't sleep for weeks," I continue. "When boarders started drifting away and nobody wanted to say out loud that we were losing them." I pause, jaw working. "I was here when things got tight and there was no one to call."

Her eyes shine, but she doesn't interrupt.

"I didn't get the luxury of leaving," I finish. "So yeah. I'm careful with where I put my trust now."

Something softens in her expression. Not weakness. Understanding.

"That doesn't mean I'm the enemy," she says quietly.

I swallow.

"No," I admit. "It doesn't."

The space between us stretches again. Thinner now. More dangerous.

She exhales slowly. "Then stop treating me like one."

I look at her for a long moment.

At the dirt on her boots. The steadiness in her stance. The way she's not asking me to forgive her. Not yet. Just asking me to stand beside her again.

That's what guts me.

Because standing beside her has never been the hard part.

But I can't. Not like this. Not when the ground beneath us is still uncertain. Not when every instinct in me warns that she's already halfway gone again, even if she doesn't know it yet.

"How long are you here, Hazel?" I ask quietly. "Because this ranch needs more than a bandage."

The words land exactly where I aim them.

She hesitates.

Just a fraction of a second. Long enough for guilt to flicker across her face before she smooths it away.

Good. She should feel that.

I step closer despite myself, drawn forward by something stronger than reason. The space between us narrows to inches. Close enough to see the pulse jump at her throat. Close enough that the heat between us feels dangerous. Close enough that I could reach for her if I let myself.

She tilts her head up to look at me, and something in her expression shifts. Softens at the edges, even as her breath catches.

"Eli," she says, quieter now. Uncertain. "I don't know what I'm doing. I need you. I need your help. I can't figure out what's next without you."

The words hit me square in the chest.

I need you.

My gaze drops to her mouth before I can stop it. To the curve of her bottom lip. To the way her breath comes shallow and quick.

God, I want her.

Not just the physical pull, though there's plenty of that. I want *her*. The girl who raced me across open fields. The woman asking me to trust her again even though she broke me the first time.

I've wanted her for years. Through the anger. Through the silence. Through every moment she was gone and every moment since she came back.

And that's exactly why I can't do this.

Because wanting Hazel Clark has only ever led to one place—watching her leave.

The temptation hits hard and fast. To close the last few inches between us. To remind both of us how easy it once was to fit together. To kiss her the way I've wanted to since the moment she stepped into that bar and back into my life.

It takes everything in me not to reach for her.

My hands curl into fists at my sides. My jaw locks. I force myself to memorize this moment—the way she's looking at me, the way her body leans toward mine without seeming to realize it, the way the air between us feels charged and fragile all at once.

Then I step back.

The movement costs me. But I do it anyway. I put space between us deliberately, anchoring myself in practicality, in work, in anything that isn't the way she makes me feel.

"Fine," I say, the word firm. Controlled. "Tomorrow we're moving stock to the upper pasture. Rotation's overdue." I hold her gaze. "Be here and ready by four. It's going to be a long day."

Her eyes widen slightly, surprise cutting through the tension.

She nods once. No argument. No pushback. Just acceptance.

"Okay," she says.

I stand there long after she's gone, hands clenched, chest tight, heart pounding.

Letting Hazel Clark back into my orbit is a mistake. One that could cost me everything.

Chapter Eleven

Hazel

The ranch wakes up in pieces. Lantern light cuts through the dark, yellow halos drifting across the corral. Horses shift and stamp, breath fogging, leather creaking as tack settles. Beyond the fence line, a gate bangs once, then stills.

The sky is still deep blue. The hour before sunrise.

I ride in as the last gate is being checked.

I don't announce myself. Don't hurry to catch up or slow like I'm a guest. Blaze moves beneath me with an easy, familiar cadence, ears forward, steps sure. The sound of his hooves on packed dirt steadies something in my chest.

I'm wearing the right jacket. Not the clean one I almost grabbed before thinking better of it, but the worn canvas I've used for years. Gloves already on. Hair pulled back tight enough it won't come loose the first time the wind kicks up. No one told me what to bring.

My pulse ticks. Not nerves exactly. Awareness. The sharp kind that comes when I step into a space that used to be mine and I'm not sure yet if it still is.

Eli sees me immediately.

I feel it before I see him looking—a subtle shift of attention, like a line tightening across the dark. He doesn't stare. Just a brief, measuring glance, the same way he checks everything else this early. Position. Readiness. Whether something will hold.

I meet his gaze without flinching, even though the urge to fill the moment presses hard at my ribs. To say something. A quiet acknowledgment of last night.

He gives a single nod. Acknowledgment, nothing more.

I let out a breath I hadn't realized I'd been holding and nudge Blaze forward. The crew moves around us without ceremony. One of the day hands we brought on for the drive swings up onto his horse and takes the far flank. Another checks the fence line with a practiced eye. Chace settles in close to the rear, posture loose, reins slack, attention already tracking movement like he was born doing this.

I guide Blaze into position without waiting to be told.

Not too close to Eli. Not tucked safely behind, either. Where the work will matter. Where mistakes won't be forgiven.

Chace glances my way, just briefly. Curious, but not surprised.

I ignore it and focus on the cattle. The low hum of sound rippling through the herd as they sense pressure shifting. Heads lift. Bodies angle. Dust stirs under hooves, faint and dry.

Eli mounts and rides out first.

The cattle begin to move almost immediately, the mass responding to the subtle shift of riders like water finding its path. I feel it settle into my bones the way it always used to. The rhythm. The balance between pushing and guiding. The delicate line between force and patience.

I loosen my grip on the reins and let Blaze do what he knows how to do.

My thighs burn faintly as I adjust my seat, the old muscle memory waking like it never went dormant. When a steer drifts left, I angle just enough to redirect it without forcing the issue. Pressure on. Pressure off.

No one calls instructions.

They don't need to.

The line stretches as we move toward the lower pasture, the dark thinning slowly as the sky begins to pale at the edges. I stay aware of Eli's position without staring at him, adjusting instinctively when he shifts.

Once, when the herd slows at a narrow point between two rises, we end up riding side by side for a stretch.

Close enough I catch the scent of him—leather and sweat and wind and something distinctly Eli beneath it all. Close enough to feel the heat coming off his horse. Close enough that if either of us shifted in the saddle, our legs would brush.

He doesn't look over. Neither do I.

But my pulse kicks up anyway, and I know—somehow I know—he feels it too. The awareness humming between us like a live wire neither of us is willing to touch.

Then the passage widens and he pulls ahead, and I can breathe again.

Once, he glances back over his shoulder.

I'm already moving.

Covering a gap that opens when the ground dips unexpectedly. Blaze responds before I fully ask, stride lengthening, shoulder cutting just enough to guide the flow back where it belongs.

Eli doesn't need to look again. But when I glance up a moment later, I catch the briefest curve at the corner of his mouth before he turns forward.

Not a smile. Not quite.

But something.

My chest goes warm.

We crest the first rise cleanly. The cattle hesitate at the change in grade, hooves testing the slope, then press on, the sound of them thickening into something solid and inevitable. I feel the buzz then, low and steady. Not adrenaline. Focus.

The quiet satisfaction of doing something that requires my whole body and leaves no room for doubt.

A young steer breaks formation near the edge.

It happens fast. Head down. Panic flickering through the line behind it.

"Shit," I mutter under my breath, already moving.

I lean Blaze into the turn harder than I plan, dust stinging my eyes as we cut across the front. For a split second, I think I've misjudged it. Think I've pushed too far, too fast. Think Eli will call out.

Nothing.

Blaze surges anyway, responding like we're one thought split in two. I lock my leg in, thigh burning as I hold the line, breath tight in my chest.

The steer checks.

Turns.

Folds back into the herd with a huff of protest like it was always meant to be there.

Chace lets out a low whistle before he can stop himself.

I glance toward Eli without meaning to, waiting for something. Anything.

He's already looking back.

Our eyes hold for a beat—long enough for me to see the slight nod. Brief. Almost invisible to anyone else watching. But there. Deliberate.

Then he adjusts the line and turns forward, and the work continues as if nothing happened.

Heat rises in my chest. Not satisfaction exactly. Something deeper. Something that settles warm and solid beneath my ribs.

He saw it.

And he let me know.

We move on as the sun finally breaches the horizon, light spilling thin and gold across the land. The ranch stretches wide and familiar, cattle flowing forward under steady pressure, the work reclaiming its rhythm.

I breathe it in. The sound. The movement. The way my body and Blaze and the land all seem to speak the same language again.

No one speaks. We don't need to.

The work continues through the morning, clean and steady. The cattle settle into their new rhythm, following the natural flow of the land as we guide them south. My muscles remember everything—the give and take, the way to read a hesitation before it becomes a problem, the patience required to let momentum do most of the work.

Later, when someone passes around water, I drink slowly and let my body catch up to itself.

Eli rides past close enough that our horses nearly brush.

"Good work today," he says without looking at me. Voice low, like it's easier to say if he doesn't have to meet my eyes.

Then he's ridden past me, heading to check the fence line before I can respond.

By the time we reach the lower pasture, sweat has soaked through my shirt beneath the jacket. My legs ache in the good way, the kind that says I've earned my place here today.

We finish the move mid-morning.

The cattle settle into the new pasture with minimal protest, spreading out to graze like they've been there all along. Dust hangs briefly in the air before the breeze carries it off, leaving the land quiet again. Too quiet.

Eli reins in near the fence line, scanning the spread with the same focused attention he's carried all morning. No smile. No nod. Just assessment. The work never really ends for him. It just shifts shape.

The crew begins to peel off naturally, riders drifting toward water troughs and shade, horses blowing out long breaths as tension drains from muscle and bone. Someone cracks a joke I don't quite hear. Another laughs.

I dismount near the gate and run a hand down Blaze's neck, loosening the cinch slowly. My legs feel solid beneath me. Used. Earned.

Eli rides past me once without slowing.

My chest dips, sharp and stupid.

Then he circles back.

He stops a few feet away, not crowding me, his eyes still on the pasture as if the conversation is an afterthought. As if the words he's about to say matter less than the land in front of us.

"Tomorrow," he says, voice level, "we'll start earlier. Push 'em further south before the heat comes up."

I look up, surprise cutting through the fatigue.

"Okay," I say, the word coming easier than I expect.

He nods once, then adds, "You handle the left flank. Chace'll take the rear."

It's practical. Efficient. Nothing in his tone suggests it means more than logistics.

It also assumes I'll be there.

I watch him start to turn his horse, the weight of that assumption settling into my chest like something solid. Something earned.

"I'll be there," I say.

He pauses, glances back. Our eyes meet for just a moment—long enough for something to pass between us that doesn't need translation.

Then he rides off.

The horses cool under the cottonwoods, reins looped loose, tack creaking softly as leather relaxes and settles back into itself. Shade pools in uneven patches along the fence line, the late-morning sun already gaining weight overhead. The work is done, but the ranch hasn't gone quiet so much as it's shifted into something looser.

Someone passes around a thermos. Another leans against the rail with a boot hooked up, talking low about nothing in particular. Laughter comes once, then fades. The cattle spread and graze like they've never known anything but this pasture, the ease of them almost insulting after the effort it took to get them here.

I drink slowly, cool water sliding down my throat, and let my body catch up to itself.

My muscles hum with that familiar post-work ache. Not pain. Proof. My hands feel steadier on the bottle than they did when I woke before dawn, the tight edge in my chest finally eased into something quieter. The land feels different under my boots now. Not foreign. Not fragile.

Just solid.

Eli hasn't joined the cluster.

He stands near the gate instead, one hand resting against the post, gaze tracking the cattle with the same focused attention he's carried all morning. He looks like he's already somewhere else. Tomorrow. The next move. The next problem waiting just out of sight.

I hesitate, then approach.

I don't announce myself. I just step into his peripheral vision and stop beside him, close enough to share the quiet without crowding it.

"They settled clean," I say.

"They did." He pauses, then adds without looking at me, "You handled that break clean too. Could've gone sideways."

Something in my chest loosens. "Almost did."

"But it didn't." He glances at me briefly. "You read it right."

The acknowledgment sits between us, simple and solid. More than I expected. Maybe more than he meant to give.

"I can check them in the afternoons," I offer.

He doesn't answer right away. The pause is brief, but I feel it—him weighing something, deciding.

"Yeah," he says finally. "That'd help."

It isn't permission. It's trust.

Something warm settles in my chest. I nod once, accepting it for what it is, and don't push for more.

The silence that follows isn't awkward. It's different than this morning. Easier. Like something between us shifted over the course of the day and we're both still figuring out what that means.

"I will see you tomorrow," he says quietly, still watching the pasture. "Same time."

"I'll be there."

He nods. Then, so quietly I almost miss it: "Good."

The word lands soft but certain. Warmer than anything he's said to me in days.

Something in my chest loosens at the sound of it.

I turn back toward Blaze, but pause when I feel Eli's attention shift.

He's watching me now.

Not openly. Not in a way anyone else would notice. But his attention is there, steady and intent, like he's measuring something new. Something that wasn't part of the plan this morning.

I meet his gaze and don't look away.

For a moment, neither of us moves. The space between us feels charged with something I can't name—something that's been building since the moment I rode up in the dark this morning. Maybe longer.

Then he nods once. Simple. Final.

See you tomorrow.

I swing up onto Blaze and turn him toward the ranch, dust rising softly behind me. The land stretches wide and familiar, full of quiet promise and quiet warning all at once. The cattle graze without concern, unaware of anything beyond the grass at their feet.

And for the first time since I came home, I feel like I'm not standing on the outside of my own life anymore.

Chapter Twelve

Hazel

Two days later, I'm driving into town.

The road hasn't changed. Same turns. Same landmarks. I could drive it blind. But making this drive regularly again—after five years of barely coming back at all—feels wrong somehow. Like muscle memory that doesn't fit the person using it anymore.

The past two days on the ranch have been different, though. Not dramatically. Just... different. Eli includes me in morning decisions now. No testing. No edge. Yesterday he asked my opinion on rotating pastures like it was the most natural thing in the world.

I'm not sure what scares me more—that it's happening, or how badly I want it to keep happening.

I park along the side street near the square and kill the engine. When Mae mentioned needing a grocery run, I volunteered. I need an hour away from the ranch.

The silence in the truck feels heavier than it should. Like the town is holding its breath right along with me.

I sit for a second, staring at the storefronts I know too well. Nothing here is new. It's just watching me differently now. Waiting to see if I'm really back or just passing through again.

I step out. Boots hit pavement. The sound is solid, familiar. I adjust my jacket and head toward the market.

A couple of people I recognize pass by. I nod. Don't stop. Boundaries, not avoidance. I'm still figuring out the difference.

Inside, the store is exactly as I remember. Narrow aisles. Faint smell of charcoal and spices. Radio murmuring somewhere behind the counter. I grab a basket and move with purpose, scanning shelves, checking labels. Building the recipe in my head.

This part feels easy.

Food has always been easier than people.

I pay. Exchange brief pleasantries with the clerk. Step back out into the sun with my bag tucked against my hip.

The town feels busier now. More voices. More movement.

I take a breath and turn toward my truck.

That's when I see him.

Eli.

Across the street near the hardware store, talking to someone I don't recognize. One hand rests on his hip. Posture easy but alert. Like he's halfway in a conversation and halfway ready to leave it.

My pulse kicks.

I shouldn't stop. Should just get in my truck and head back.

My feet don't listen.

He looks different here. More contained than he does on the ranch. Not out of place—Eli never looks out of place—but pressed into narrower lines. Like the town demands a version of him the land doesn't. Same boots. Same jacket. But there's something sharper about the way he holds himself. Aware of eyes on him in a way he never is out in the pasture.

I shift the bag in my hand and start walking again.

Very aware of the distance between us.

Very aware of the way my chest tightens just looking at him.

I'm halfway across the street when a voice cuts in from my left.

"Hazel Clark."

Cole.

His tone is warm. Almost delighted.

"Twice in one week. People are going to start talking."

I stop. Turn.

Cole Maddox stands just outside the café, hands in his pockets, expression open and pleasant in a way that makes my shoulders tense automatically. He's smiling like we're old friends. Like our last encounter wasn't layered with something I still haven't figured out how to interpret.

I smile back out of habit. Polite. Guarded.

"It's a small town, Cole. Hard to avoid anyone for long."

"True enough."

His gaze flicks to the bag in my hand, then back to my face. Assessing. Casual. Interested.

"Good to see you settling in. Been making the drive to town pretty regularly now, haven't you?"

The observation lands like he's been keeping track.

I don't answer.

He shifts his weight. Settling in like he has all the time in the world.

"So you staying, then? Or is this still just a... temporary thing?"

The question hangs.

Before I can answer, the air shifts.

Eli has gone quiet across the street.

He hasn't moved closer. Hasn't interrupted. But his attention is on us now. Sharp. Unmistakable.

I feel it settle along my spine. Steadying and unnerving all at once.

Cole follows my gaze. His smile widens.

"Eli keeping an eye on things, as usual." He says it like a compliment, but something underneath doesn't match. "Can't blame him. Running a place that size mostly solo—lot of pressure. Especially when things get tight."

I don't take the bait.

Cole steps a fraction closer. Still respectful of space, but near enough that anyone passing would assume familiarity.

"Actually, I've been hearing some things. Word around town is Clark Ranch has been struggling with timing lately. Rotations running behind schedule. That kind of thing adds up fast when margins are already thin."

My pulse jumps.

"Where'd you hear that?"

"Oh, you know." He shrugs. Easy. Unconcerned. "Small town. People talk. Feed store. Hardware store. Word gets around when operations start slipping."

The implication is clear. He's been paying attention. Close attention.

I feel the words land. Quiet. Weighted.

"Didn't realize you kept such close track of other people's business," I say carefully.

Cole laughs. The sound carries just enough to turn a couple of heads nearby.

"Not tracking. Just aware. That's how you stay competitive out here—knowing what's happening in the neighborhood." He pauses. "And when a place like Clark Ranch starts showing cracks... well. People notice."

Across the street, Eli finishes his conversation.

He doesn't look our way, but his posture shifts. Shoulders squaring. Attention narrowing.

Cole notices.

"I actually bought the Peterson place last month," he continues, voice casual. "They'd been holding on for a while, but when the margins got too tight..." He trails off. Lets the implication hang. "Sometimes it's better to sell while there's still something worth selling."

My stomach tightens. The bag handle cuts into my palm.

"Cole," I say, keeping my voice even, "are you trying to tell me something, or just making conversation?"

His eyebrows lift. All innocence.

"Just conversation, Hazel. Neighborly concern." He glances past me briefly. "Though I will say—it's interesting timing. You coming back right when things are getting tight. Makes people wonder if you're here to help turn it around, or if you're just... passing through."

The words hit exactly where he meant them to.

I open my mouth to respond.

A shadow falls across the pavement.

Eli steps in.

Close.

Close enough that I catch the scent of him. Leather and wind and something distinctly Eli.

Close enough that our shoulders nearly brush.

Close enough that anyone watching would see exactly what this is.

A claim.

My pulse jumps for entirely different reasons now.

He doesn't look at me. Doesn't touch me. But his presence is solid. Unmistakable. A line drawn without words.

"Cole," he says. Voice flat.

Cole's smile sharpens.

"Eli. Knew you'd make your way over eventually."

"Didn't mean to interrupt."

There's no apology in Eli's tone.

"You're not interrupting a thing." Cole's eyes flick between us. Satisfaction glinting there before he smooths it away. "Just catching up with Hazel. Mentioned I bought the Peterson place. Figured you'd heard."

Eli's expression doesn't change.

"I heard."

"Good piece of land. They held on as long as they could, but..." Cole shrugs. "Sometimes these old family operations just can't keep up anymore. Market's different now. Requires scale. Resources."

The silence that follows is thin. Taut.

Eli's voice stays level.

"We're doing fine."

"Sure, sure." Cole nods slowly. "Just saying—if things ever get too tight, I'm always interested in good land. Neighborly offer. No pressure."

The implication settles low in my gut.

A door opens behind us. Bell chimes. Someone steps out, glances between the three of us, slows just enough to register the tension. Keeps walking.

Eli shifts closer to me.

Still no touch. But his proximity is deliberate now. Protective.

"We're not interested," Eli says. "And we're not selling."

Cole holds his gaze. Measuring.

Then he smiles again. The easy mask sliding back into place.

"No offense meant, Eli. Just wanted to put it out there. You know where to find me if circumstances change."

He turns to me. Eyes sharp despite the pleasant tone.

"Good seeing you again, Hazel. Hope you're planning to stick around this time. Would be a shame to watch the place struggle while you're figuring out whether you want to stay or go."

He walks away. Stride unhurried. Confident. Like he's already won something I didn't know we were competing for.

I watch him go.

Heart thudding too hard.

Only when he's fully out of sight do I realize how tense my shoulders are. How shallow my breathing has become.

Eli doesn't move right away.

When I finally glance up at him, his jaw is tight. Eyes tracking Cole's path down the sidewalk even though there's nothing left to see.

"You okay?" he asks quietly.

I nod. Though the answer doesn't feel complete.

"Yeah. Just wasn't expecting that."

His mouth tightens. Not quite a smile. Not quite anything.

"That wasn't small talk," he says.

I meet his gaze. The street suddenly feels too exposed for the weight settling between us.

"No. It wasn't."

Eli exhales slowly. Then angles his body to guide us a few steps away from the storefront. Without touching me.

It's automatic. Protective in a way that makes my chest ache.

Something warm unfurls beneath my ribs. Not just gratitude. Something deeper.

The realization that he stepped in without thinking. That protecting me was instinct, not calculation.

"He likes to sound harmless," Eli says once we're out of earshot. "Makes people underestimate how much attention he's actually paying."

"And Cole's watching to see what we do."

"Yeah."

The certainty in his voice steadies me.

I nod once. Resolve settling somewhere behind my ribs.

"So he's not just a problem. He's actively working against us."

Eli's expression doesn't change, but something flickers across his face. Too fast to name.

"He's been working against us for a while now. This is just the first time he's said it to your face."

I process that.

The implications stacking up faster than I can sort through them.

Cole didn't just take clients when Dad died and I left. He's been holding onto them deliberately. Watching to see if we'd fail completely or try to rebuild.

"We should talk," I say. "About all of it. Not here."

Eli nods. Then finally looks at me directly.

The intensity in his gaze catches me off guard. Not anger. Something deeper. Something that looks almost like concern.

"Later," he agrees.

For a moment, we just stand there.

The space between us feels different than it did two days ago. More solid. Less guarded.

Like working together in the pre-dawn quiet changed something neither of us is ready to name yet.

I'm the one who breaks eye contact first.

"I should get back," I say.

"Yeah."

I turn toward my truck. Then pause.

"Eli?"

He looks at me. Waiting.

"Thanks. For stepping in."

His expression softens. Just barely.

"Didn't think about it."

That's what scares me.

I climb into the truck and pull away. Watching him in the rearview mirror until the town swallows him whole.

My hands are steady on the wheel.

But my pulse hasn't settled.

Not from Cole's veiled threats.

From the way Eli stepped in without hesitation. The way his presence beside me felt like protection and promise and danger all wrapped into one.

Cole isn't just watching to see if we fail.

He's waiting to make sure we do.

And I'm done letting other people decide whether I belong here.

The road stretches ahead. Wide and open.

I press the gas and head home.

Chapter Thirteen

Eli

By the time Hazel comes back to the ranch, the light has shifted.

It isn't evening yet, but the sun has dropped low enough to stretch the shadows long across the corral, turning the dust soft and gold instead of harsh and white. I've been expecting her. Not because she said when she'd be back, but because I know the look she wore when she drove off. Purposeful. Set. The kind that doesn't lead straight home.

I hear the truck before I see it, the familiar rattle slowing near the fence line. I keep working, hands steady on the halter rope, attention fixed on the colt. He's young. Too much leg, too much opinion. Smart enough to resist, not experienced enough to know why he shouldn't.

"Easy," I murmur.

I've spent the better part of the afternoon with him, letting him burn off nervous energy without turning it into a fight.

Her door shuts behind me.

I don't turn right away.

She walks closer, boots crunching softly over the dirt, stopping just outside the rail. I feel her there the same way I always do. A shift in the air. A change in weight.

For a moment, neither of us speaks.

The Cole encounter sits between us—unspoken but present. His threats. The way I stepped in. The conversation we said we'd have later.

Later.

Not now.

She leans her forearms on the fence, watching the colt. "He giving you trouble?"

"Has been all day," I say. "Wants to do everything except what I'm asking."

She smiles, faint but real. "Sounds familiar."

That gets me. Not enough to laugh, but enough that the tension eases a notch.

"You want in?" I ask.

She doesn't hesitate. "Yeah."

I unlatch the gate and step back so she can enter first, watching the way she moves. Careful, but not tentative. Aware of the animal without flinching from him. I clock it all, the same way I always do when someone steps into a pen. Fear shows itself fast if it's there.

She doesn't have it.

"What's his issue?" Hazel asks.

"Trust," I say simply. "Same as always."

I hand her the lead, keeping hold of the line between us. "Don't try to control him. Just keep him with you."

She nods, adjusting her grip. The colt snorts, head tossing, hooves scraping as he tests the pull. She holds firm, but not stiff. I watch her shoulders, the set of her spine, the way she matches the colt's movement instead of fighting it outright.

"Good," I say. "Let him feel you there."

She does. For a few seconds, it works.

Then the colt spooks. Not full panic, just enough of a sideways jolt to catch her off guard. The rope burns across her palm as she stumbles, boots sliding in the dirt. I move without thinking, closing the distance in two strides.

"Hazel," I say, voice even. "Don't let go."

She doesn't. She digs in instead, breath sharp, surprise flashing across her face before determination replaces it. The colt rears slightly, front hooves lifting before slamming back down.

She loses her balance.

I catch her at the waist, one arm firm around her middle, the other steadying the rope with practiced ease. I don't yank. Don't rush. I just anchor us both until the colt settles, his movements slowing as the tension bleeds off him in small, reluctant increments.

"Easy," I murmur again.

She sucks in a breath, and for a second we're locked there. Her back against my chest, my arm solid around her ribs. The heat of her cuts through denim and cotton like they're nothing at all.

I can smell her. Dust and sweat and something underneath that's just Hazel. Something I'd recognize anywhere.

I feel the moment her pulse jumps, fast and startled, under my forearm. Or maybe that's mine. Hard to tell when we're this close.

Then she steadies. Her breathing evens out, but she doesn't pull away immediately.

Neither do I.

For half a second, it would be easy to forget why I'm keeping distance. Why this can't be simple.

I step back, hands dropping to check her stance, nudge her feet into better position with my boot. Practical. Necessary.

Safer.

Her eyes find mine, still bright with adrenaline, and something else underneath I don't let myself name.

"You okay?" I ask.

She nods. "Yeah. Just wasn't expecting that."

"None of them announce it."

She huffs a breath that might be a laugh. "Figures."

I hand her the lead fully this time. "Try again. He felt you hesitate, but you didn't quit. That matters."

She flexes her hand, then squares her shoulders. "Okay."

We work the colt in a slow circle, and I think out loud as we go — not instructions, just the rhythm of it. Where the pressure is. What the twitch along his flank means before it becomes movement. She already knows. But sometimes it helps to hear it said.

"Don't anticipate," I say. "React."

She listens. Really listens. I see it in the way she adjusts, the way her breathing steadies, the way her grip changes from defensive to confident.

The colt tests her again. She holds.

By the third pass, his head drops a fraction. His steps even out.

Progress.

She catches it too. Her mouth curves, satisfaction flickering across her face. "He's calmer."

"He's learning," I say. "So are you."

She glances at me. "You saying I forgot?"

"I'm saying time off shows. So does commitment."

She doesn't argue that.

The colt finally halts, standing still in the center of the pen, sides heaving lightly. She exhales, long and slow, and reaches out, palm open, letting him sniff her fingers before she touches him. The horse doesn't pull away.

Something settles in my chest that's been tight since town.

"That's it," I say quietly. "You've got him."

She rests her hand against the colt's neck, eyes soft now, wonder threading through her relief. "Feels good to remember how."

I watch her, the animal, the way trust is taking shape in real time. Not perfect. Not finished. But real.

"Yeah," I say. "It does."

The sun dips lower, throwing our shadows long and tangled across the dirt. The colt shifts closer to her, choosing her space without being asked.

I don't miss it.

Neither does she.

She looks up at me then, and for a second she's unguarded. That smile she used to give me when something went right and she wanted me to see it first. It spreads slowly, like she's trying not to let it show too much, but the pride leaks through anyway.

For a second, she looks lighter. Not careless. Just present.

I feel it land low in my chest.

"You always had a feel for this," I say before I think better of it. I nod toward the colt, calm now beside her. "Just like your dad."

The shift is immediate.

Her smile doesn't disappear, but it falters, like a muscle that catches unexpectedly. Her gaze drops to the dirt at her feet. Not dramatic. Just enough. I see it pass across her features, that brief, private grief she never announces. The kind that shows up in the smallest ways. A tightening around the mouth. A breath taken a little too carefully.

She swallows.

"Yeah," she says softly.

For a moment, I wish I hadn't said it. Not because it isn't true, but because some truths carry weight whether you mean them to or not.

Then she adjusts her stance, grounding herself the way she always has. She brushes her hands together, dusting off nothing, and lifts her head again. The sadness doesn't vanish, but it settles. Makes room for something else.

She's quiet for a beat, gaze drifting out toward the pasture where the land rolls open and wide.

"I've been thinking about the ranch," she says finally. "About what it used to be. What it could be again."

I still.

She keeps going, eyes on the horizon. "I want to understand how it all worked. What Dad built here. The whole operation."

I study her then. Really study her.

The way she's speaking now isn't casual. It isn't reactive. It's deliberate. She's thinking ahead. Planning.

"Good," I say. The word is simple, but I mean it. "That'll help."

She glances back at me. "You think people would come back? If we rebuilt what he had?"

"Maybe," I reply. "Better to know what you have before someone tries to take it."

She nods, absorbing that. "That's what I figured."

She's quiet for another beat, then adds, "I'm going to go through his notebooks. The ones in his office. See what he kept track of. Maps. Rotations. Anything that might help."

Something eases in my chest at that. Respect, mostly.

"He was thorough," I say. "If anyone kept notes, it was him."

"That's what I'm hoping."

I nod once. "If you want another set of eyes, let me know."

She looks at me then, full-on. The gratitude there isn't dramatic. Just real. The kind that doesn't need words to make it bigger than it is.

"Thank you," she says.

Her smile comes back, softer this time, quieter, but no less warm. It hits me the same way it always has—like something I misplaced and only just realized I'd been missing.

She glances toward the house, the porch light just starting to glow as the sun dips lower. "I should probably head in. Help Mae with dinner."

"Yeah. She'll put you to work."

She laughs under her breath. Then she hesitates. Just a fraction longer than necessary.

"You could come in," she says. Doesn't quite meet my eyes. "For dinner."

The invitation settles between us, heavier than it has any right to be.

I picture it easily. The kitchen. Mae bustling around, pretending not to notice anything while noticing everything. Hazel moving through the space like she belongs there, because she does. The easy rhythm of it. The way it would feel to slide back into that orbit without resistance.

It would be easy.

Too easy.

"I better not," I say finally. "Still got a few things to check before it gets dark."

She searches my face, then nods, accepting the answer without pushing. "Okay."

She turns and walks toward the house, her stride unhurried, confidence settled back into her bones. I watch her go, same as I always have. The way she fits into the landscape like she never left it. Like the land recognizes her even if the town hasn't yet figured out how to.

I stay where I am long after she reaches the porch.

It would be easy to follow her. To step inside, let familiarity carry me forward. Easy to forget why distance matters.

Hazel has always been gravity for me. Not a choice. Just pull.

Dangerous if I let it be.

She left once without looking back. Grief, probably. Fear of a future she didn't choose yet. I stood too close to that future—already rooted, already certain. She needed to run and I was in the way.

I get it.

Doesn't mean I'm ready to stand there again.

I exhale slowly and turn back toward the pen. The colt waits in the fading light.

Trust, earned inch by inch. Not rushed. Not assumed.

Some things, once broken, need space to mend.

Even if part of me still wants to chase what once felt like home.

Chapter Fourteen

Hazel

The house smells like onions and something simmering low and patient.

I step inside and shrug out of my jacket, hanging it on the peg by the door out of habit. Dust still clings to my cuffs. My muscles carry the good kind of ache, the kind that comes from work done with intention. From being useful.

Mae stands at the stove, back to me, wooden spoon moving slow through a pot that doesn't look fancy or celebratory. Just dinner. Practical. Sustaining.

"You get back alright?"

"Yeah." I move to the counter, wash my hands under warm water. "Town was busy."

Mae glances over her shoulder. "Get what you needed?"

"Yeah. Stuff for the barbecue." I dry my hands. "Worked the colt with Eli after."

That gets Mae's attention. She turns, leaning a hip against the counter. "The new one?"

"Yeah. He's got opinions."

Mae smiles faintly. "They always do."

"He settled though. Took some time, but he did."

"Good." Mae stirs the pot again, slower now. "Eli's good with them."

"He is."

Mae nods once, like that confirms something she already knows. The kitchen settles back into its quiet rhythm. Spoon against pot. The low hum of the overhead light. Outside, the last of the daylight slips away.

Mae reaches for the salt, sprinkles a careful amount into the pot, then pauses.

"I swear," she says, more to herself than anything, "every time I go to the store lately, something's gone up again."

I look up from where I'm stacking the groceries I brought in. "Yeah?"

Mae shrugs. "Groceries. Fuel. Doesn't seem to matter what." She sets the salt down and wipes her hands on a towel. "Been spacing out the supply orders. Trying to stretch things."

I still.

It isn't what Mae says. It's how she says it. Casual. Offhand. Like a comment about the weather. But I catch the way her eyes don't quite meet mine after. The way the spoon rests longer on the counter than necessary.

I file it away. I don't say anything yet.

"Want me to chop something?" I ask instead.

Mae shakes her head. "Almost done."

I lean back against the counter, watching her. Waiting. I don't push. Mae has always talked when she's ready. Anything forced just stays shut longer.

We work in silence for a minute. Mae plates the food. I set the table. The clink of dishes sounds louder than it should.

When Mae finally sits down, she doesn't eat right away. She rests her hands on the table, fingers curled loosely, gaze fixed somewhere just past my shoulder.

"Things are tighter than they used to be," she says.

The words land without drama. No sigh. No warning. Just fact.

I look at her. Really look. "How tight?"

Mae's mouth presses into a thin line. She hesitates, just long enough for me to see the calculation there. Then she exhales.

"Feed's up. Fuel too." Mae sets down her fork. "When things run late, even a day or two, it stacks fast. Payments don't line up like they used to."

I nod slowly, letting that settle. "Is it bad?"

"No," Mae says immediately. "No. We're fine." She holds my gaze, firm. "I don't want you thinking otherwise."

"I'm not," I say. "I just want to understand."

Mae relaxes a fraction. "It's tight weeks, not a collapse."

I glance down at my plate, appetite gone. "Is Eli—"

Mae cuts me off gently. "Eli's done everything right."

There's no hesitation in that. No softening. Just certainty.

"He's kept things moving," Mae continues. "He's careful. He plans. He stretches every dollar farther than most people would." She shakes her head. "This isn't about him."

I absorb that. Let it settle. The image of Eli in the corral earlier flickers through my mind. Calm. Focused. Holding tension without letting it turn sharp. The way he stepped back when I invited him to dinner—like he knew better than to let things get easy between us.

"So it's timing," I say.

Mae nods. "Mostly. When things move on schedule, we're fine. When they don't..." She trails off. "It narrows fast."

I sit back in my chair. I don't say what I'm thinking yet. About the pasture. The cattle. The way the days have felt compressed lately, like everything is leaning toward a deadline no one has named.

Mae reaches across the table and touches my wrist briefly. Not pleading. Just grounding.

"I didn't want this on you. Not right when you got back."

I cover her hand with mine. "It's not."

Mae studies me, then nods. "Good."

We eat then, quietly. The food is good. Familiar. But the air between us has shifted. The door Mae opened doesn't slam wide. It just stays ajar, letting in a draft I can't ignore anymore.

And I don't want to.

The silence stretches longer than comfortable.

I hear myself speak before I've fully decided to.

"What can I do?"

The words come out even. Practical. Like I'm asking where the extra towels are kept or whether Mae needs help clearing the table. No drama. No promise wrapped inside it. Just a question with weight to it.

Mae looks at me then. Not quickly. Not with surprise. She studies me the way she always has when something important is on the table, gaze sharp and searching, like she's looking past the words to whatever sits underneath them.

Mae doesn't answer right away. She leans back in her chair, fingers lacing together, considering.

"I didn't want you worrying about all this," Mae says finally. Voice gentle but firm. "Not yet. You've got enough to figure out without the ranch stuff too."

I rest my forearms on the table. I don't argue. Don't rush to soften the moment.

"It's my worry if I'm here," I say quietly.

Mae's brow furrows.

"And I'm here."

Mae searches my face. Not for guilt. Not for obligation. For intention.

I don't offer sympathy. I don't frame it as helping out or easing a burden. I don't promise to fix anything. I'm offering capacity. Time. Attention. A set of hands that knows the land well enough not to slow things down.

Something shifts.

Mae's shoulders ease a fraction. Not relief. Acceptance.

She nods once. A single, decisive motion.

"Alright," she says.

It isn't permission. It's acknowledgment.

I feel it in the way the air changes between us. In the way Mae's gaze lingers now without caution, measuring me not as someone passing through, but as someone standing in place.

I'm not visiting anymore.

I'm back in the room.

After we clear the plates, I stand at the sink long enough to rinse the last dish twice, more for the steadiness of the routine than because it needs it. Mae moves around me in the kitchen with quiet purpose, putting leftovers away, wiping the counter, the evening folding itself into its usual shape even though I can feel the shift underneath it.

The conversation with Mae sits heavy in my chest, but not in a bad way. More like weight I'm choosing to carry.

When the kitchen is finally clean and the house settles, I dry my hands on a towel and glance toward the hallway.

"I want to check something," I say.

Mae looks up from where she's stacking containers. "Now?"

I nod. "Yeah. Just... Dad's office."

Her expression softens, but she doesn't ask questions. She gives a small nod toward the back of the house, an unspoken permission. "Light's on if you need it."

I move down the hall, the floorboards creaking in the same places they always have. The house feels different at night. Smaller. Warmer. The sounds contained. My childhood bedroom door sits half closed, a thin stripe of darkness behind it, and I keep walking.

The office door opens with quiet resistance, like it hasn't been used much lately but hasn't been forgotten either. Inside, the air is cooler. Dust and old wood and the faint trace of aftershave, or maybe just memory.

I flick on the lamp.

The light pools across the desk, catching on the edges of stacked folders and a couple of notebooks Mae must have moved to one side for safekeeping. The room isn't preserved like a shrine. Just unused. Mae's kept it available even if no one sits here anymore.

I pull the chair out and sit. The wood creaks under my weight, a sound that hits harder than it should. I rest my hands on the desk for a moment, palms flat, feeling the grain beneath my skin.

Then I open the top drawer.

A worn spiral notebook lies inside, cover bent, the corner softened from years of being handled. I lift it out and turn it over. My father's handwriting stares back at me from the front in thick black ink. Blocky. Certain.

My throat tightens.

I don't stop.

I open it.

The pages are filled edge to edge. Dates. Names. Weather notes. Short observations written in the margins. It isn't pretty. It isn't organized in a way I would have recognized back then. But now, sitting here with Mae's words still in my ears, it feels like a map.

Timing discipline. Not perfection. Just the steady, relentless management of days.

I flip through and find a section where the handwriting changes slightly, more hurried, as if he'd been jotting notes on the fly.

Move cattle early if heat hits by noon. Don't wait for the perfect day, you'll lose the window. If you're behind, you'll stay behind.

My fingers pause on the page.

I can hear his voice in the bluntness of it. Not unkind. Just clear. My father was never a man who pretended the land would forgive you if you forgot about it for a week.

I flip again. More notes. Rotation reminders. Grazing days counted out. A scribbled line about storms rolling in early one year, forcing a change in plans.

I keep going until something else appears.

A list of names.

Not cattle. People.

Boarding: Collins mare, full care Training: Roper gelding, tune-up Lessons: Tues/Thurs evening

I stare at it longer than the rest.

My dad's handwriting has always been all over the ranch. But this—this is a part of the operation I haven't thought about in years. I can picture it now with sudden clarity. The extra trailers parked along the side. The visiting riders. The steady stream of town kids showing up for lessons in summer, their helmets too big, their excitement loud enough to carry all the way to the house.

The boarding and training program was an entire income stream.

And it's gone now.

I swallow, the reality of it settling in.

Of course it is. He was the one with the reputation. The one people trusted with their horses. The one who could take a nervous colt and turn him into something steady. Who could tune up a barrel horse, troubleshoot a problem, teach a teenage girl how to sit deep and stop yanking on the reins.

I helped sometimes. I was around it. I even loved it. But I didn't understand what it meant financially.

Back then, I was young. Living in the moment. The ranch was the background to my life, not the fragile machine keeping the lights on. I cared about the horses and the work and the way the sun felt on my shoulders after a long ride, but I didn't care about invoices or deposits or how a boarding fee paid for diesel and feed.

I didn't pay attention back then.

I flip farther and find a page where my father has written numbers down the side in neat columns.

Boarding fees. Lesson fees. Training packages. Names beside them. Payments marked with small checkmarks.

My chest tightens.

I can almost see the sequence of loss. How that income stops in one abrupt, brutal moment. How the ranch would have felt it immediately. How Mae would have taken over what she could. How Eli would have taken over what he had to. How the cattle operation alone carries them, but not with the same cushion. Not with the same margin for a late season or a missed window.

I lean back slightly, the chair creaking again, and stare at the desk lamp's circle of light.

So much of this has been happening while I'm elsewhere, believing the ranch is simply... the ranch. Constant. Permanent. Like land can't be vulnerable.

I turn the page again and find more of what I need. Notes about when my dad moved cattle to avoid a cold snap. A reminder to repair a fence before a storm line hit. A sharp, underlined sentence that feels like it was written after a mistake.

Losing days costs money. Losing horses costs the ranch.

I run my thumb along the edge of the paper.

The colt earlier comes back to me. The way it took patience and steadiness to keep him from turning fear into fight. The way he finally softened, finally chose to stand.

Trust, earned slowly.

Timing, managed relentlessly.

And the piece I've been missing until this moment.

They don't just need to catch up. They need income that isn't tied to the cattle clock alone. They need something that can steady the ranch when weather steals a week or the market dips. They need what my dad built with his hands and his reputation.

I stare at his handwriting again.

I have his blood. I have the skill. And I've spent years not using it.

I reach for the next notebook. This one's thinner, more recent. I flip through quickly—more of the same. Rotations. Weather patterns. Client names that thin out toward the end, then stop altogether around the time he died.

The last entry is dated two weeks before the heart attack.

I close it and set it aside.

I don't need to read every page to understand what happened here. What was lost. What needs to come back.

I close the final notebook gently and stack it with the others, my palm resting on the cover for a moment like I'm making a promise I don't need to speak out loud.

Not yet.

But soon.

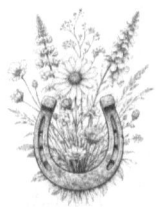

Chapter Fifteen

Hazel

The colt sidesteps again, ignoring the cue I know I'm giving correctly.

Or correctly enough that it should count.

It doesn't.

I've been at this for nearly two hours. Sweat dampens the back of my shirt. Dust clings to my boots, my jeans, my hands. The colt's ears flick back, then forward, attention scattering everywhere except where I need it. I exhale through my nose and reset, frustration creeping in where confidence should be.

I want this to work.

Not just today. Not just with him.

I want to prove the ranch still has what it takes. That it didn't lose its edge when my dad died. That the knowledge he poured into it didn't disappear with him, leaving behind only land and memory and a version of myself that never quite felt finished.

Patience, Hazelnut. That's all it takes.

My dad's voice echoes in my mind.

My mind drifts, unhelpful and persistent. To the books I pored over last night, pages dog-eared and smudged with dust. To the years when boarding and training kept this place moving, steady income flowing in even when cattle prices dipped or repairs stacked up faster than checks cleared. Horses have always been the quiet backbone of the ranch. The part that worked even when everything else strained.

If we can train this colt well, really well, it could mean something. A win. A name getting passed around again. Boarders coming back, trailers lining the drive like they used to.

My phone buzzed this morning. Denver. My boss checking in, careful and neutral, reminding me the time was there without pressing on it. I didn't call her back.

The colt spooks at nothing, jerks sideways, and I barely catch it in time. My reaction is slower than it should be.

That scares me more than his resistance does.

"Hazel."

The voice comes from closer than I expect. I startle, reins tightening instinctively as I turn.

Eli stands just inside the fence line, hat low, arms relaxed at his sides like he's been there longer than I realized. His gaze is on the colt, not me, reading the tension like it's written plainly across muscle and breath.

"If you keep thinking about other things while working him," he says, calm but certain, "you're never going to get through to him."

I still. The colt shifts, sensing the pause.

Of course he knows.

I don't have to say a word. Don't have to explain the spiral, the pressure from Denver, the leaving that's already half-built in my head. Eli has always known when I'm somewhere else, even when my body stays put.

That used to feel normal. Easy.

Now it lands heavier.

I draw a breath and bring my focus back where it belongs. On the colt. On the line of his neck, the tension in his shoulders, the way his weight shifts before his feet do. I soften my hands, ease the pressure I hadn't realized I was holding.

The change is immediate. Not dramatic. Just enough.

The colt flicks an ear back toward me, then forward again. Listens.

"That's it," Eli says quietly.

I adjust, try again, slower this time, less force, more intention. The colt hesitates, then gives me a half step of what I'm asking for. My mouth curves before I can stop it.

Eli moves closer, boots crunching softly in the dirt. "You don't need to crowd him," he says. "Just be clear."

I nod, eyes still on the colt. "I know."

"I know you do."

The colt spooks again, smaller this time, more uncertainty than defiance. I shift to correct him, but my footing slips on loose dirt. For half a second, everything tilts.

Eli's hand comes to my waist without hesitation. Solid. Grounding. Another hand catches my arm, steadying me before I even fully stumble. It's brief. Practical. Exactly what it needs to be.

"Got you," he says.

I regain my balance and straighten, pulse loud in my ears. I turn my head, meet his eyes.

We hold.

Just a second too long for it to be nothing.

Eli lets go first, hands dropping back to his sides like they were never there. The space between us resets, but the heat doesn't disappear. It lingers, low and quiet, tucked under the work waiting to be done.

I swallow and refocus, guiding the colt through the movement again. This time, he follows through fully. Clean. Responsive.

I exhale, something loosening in my chest. Progress. Real progress.

An image forms without effort. Trailers in the drive again. Horses in the paddocks that aren't mine. Riders coming in from out of town. Lessons. Training. The steady, patient work my dad built this place on—not flashy, but reliable. Profitable.

I work the colt through another pass, then another, confidence threading back into my hands. When I glance over, Eli is watching me now, not the horse. His expression is unreadable, but there's something settled in it. Something like recognition.

He doesn't say anything.

He doesn't need to.

He sees it in the way I move. In the way I don't rush. In the way I stay with the colt even when it's hard.

Action, not promise.

We work the colt like that for the next hour.

Not perfectly. Not effortlessly. But together.

I settle into the rhythm of it, the quiet exchange of pressure and release, correction and reward. Eli doesn't crowd me. He circles when needed, steps in only when something small could turn into something wrong. A reminder to soften my hands. A murmur to wait half a beat longer. Each adjustment lands cleanly, not as instruction but as confirmation of things I already know.

The colt responds. Slowly at first. Then with more consistency. His steps even out, ears less restless, attention lingering where it had skittered before. I feel it in my hands, in the way his movement starts to flow instead of fight.

It feels good.

Not just the progress. The doing. The steadiness of it. The way my body remembers before my doubts can interfere. Sweat runs down my spine. Dust coats my boots. Purpose settles in my chest like something reclaimed.

By the time we finish, the colt is calmer, head lower, breath steady. I lead him back to the barn, unsaddle with practiced motions, muscles easing as routine takes over. I run a curry over his coat until the dust lifts and his skin ripples beneath it. Check his legs. Pick out each hoof carefully, tapping stones loose, brushing shavings away.

I lead him into his stall, spread fresh shavings, fluff the hay, top off the water. He lowers his head immediately, content enough to eat.

Routine. Familiar. Grounding.

I latch the stall door and lean back against the rail, my breathing slowing, the echo of work still humming through me. Eli stands a few feet away, arms resting on the top board, watching the colt settle like he's checking more than just the horse.

I wipe my hands on my jeans. Hesitate. The moment stretches, waiting for me to either speak or let it pass.

"I've been thinking about the boarding program," I say finally. "What my dad had going before."

Eli's attention sharpens, his posture changing in a way I recognize immediately. "Yeah?"

"We could bring some of that back. Training. Boarding." I push on before doubt can catch up. "Get this colt ready and have Addie show him at the Fall Classic."

He stills.

"He's good. You know he is." The words come faster now, momentum building. "If we can show the progress—prove what we can do with a horse like him—it brings attention back to the ranch. Clients. Income that isn't just cattle."

Eli stays quiet. Too quiet.

"I've been looking at the numbers," I continue. "The years before things started slipping. That side of the ranch kept things afloat even when cattle prices dipped. Even when repairs stacked up."

I meet his eyes now, tentative but steady. "If we could build a reputation again—"

"How long are you planning to stick around for this?"

The words land heavier than I expect, cutting straight through the momentum I've built.

"That's unfair," I say, too quickly.

He straightens, jaw setting. "It's a legitimate question."

"I'm here now, aren't I?"

"For how long?" Eli steps closer, the careful restraint he's held cracking just enough to let the truth through. "A month? Two? Until your boss calls one more time and you realize you miss the city?"

"That's not—"

"You don't get to breeze back in here like you didn't take off," he says. "Like you didn't leave all of this behind."

The barn feels smaller suddenly, the space between us filled with everything we haven't touched yet.

"You don't know what it was like," I say, quieter now but holding my ground. "Being here after he died. Everywhere I looked—"

"I know exactly what it was like." His voice is rough now, raw. "I was here too, Hazel. I stayed."

The words hit like a physical blow.

"You think I didn't grieve him?" Eli continues. "You think watching you fall apart didn't gut me? You think I wouldn't have done anything to make it easier for you?"

"I didn't ask you to—"

"No. You didn't ask for anything. You just left." He looks at me then, really looks at me, eyes dark with something that's been waiting a long time to be said. "Do you have any idea what the last five years have been like? Holding this place together on my own? Watching Mae try to pretend everything was fine when it wasn't?"

"I know I hurt you—"

"You're not the only one who lost your dad."

The words sit between us.

He looks away first. Jaw tight. Something working behind his eyes that isn't anger.

"I taught myself not to think about him," he says, quieter now. "Because every time I did, I'd think about you too. And that was worse."

My chest tightens. "I understand how I left was wrong."

"Do you?" Eli's hands curl into fists at his sides. "Because you're standing here right now talking about building something back up, and you can't even tell me if you're staying long enough to see it through."

"It's not that simple."

"It is that simple." He steps back, the distance between us suddenly a chasm. "Are you staying or not?"

The question hangs in the air, waiting.

I open my mouth. Close it. The answer should be easy. Yes or no. But my throat closes around the words, and nothing comes out.

"That's what I thought," Eli says quietly.

"I have a life in Denver," I say finally, the words scraping out. "A job. A career I worked for. I can't just—"

"I'm not asking you to throw your life away." His voice is tired now, the anger draining into something worse. Something that looks like resignation. "I'm asking if you want to be here. If this place matters enough to fight for it."

"Of course it matters—"

"Then prove it." He holds my gaze. "Don't talk about training programs and Fall Classics and building reputations if you're just going to leave again when it gets hard."

"That's not fair."

"None of this is fair, Hazel." Eli's jaw works, like he's holding back more than he's saying. "I'm not saying you staying would've changed everything. But it would've made the burden easier to carry."

The truth in that sits between us, impossible to argue with.

Before I can find a response that doesn't sound like defense, before I can explain the leaving or the fear or the way I hadn't known how to stay without breaking, Eli turns and walks away. His boots crunch against the dirt as he heads toward the far side of the barn, shoulders tight, back rigid.

I stay where I am.

The colt shifts softly behind me, hay rustling. Dust settles around my boots. The quiet stretches, broken only by the sound of Eli's truck starting outside, gravel crunching as he drives away.

My hands grip the rail, knuckles white.

I still don't have an answer to his question.

Chapter Sixteen

Eli

I shouldn't have just walked away like that.

The thought hits me for the hundredth time as the shovel drives into hard earth. I reset my grip, muscles protesting, and thrust again. The post along the west wall has been shifting for months, ground too soft from last week's weather. Should've fixed it sooner.

Temporary fixes. That's how everything's been run lately.

I wipe sweat from my forehead, jaw tight. The barn looms behind me, empty and quiet. I've been working alone since yesterday.

Since the fight.

Two days since Cole made his offer in town. One day since Hazel proposed rebuilding the training program and I asked the question she couldn't answer.

And now this.

You're not the only one who lost your dad.

I'd watched her face when I said it. Watched the words land like a physical blow. And I'd meant them—every one of them. The way her expression crumpled before she locked it down made something in my chest twist sideways.

She'd stood there, mouth opening and closing, trying to find a response. And then I'd walked away like a coward.

Part of me wants to find her. Tell her I didn't mean it like that. That I wasn't trying to weaponize her grief against her.

But I was. And she needed to hear it.

Even if it makes me feel like shit.

I drive the shovel down again, harder this time.

The problem is, she still didn't answer my question.

Are you staying or not?

That's what this comes down to. Not whether she's sorry. Not whether she understands what the last five years cost us. Whether she's willing to stay and do the work.

And she couldn't even say it.

I'd seen it in her eyes—the panic, the doubt, the way she looked at me like she wanted to but couldn't make the words come out. That hesitation told me everything I needed to know.

She's already halfway gone.

The realization sits heavy in my gut, familiar and cold. I've been here before. Watching her pack herself up piece by piece until there's nothing left but the shape of her absence.

I'm not doing it again.

I straighten, testing the post. Still loose. Needs more depth. I dig again, letting the rhythm take over, focusing on the bite of metal in dirt, the strain in my shoulders, the way my breath evens out when there's work between me and my thoughts.

The air sits heavy and wrong, pressure building behind my eyes. Storm weather. The kind that makes the horses restless and the cattle skittish. The sun climbs higher, but the light feels strange. Muted. Sweat dampens my shirt despite the wind picking up, carrying the smell of rain that isn't here yet.

This is what I'm good at. Fixing what's right in front of me. Holding things together even when they're worn thin.

Even when they don't want to be held.

I reset the post, pack dirt back in around the base, tamping it down hard. The work steadies me. Brings my pulse back under control.

Chace comes across the yard at a near-run, easy grin nowhere in sight.

I clock it before the words land. Chace doesn't run unless something's wrong.

"What?" I ask, straightening.

Chace stops a few feet away, hands on his hips. "Looks like a line got cut on the east pasture sometime last night."

My chest tightens. "How bad?"

"Hard to say yet," Chace says. "But it's where the fence dips near the tree line. If they pushed through there..." He exhales. "We're missing cattle."

"How many."

Chace exhales. "At least twelve. Could be more."

I swear under my breath, the sound rough and immediate. I drop the shovel where it stands, metal clanging against dirt.

"Damn it."

The east pasture. We'd moved that group out there days ago. Fresh grass. Plenty of room. I'd walked the line myself before dark.

"How long you think they've been gone?" I ask, already moving.

"No telling," Chace says, falling into step beside me. "If they got out early enough, they could've covered miles by now. Especially if something spooked them."

My mind is already running through it. Terrain. Water sources. If they broke as a group or scattered. Whether someone drove them or just let them bolt.

"Alright," I say, decisive. "We saddle up. Grab a couple guys from my place who can ride and track. No point throwing bodies at it if they don't know what they're doing."

Chace nods. "I can get Caleb and Mark."

"Do it," I say. "Tell them to bring ropes, extra tack, and water. We're not chasing shadows."

I cut toward the barn, pace quickening. "I'll call Addie. She's got good eyes and she knows the land."

Chace glances at me. "You think she's up for that?"

I don't slow. "She'll want to be."

I pull my phone from my pocket as I go, already dialing. The barn doors loom ahead, red paint dulled and flaking, hinges creaking as I shove one open.

"Addie," I say the second the line connects. "We've got cattle out."

I listen, jaw tight.

"East pasture. Fence was cut. We're missing at least a dozen."

A pause. Then: "Yeah. I know."

I duck into the tack room, muscle memory taking over. Saddle off the rack. Cinch checked. Bridle in hand. My horse lifts its head from the stall, ears flicking forward like it senses the shift.

I continue. "No telling how far they've gone. I need you geared and ready in twenty."

Another pause.

"Good," I say. "Bring extra water and whatever you think you'll need. This could take a couple days."

I hang up and slide the phone back into my pocket, already moving. The barn fills with sound as I work—leather creaking, metal clinking, hooves shifting impatiently in stalls.

This isn't an accident.

That thought settles cold and certain in my gut.

A clean cut. No break. No storm damage. Someone took the time to do it right.

The question is who.

Cole's land runs along that fence line.

The thought hits immediately, sharp and unwelcome. The Peterson place he just bought sits right there. And the timing—right after he made his "neighborly offer" to buy us out in town.

Too convenient.

I push the thought aside. No proof. Could've been anyone—kids, drifters, someone cutting through and not giving a damn about fixing what they broke.

But Cole's face flashes in my mind. That satisfied smile when he walked away from Hazel. Like he'd already won something.

The timing feels wrong.

Everything about this feels wrong.

Mae appears on the porch, hand shading her eyes against the strange light. "Eli?"

"Fence got cut," I call back, not slowing my pace. "We're going after them."

Hazel steps out behind her, already dressed for riding. She must've been inside helping Mae when Chace found me. Her hair is pulled back, jacket on, boots laced tight.

She's ready.

Mae's face tightens with worry, but she nods. "Be careful."

"Always am," I say.

Mae's eyes flick between us—me in the barn doorway, Hazel on the porch. Whatever she sees there makes her mouth press into a thin line, but she doesn't comment. Just turns and goes back inside, leaving us alone.

Hazel crosses the yard toward me, moving with purpose. Her expression is set, that familiar mix of concern and steel I've seen a thousand times.

She looks like she didn't sleep either.

Good. At least I'm not alone in that.

"What's going on?" she asks.

I don't dress it up. "Fence got cut on the east pasture. We're missing cattle."

Her expression sharpens instantly. "How many?"

"At least twelve. Could be more."

She exhales, hard. "When?"

"Sometime last night." My gaze flicks past her, tracking the sky, the men moving, the way the day has already gone wrong. "We're heading out now."

"I'm coming with you."

"No."

The word is out before I think about it. Flat. Final.

Hazel stills. Her jaw sets. Eyes flash.

"Excuse me?"

I exhale through my nose, irritation threading through the urgency. I don't have time for this. Not after yesterday. Not with everything unsettled between us. "You're not riding out into this."

She steps closer. Too close. Close enough I can see the stubborn set of her mouth. The fire in her eyes that I know too well.

"Eli—"

"No," I cut in, jaw tightening. "This isn't—"

"Eli Dawson," she says, voice low and dangerous, "this is my ranch."

The words hit harder than I expect.

Harder than *You're not the only one who lost your dad* hit her.

We're standing close enough that anyone watching would see this for what it is. Not just an argument. A line being drawn.

Her chin lifts. Doesn't back down an inch.

I hold her gaze, feel the pressure of it, the truth she's throwing in my face whether I like it or not. "This isn't about ownership."

"It damn well is," she says. "Those cattle are mine. That fence is mine. And whoever cut it did it on my land."

The wind picks up harder now, rattling metal somewhere near the barn. Dust swirls across the yard. The storm sits heavy on the horizon, waiting.

Neither of us moves.

"I know this land," she continues. Voice steady. Certain. "I know where they'll head. I'm not sitting on the porch while you go chasing my family's livelihood."

I scrub a hand over my face, frustration flaring hot.

I want to tell her she gave up the right to call it "her ranch" when she left five years ago. Want to throw yesterday back in her face—all her careful talk about training programs she might not stick around to see through.

But standing here now, watching the set of her jaw, the way she's already dressed for work, boots laced, jacket ready, I see something else.

She's not asking permission.

She's telling me.

I remember the cattle move last week. The way she handled the left flank without question, read the herd, didn't hesitate. She knows what she's doing out there. Has always known.

That doesn't make this easier.

And part of me—the part that's too tired to keep fighting her—respects the hell out of that.

"Damn it," I mutter.

I look at her again and see it—the resolve. The refusal to be sidelined. The same stubborn streak that's always made me respect her and curse her in equal measure.

The same stubborn streak that made me fall for her in the first place.

"Fine," I say finally.

Her shoulders ease just a fraction.

"But you hurry the hell up," I add immediately. "Pack like you might be gone overnight. Warm clothes. Water. Whatever you think you need." My eyes harden. "We don't turn back just because it gets uncomfortable."

She meets my stare without blinking. "Wouldn't dream of it."

I nod once, sharp. That's all I've got time for.

Then I turn and march back toward the barn, jaw set, stride hard.

Maybe she'll leave after this. Maybe she won't.

But right now, we've got cattle to find.

And for once, she's not running.

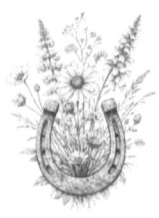

Chapter Seventeen

Hazel

The sun hangs low but stubborn, all gold and fire along the ridge as I snug Blaze's saddle into place. The leather creaks under my hands, warm and familiar.

Eli stands a few yards off, checking his cinch.

We haven't spoken since the fight.

Not about yesterday. Not about the cattle. Not about anything.

The silence sits between us like something solid, heavy with everything we're not saying.

All I know is what Chace barked across the yard a half hour ago. A line cut. Cattle missing. East pasture. That's it. No numbers, no details, just the kind of clipped urgency that turns your stomach cold.

One day after the fight that left everything broken between us.

One day after I couldn't answer his question: are you staying or not?

And now we're riding out together anyway, because the cattle don't care about our problems.

I glance past Blaze's neck and see Addie and Chace riding up from the barn, their horses tossing their heads, restless. Addie's ponytail flashes against the fading sky.

"East fence makes more sense," Addie is saying. "If they slipped through there, they'd push downhill, not up."

Chace snorts. "You don't know that. Whoever cut it might've been herding them toward the creek."

They're still bickering when Eli steps forward, his jaw tight, eyes already scanning the horizon like he's measuring the land.

"We're heading south," he says, sharp enough to slice clean through them. "Tree line first. Then we work our way back."

No debate. No discussion.

Just orders.

Addie lifts a brow but says nothing. Chace tips his hat, already turning his horse.

I feel that old pull settle in—the way Eli steps in and the world adjusts around him, everyone falling into place. Including me.

I don't say anything either.

We start riding.

The land rolls out in endless waves of gold and green, broken by dark stands of pine and the silver thread of the creek winding through the low points.

We split up at the first creek crossing. Addie and Chace take the east ridge, Eli and I follow the creek bed south. The theory is simple: cattle need water. If they bolted through that cut fence, they'd eventually circle back looking for it.

But the creek is empty. No tracks. No fresh dung. No sign they've been through here at all.

For a moment, I think I see movement on the ridge—dark shapes against the grass. My heart kicks.

"There," I say, pointing.

Eli follows my gaze, then shakes his head. "Shadows."

He's right. Just wind through tall grass.

We keep moving, following the creek as it curves east. My legs ache from hours in the saddle, thighs burning. I take a swig from my water bottle—almost empty—and taste dust.

Still nothing.

We round a bend and I pull Blaze to a stop.

"Wait," I say.

Eli turns, impatient. "What?"

I dismount. The grass here is trampled, bent in a direction that doesn't match the wind. Fresh. I crouch, fingers brushing a partial print in soft earth.

"They came through here," I say. "Maybe six, eight hours ago."

Eli rides back and looks down. His jaw tightens, but he nods.

"Which direction?"

I stand, following the bent grass with my eyes. "South. Toward Hollow Creek."

Something shifts in his expression. Not quite approval. But acknowledgment.

He doesn't thank me. Just turns his horse and follows the trail I found.

But he doesn't question me either.

We regroup with Addie and Chace an hour later at the split oak where the property line angles west. The clouds that looked threatening earlier have shifted north.

Addie and Chace ride up from the east ridge, their horses breathing hard.

"Nothing," Addie reports, frustration clear in her voice. "Not a damn thing."

"Shocking," Chace says. "Almost like the cattle didn't consult a map before wandering off."

Addie shoots him a look that could strip paint. "Do you ever shut up?"

"Not if I can help it." Chace grins, unrepentant. "Silence makes you twitchy."

"You make me twitchy."

"See? I'm consistent."

Despite everything, I almost smile.

"Hazel found tracks," Eli says, cutting through their banter. "Heading south toward Hollow Creek."

Addie straightens in her saddle. "How old?"

"Six to eight hours," I say. "Maybe more."

Chace whistles low. "That's a lot of ground they could've covered."

"Then we keep moving," Eli says. He checks the sky, calculating. "We've got maybe two more hours of good light."

We ride south together now, all four of us in a loose line, eyes scanning the horizon. The sun drops lower, painting everything in shades of amber and shadow.

The trail I found peters out near the rocky ground above Hollow Creek. We split up again, covering more ground, checking every draw where cattle might shelter.

The light fades from gold to gray.

Eli rides back toward me as the sun finally drops behind the ridge.

"We need to set camp," he says. "Can't track in the dark."

I want to argue. Want to keep searching. But he's right.

"Alright," I say quietly.

His eyes flick to mine for just a second, then away.

Dusk settles in slow and blue as Eli picks a rise of ground just above the tree line. High enough to keep us visible. Close enough to shelter the horses from the wind.

We make camp without much talk.

Chace gets the fire going while Addie stakes the tents. I unsaddle Blaze and lead him to where Eli has already tied the other horses, close enough to the trees for shelter.

Eli's back is to me, his hands working over his horse's legs, checking for injuries, stones, anything that might slow us down tomorrow.

I do the same with Blaze, working in silence a few feet away.

"There's extra grain in my pack," Eli says without looking at me. "They'll need it."

It's the first practical thing he's said to me since the fight.

"Thanks," I say quietly.

He doesn't respond.

I grab the grain and measure it out carefully. Blaze dips his head immediately, content. I run a hand down his neck, feeling the warmth and muscle beneath his coat.

When I turn back, Eli is already walking toward the fire.

Dinner is canned beans heated over the fire and coffee that tastes like dirt and salvation in equal measure. No one talks much. We're too tired. Too worried.

I sit on a log across from Eli, the fire crackling between us. He eats mechanically, staring into the flames.

Once, our eyes meet across the fire.

For half a second, I think he might say something.

Then Chace asks about tomorrow's route, and the moment passes.

The sky above us deepens from blue to black. Stars appear, one by one, until the whole dome is scattered with light.

"First watch?" Addie asks, looking at Eli.

"I'll take it," he says.

"I can—" I start.

"I've got it," Eli cuts in, his tone making it clear the discussion is over.

I bite back the argument. Not everything has to be a fight.

Addie yawns and stands, stretching. "Wake me in four hours."

"Will do," Eli says.

Chace is already heading toward his tent. Addie follows, her silhouette disappearing into the dark.

That leaves me and Eli.

Alone.

The fire pops, sending sparks spiraling up into the night. I should go to my tent. Should leave him to his watch.

But something holds me in place.

I open my mouth to say something—anything—but the words tangle before they reach air.

The fire pops. A log shifts, sending sparks up into the dark.

"You did good today," I say finally. Safe. Neutral.

It's not what I meant to say, but it's something.

Eli's jaw works. He stares into the flames like they might give him an answer he's not finding on his own.

"You always could read the land better than anyone," he says quietly. "Even when we were kids."

The past tense lands heavier than it should. Like he's talking about someone who doesn't exist anymore.

But I'm right here, I want to say. *I'm still me.*

Except I'm not sure that's true.

"You remember that time we lost your dad's prize heifer?" I ask. "We were what, fifteen?"

His mouth curves. A real smile, brief but genuine. "Sixteen. And it wasn't lost. It got stuck in the ravine past Carson's property."

"You wanted to tell your dad. I made you wait."

"Because you were sure you could find her." He shakes his head, but there's something softer in it now. "Dragged me through half the county looking."

"We found her."

"We did." He pauses, then adds, "Took us all night. We fell asleep by the creek waiting for her to calm down enough to move."

The memory surfaces fully now. Both of us exhausted, covered in mud, his jacket draped over both our shoulders because I'd left mine behind. The stars overhead just like tonight. The way he'd kept watch even then, making sure I was warm enough, safe enough.

The way it had always been easy with him. Uncomplicated.

Until it wasn't.

"I miss that," I say before I can stop myself.

His eyes lift to mine across the fire.

The air between us shifts. Tightens.

"Miss what?" His voice is low. Careful.

Us, I want to say. *When it was simple. When I didn't ruin everything by taking more than I could handle.*

But the words stick in my throat.

Because he was there that night too. The night everything changed. The night I reached for him in the dark and he reached back and for one perfect, terrible moment, I thought maybe I could stay.

And then the sun came up and I ran.

"I miss knowing what to say to you," I manage finally.

Something flickers across his face. Pain, maybe. Or recognition.

He stands abruptly, his shadow cutting long across the firelight.

"You should get some sleep," he says, and this time it sounds less like an order and more like self-preservation.

I nod. Stand. Brush the dirt from my jeans.

I make it three steps toward my tent before I hear him again.

"Hazel."

I turn.

He's still standing by the fire, his back to me now, shoulders tight.

"For what it's worth," he says quietly, not looking back, "I miss it too."

The words hit harder than anything he's said to me since I came home.

I don't trust myself to respond. So I just nod—even though he can't see it—and walk to my tent before I do something stupid like cry.

Or stay.

Inside, I lie on top of my sleeping bag, fully dressed, staring at the canvas above me. The fire's glow filters through the fabric. Orange. Shadow. Orange.

Outside, Eli's boots crunch softly. Wood crackles as he adds to the fire.

Keeping watch.

Protecting what's left.

Like he always has.

The thought lands heavier than I expect.

I was scared. That's why I left. Drowning in grief and terrified of the way he looked at me—like I was something worth holding onto when I felt like I was breaking apart.

If I'd stayed, I would've failed him. Disappointed him. Become one more thing on this ranch that couldn't be saved.

So I ran.

And I've been running ever since.

Even now, lying here, part of me wants to keep running.

But there's nowhere left to go.

I pull the sleeping bag over my shoulders and close my eyes. Tomorrow we'll search again.

But tonight, I let the exhaustion pull me under, grateful for the temporary reprieve.

Chapter Eighteen

Hazel

By noon the next day, we find them.

Twelve head, all bunched up in a shallow draw a mile past the tree line, grazing like nothing in the world has ever gone wrong. No injuries. No blood. Just spooked, the way cattle get when something startles them hard enough to break instinct.

Relief comes first, sharp and dizzying.

Then the anger follows, slow and hot.

Because fences don't cut themselves.

We spend the better part of the morning pushing the herd back through the pasture, dust rising around hooves, the air full of lowing and the creak of saddle leather. Eli moves the way he always does when he's focused, steady and sure, cutting off strays before they can wander. I watch him without meaning to.

Something about the way he handles the land and the animals still reaches straight through me.

Once the cattle are secured in the north pasture, we stop at the east fence line on the way back.

The wire dangles loose, cut clean through. No fraying. No rust break. No storm damage. Someone used wire cutters and knew exactly what they were doing.

Eli dismounts and crouches beside it, running his fingers along the severed edge. His expression hardens.

"Deliberate," he says quietly.

Cole's land runs right along this fence line. We both know it. Neither of us says it out loud.

The ride back to the ranch is quiet. Not strained. Not hostile. Just full. The kind of quiet that sits heavy between people who have too much to say and no idea where to start.

I can ignore the way my pulse kicks when he glances back at me. Ignore the tension that hasn't faded with time. I can set all of that aside if it means getting him back. The Eli from before everything cracked open.

Part of me wonders if nothing actually changed back then.

If I just finally saw what was already there and got scared enough to run.

The thought makes my stomach twist.

Back at the ranch, we unsaddle in the late-afternoon light, the sun slipping low and gold behind the hills. Leather thumps softly as gear is pulled free. Blaze nudges my shoulder, impatient for his grain, and I laugh despite myself, the sound small but real.

Eli works beside me in silence, efficient and controlled. When our hands brush passing a saddle blanket, the contact sends a spark through me that I pretend not to feel.

We lead the horses toward the barn, the smell of hay and warm animals wrapping around us like a memory.

That's when the sound of tires on gravel cuts through it.

I turn, one hand still on Blaze's reins, as a truck comes down the long drive. Slow. Deliberate.

Eli goes still beside me.

"Who is that?" I ask.

He doesn't answer. But his jaw sets in a way I recognize.

He knows.

The truck settles to a stop at the edge of the yard, dust lifting around the tires before drifting back down.

For a second, everything feels suspended.

Then the door swings open.

Cole Maddox steps out, all boots and hat tipped low, that practiced half-smile already in place.

"Hazel," he says, his gaze landing on me with easy confidence. "I heard you've been working hard helping Eli."

Eli is beside me before I even register him moving. Not touching, not quite, but close enough that I feel him there, solid and steady at my back. Whatever tension has been eating at us all day vanishes the second Cole opens his mouth. This isn't between me and Eli anymore.

This is something else.

Cole's eyes flick to Eli, linger, then come back to me. "That's real good of you, considering you've got that job waiting in Denver."

The implication lands clean: You're temporary.

"I'm here as long as Mae needs me," I say.

"Is that right." His smile doesn't waver. "Well, that's sweet of you. Mae's lucky to have family stepping up." He pauses, just long enough. "Even if it's just for a visit."

Heat creeps up my neck.

"Watch it," Eli says flatly.

Cole just laughs, soft and easy. "Relax, Dawson. Just making conversation." He looks back at me. "Though I gotta say, Hazel, it's interesting timing. You show up right when things are getting tight around here. Almost like you knew."

"Knew what?" I ask.

"That Mae might need to make some hard choices."

Something in Eli shifts. I feel it more than see it—the way his body goes still, dangerous quiet settling over him.

Before it can go any further, the front door opens.

Aunt Mae steps out onto the porch, eyes sharp, posture calm. She takes in the scene in a single glance and misses nothing.

"Cole," she says pleasantly. "Please, come inside."

The words are polite.

The invitation is not.

Cole's smile widens. He gives me one last look, all easy confidence and calculated patience, then turns toward the house like he's already been invited to stay.

I watch him go, my pulse loud in my ears, then turn to Eli.

"What the hell was that about?"

He goes still for a beat. His gaze cuts once toward the house, then back to me, dark and closed off.

I catch his arm before he can walk away.

"Eli—"

"I can't go in there." His voice is tight, controlled. "Not with him."

I understand. If Eli's in that room when Cole starts talking numbers, it'll end with someone bleeding.

"I'll tell you everything," I say.

He nods once. Then heads for the barn, shoulders rigid, hands already curling into fists.

I hesitate for half a second.

Then I turn and go after Cole, my steps quickening as unease curls low in my stomach.

I push through the front door just in time to hear Aunt Mae's voice carrying down the hallway.

"Right this way, Cole."

Footsteps move toward my dad's old office, the sound muffled by thick rugs and years of use. I slow, instinct prickling, and follow at a distance.

The house feels different with him in it. Tighter. Like something unwelcome has been let past the threshold.

By the time I reach the office doorway, Cole is already inside, hat in hand, posture easy and respectful in a way that barely resembles the man who was just needling me in the yard. His voice is smooth now, measured.

"I appreciate you making time for me, Mae. I know things have been... complicated lately."

Aunt Mae gestures him toward one of the leather chairs. "Sit. Let's hear what you came all this way for."

I hover just outside the doorframe, watching him shift seamlessly into something else. No swagger. No barbs. Just confidence, polished and professional.

It makes my stomach turn.

This version of Cole is worse somehow. Sharper. More dangerous than the one who throws pointed comments in the yard. This one smiles with purpose.

He sits, folding his hands loosely in front of him. "I'll get right to it. I think there's a way we can both come out ahead here."

Aunt Mae's gaze flicks toward me.

Slow.

Weighing.

For a moment, I think I might be sent away. The idea of it—of being shut out of something that has my dad's name all over it—makes my chest tighten.

Finally, Mae speaks.

"Haze, you know things aren't getting any easier around here." Her voice is steady, but there's tiredness beneath it. "I need to make some hard choices about the ranch. Cole has a proposal for me, and I invited him here to tell me what's on his mind." She meets my eyes. "I reckon you can remain respectful, or you can go to the barn with Eli. Yes?"

The words land harder than I expect.

Cole Maddox. Of all people.

I swallow. I don't trust myself to speak.

So I nod.

Cole's mouth curves faintly, that polite, practiced expression still in place, and I hate how easily he wears it.

I take a step farther into the room and wait to hear what he's come to say.

The office still smells faintly like my dad. Old leather. Paper. The clean, dry edge of aftershave that no amount of time has ever fully erased. I stand just inside the door, hands folded tight in front of me, as Cole settles deeper into the chair across from dad's desk.

He rests his hat on his knee, posture relaxed, respectful. It's unsettling how easily he fits in the room.

"I'll keep this simple," Cole says. "Clark Ranch is carrying more weight than it should be. Feed costs, labor, repairs, auction schedules. Things are tight. Tighter than you let on."

Mae doesn't respond. Just watches him, eyes steady.

"I'm not here to make that worse," he continues. "I'm here to offer breathing room."

My spine stiffens.

"By buying us," I say. "You mean taking what isn't yours."

Cole's gaze slides to me, mild and measured. "I prefer to think of it as investing, Hazel. Keeping Clark Ranch in the family—with outside support."

Mae lifts a hand. "Hazel."

I fall silent, chest too tight to breathe.

Cole continues. "I'm offering to purchase a majority stake. You keep running it. You keep the Clark legacy intact. The name stays on the gate. I take on the financial risk."

"And what do you get?" Mae asks.

"A return," he says easily. "And a say. Nothing unreasonable."

I stare at him. "You think owning half of my family's ranch is nothing unreasonable?"

"Mae's the one carrying the weight," he says simply. "I'm here to help lighten that load."

The words hit harder than I expect. He doesn't raise his voice. Just lets the truth sit there, sharp and clean.

Mae hasn't moved. Her hands rest on the desk, fingers laced. Thinking. Weighing.

"You're asking me to sell my brother's life," Mae says quietly.

"I'm asking you to save it," Cole replies. "Before the bank decides to do it for you."

Silence stretches.

I feel like I'm standing in the middle of something fragile. Something already cracking.

A folder slides out from under his arm and onto the desk. Neat. Organized. Official.

"I always come prepared."

Mae doesn't touch it.

For a long moment, no one speaks.

Then she exhales slowly and straightens. "Thank you for your time, Cole. I'll review the terms with my lawyer and be in touch."

My stomach drops.

She's not saying no.

There's no commitment in her voice. But there isn't dismissal either.

Cole stands, smooth and unhurried. "That's all I ask."

He gives me a small, unreadable smile as he takes his hat. "Good seeing you again, Hazel."

I can't bring myself to answer.

He leaves the room with the same quiet confidence he brought into it.

The door clicks shut.

For a second, I can't move. Can't breathe.

Mae is actually considering it.

The realization hits like a physical blow.

I spin toward my aunt.

"You can't possibly be considering this." My voice cracks. "Aunt Mae. Daddy would roll over in his grave. So would Grandpa. Selling controlling stakes to the Maddoxes? How can you even think about that?"

Mae draws a slow breath, the kind that comes from deep in her chest.

"Haze," she says gently, "I know this is hard. But I'm not getting any younger." She rests her hands on the desk, fingers splayed. "And as you've noticed, I can't maintain this land the way it needs anymore. I was never the trainer. That was your daddy. He was the one who could bring a horse along, who could turn nothing into something worth betting on."

Her voice doesn't break, but something fragile lives underneath it.

"We don't make enough with cattle alone to sustain this operation. Not anymore. We've already cut down to a skeleton crew. You see the roofs that need patching, the fences we can't afford to replace, the equipment that keeps breaking. I just..." She exhales. "I don't see a way out."

I shake my head, panic rising fast and sharp.

"I have a plan," I say. "We train the colt. Get Addie to ride him at the Fall Classic. It won't solve everything overnight, but if we place well, we can use that momentum to start calling former clients. A good showing gives us credibility again."

Mae's expression doesn't change.

"I know it's not immediate money," I continue, faster now. "But Cole's offer won't close tomorrow either. Deals like that take weeks, maybe months. This buys us time. And if it works—if we can show the boarding program is viable again—you have leverage to say no."

Her gaze lifts to me.

There's a question in it she doesn't say out loud.

I see it anyway.

I look away.

"Just let me try," I say, desperation creeping in. "We can train the colt. Get Addie to ride. If people see we're producing show horses again, if they see we have riders and talent here, maybe the boarders will come back. Maybe the money will follow."

Mae studies me for a long moment.

Then she nods.

"All right," she says quietly. "Let's see what you've got."

I don't wait for anything else.

I turn and run for the barn, boots hitting the floor hard, heart pounding with something that feels dangerously close to hope.

If I'm going to save this ranch, I can't do it alone.

I need Eli.

Not just as foreman. As partner.

The way it should have been from the start.

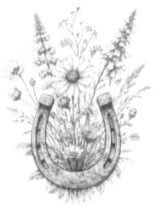

Chapter Nineteen

Hazel

I cut across the yard instead of going around it.

The late afternoon sun sits low over the barns, spilling gold across the packed dirt and catching in the dust that hangs in the air. Somewhere near the back fence a horse snorts, the sound lazy and familiar. The ranch looks almost peaceful, which feels like a lie.

My mind is already racing ahead of my steps, lining up what I need to say. If I'm going to save this place, I have to start now. The colt is green but promising. Addie has the seat for it, the patience too. The Copper Ridge Fall Classic is four weeks out—trail class division, or ranch horse if we can get him solid enough. The first show that really matters before winter sets in.

Four weeks isn't much time, but if we can get the colt ready, if Addie can put in a clean ride, people will notice. Word spreads.

Boarders might come back. It's not a magic fix, but it's a starting point.

And then what?

The question sits in my chest, uncomfortable and unavoidable.

I don't know. I honestly don't know.

Part of me wants to stay here, rebuild what Dad built, prove I can do this. Another part keeps thinking about Denver, the career I worked so hard for, the life I built there. Five years of climbing, learning, becoming someone who isn't just John Clark's daughter.

I can't just throw that away.

Can I?

Eli will understand. He has to. Once I explain the plan, show him it could work, he'll see I'm trying. That has to count for something.

I cross the space between the house and the barn at a quick pace, boots kicking up small clouds of dust. As I draw closer, I hear the steady rush of water from around the back side, rhythmic and loud against the quiet of the afternoon.

Watering the horses, I assume.

I round the corner of the barn—

And stop dead.

Eli stands under the wash hose, head tipped back, water streaming down bare skin. No shirt. Just him and the water and late afternoon light turning everything gold.

Heat hits me so fast I forget how to breathe.

He's all lean muscle and sun-darkened skin, water sliding down his back, his shoulders, catching in the hollow of his spine. His jeans are soaked, clinging low on his hips, and I can't—I shouldn't be staring but I can't make myself look away.

My hands clench at my sides. My pulse kicks into a rhythm that has nothing to do with the walk over here.

He shuts off the hose. Silence drops like a weight.

My pulse is everywhere. Throat, chest, low in my stomach where warmth pools insistent and impossible to ignore. Everything feels too warm, too tight.

He rolls his shoulders, slow and easy, water dripping from him in the quiet. Then turns.

Not startled. Deliberate. Like he knew I was there the whole time.

Our eyes meet.

The air between us feels electric. Too close.

Heat crawls up my neck, floods my face. He sees it. I know he sees it.

My eyes drop—I can't help it—to his chest, his stomach, the soaked waistband riding low enough that—

"How'd the meeting go with Cole?"

The words register slow. Too slow.

I blink, trying to process, my brain still cataloging the way water clings to his skin, the way his chest moves when he breathes, how unfairly good he looks dripping wet and half-dressed in barn light.

"I—" I start, then stop.

He's still looking at me. Like he knows exactly what he's doing.

I shift my weight and his gaze tracks the movement. Drops briefly. Comes back up.

I try again. "I—"

Nothing.

Eli doesn't move. Doesn't reach for the towel two feet away. Just stands there, water dripping, and watches me fumble for words.

"I'm sorry," I blurt finally, jerking my gaze away. My face is on fire. "I didn't—I was just—I thought you were—"

I spin halfway toward the door.

Behind me, he laughs. Low and surprised, the sound making my stomach flip.

"It's fine," he says, and I hear fabric shifting as he reaches for his shirt. "You look like you walked in on a crime scene."

I force myself to turn back.

He's pulling the shirt over his head now, damp hair falling forward. Water immediately darkens the collar, makes the fabric cling to his shoulders, his chest.

Still unfair.

"There's showers in the bunkhouse," I say, trying for casual and landing somewhere between nervous and strangled. "You know. With doors."

"Shower's been broken for weeks," he says flatly.

Right. Of course it has.

I clear my throat. Try to find the thread of why I came here in the first place.

The list. The plan. The colt. Mae. Cole's offer. The Fall Classic.

Four weeks.

The words come back slowly.

"I know things have been... difficult between us," I say finally. My voice is steadier than I expect. "And I know we have a lot to talk about."

Eli's hands still on the hem of his shirt.

"But right now, I need your help," I continue. "I need us to work together if we're going to save this place."

He doesn't interrupt. Doesn't look away.

Just listens.

"I know it means as much to you as it does to me," I say quietly. "Maybe more."

That lands.

I see it in the way his jaw relaxes, the way something shifts in his expression.

I take a breath and keep going.

"There's a show in four weeks. The Copper Ridge Fall Classic. Trail class or ranch horse division." I meet his eyes. "It won't solve everything overnight. But if we can place well, we use that to start calling Dad's old clients. The Hendersons. The Collins family. A good showing gives us credibility again. Proof we can still train."

He's silent for a long moment.

"Mae's actually considering Cole's offer," I continue. "She's got eight, maybe ten months before things get critical. This buys us time. We train the colt, compete, bring boarders back. Build the program over the next six months. But we have to start now."

"And you'll be back in Denver by then."

My stomach drops.

Actually, it's sooner than that. "Two weeks," I correct quietly. "My boss gave me three weeks. That was a week ago."

Eli goes still. "So you're already—"

"I'll ask for an extension," I say quickly. "Tell them I need more time. They'll understand."

I hope.

His expression tells me exactly what he thinks about that plan.

"I can make it work," I continue, pushing forward. "Four weeks to get the colt ready, get Addie riding him. We don't even have to win. We just have to show we're producing solid horses again. Then we—"

"And then what?" he cuts in. "You go back to Denver and we hire some stranger to keep it going?"

The question sits between us, sharp and unavoidable.

I don't have a good answer.

"I don't know yet," I admit. The honesty scrapes out of me. "I want to help. I want to save this place. But I don't know if I can just... throw away five years of work. A career I built. A life—"

"A life that wasn't here," he finishes quietly.

"Don't do that."

"I just need the truth, Hazel." He steps closer. "I need to know if you're going to disappear again."

My chest tightens. "I'm here now. I'm asking for your help instead of running."

"For four weeks."

"For as long as it takes."

"Until Denver calls." He watches me. "You haven't quit that job, have you."

It's not a question.

I look away.

"That's what I thought," he says quietly.

Silence stretches between us, thick and uncomfortable.

"You can't do this halfway," he says finally. "You can't set something in motion and then disappear. Mae needs someone who'll be here. Not someone counting down days until they can leave."

The words land harder than I expect.

"I'm trying—"

"I know you are." His voice softens slightly. "But trying isn't the same as committing."

I swallow hard.

Eli is quiet for a long moment. I can see him weighing it—my offer to help against my refusal to promise anything.

"Four weeks," he says finally. "We train the colt. Get Addie ready. You do what you came here to do."

Relief floods through me.

"But," he continues, and the word cuts sharp, "you're going to have to choose. For real this time."

"I know—"

"Do you?" He holds my gaze. "Because once we start this, once we bring clients back and get Addie competing, this ranch needs someone committed. Not someone with one foot out the door."

The weight of that settles in my chest.

"After the Fall Classic," he says. "Four weeks from now. That's when you decide. You tell me—and Mae—if you're staying or going. Face to face. No more 'maybe' or 'I'll figure it out.'"

A deadline.

He's giving me a deadline.

"Okay," I say quietly.

"Okay?"

"I'll decide. Before I leave for Denver. I promise."

He studies me like he's trying to decide if that promise means anything.

"If I say the colt's had enough, we stop," he says. "If Addie isn't ready, we don't push her. And if you decide halfway through that Denver is more important, you tell me. You don't just disappear."

"I won't."

"You did before."

The truth of that sits between us, undeniable.

"I know," I say. "And I'm sorry. But this time is different."

"Is it?"

"I'm trying to make it different."

He looks at me for a long moment. Then nods once, sharp and final, like the decision cost him something.

"We start tomorrow," he says. "Four a.m. Colt needs consistent work if we're going to make this timeline."

"I'll be there."

He turns toward the parking area, boots crunching over gravel.

At his truck, he pauses.

Looks back.

"It's not that I can't stand being around you, Hazel," he says, his voice low and stripped of its usual edge. "It's that it feels too easy when I am."

Then he climbs into his truck and drives off down the ranch road, heading toward Dawson Ranch, leaving me standing in the fading light with my heart pounding and his words settling slowly into my chest.

Four weeks.

Four weeks to prove I can do this. To save the ranch. To figure out what I actually want.

Four weeks to decide if I'm brave enough to choose.

Chapter Twenty

Hazel

I find Mae in Dad's office.

She's at the desk with the ledger open, reading glasses perched on her nose, pen tapping against the page in that absent rhythm she does when the numbers aren't adding up the way she wants.

The afternoon light slants through the window, catching dust motes and turning them gold. The room still smells like him—old leather, paper, the faint ghost of aftershave that five years hasn't managed to erase.

I knock on the doorframe even though the door's open.

Mae looks up, eyes tired but warm. "Hey, honey."

"Got a minute?" I ask, laptop tucked under my arm.

"For you? Always." She sets the pen down and leans back in the chair. It creaks—the same sound it made when Dad sat there, the same protest of old wood and older springs.

I cross to the desk and pull up the Fall Classic registration page on my laptop. "I'm ready to register. Just need the ranch account info to pay the entry fee."

Mae's expression doesn't change immediately. But something shifts behind her eyes. A hesitation. A weight.

"Sit down, Haze."

My stomach drops.

Those three words carry more than they should. I lower myself into the chair across from her, the leather cold even through my jeans.

Mae takes off her glasses and sets them carefully on top of the ledger. For a long moment, she just looks at me. Not unkind. Just... tired. The kind of tired that lives in your bones and doesn't leave.

"How much is the entry fee?" she asks quietly.

"Eight hundred dollars." I say it like it's nothing. Like it's reasonable. "For both classes—trail and ranch horse."

She nods slowly. Doesn't say anything right away.

The silence stretches.

"Mae—"

"I know this plan matters to you," she says, cutting me off gently. "I know you and Eli have been working hard. I see it. I see you out there every morning before the sun's up, putting in the hours."

"But?"

She exhales, the sound heavy. Then she reaches for the ledger and turns it toward me.

Numbers fill the page in her careful handwriting. Columns of them. Income. Expenses. Red ink in places there shouldn't be.

"We're three months behind on the grain bill," she says. "Vet expenses from last quarter are still unpaid. The fence repair we've been putting off is going to cost more the longer we wait. And the equipment—" She stops. Shakes her head. "It's breaking faster than I can fix it."

I stare at the numbers. They blur slightly.

"I can't justify eight hundred dollars for an entry fee when we're this far underwater, Haze." Her voice cracks just slightly on my name. "I want to. God, I want to. But I don't have it to give."

My throat tightens. "But this is how we save the ranch. This is the plan. We place well, we get attention, boarders come back—"

"I know," she says, and the exhaustion in her voice makes me stop. "I know what it could do. But 'could' doesn't pay the feed bill that's due next week."

I close my eyes.

This can't be happening.

"Cole called again yesterday," Mae says quietly.

My eyes snap open. "What?"

"I didn't tell you because I didn't want to worry you. Didn't want to make you feel like—" She stops. Starts again. "He's been patient. Kinder than I expected, actually. But he made it clear the offer won't stay on the table forever."

The room feels smaller suddenly. Too warm.

"How long?" I ask.

"He said he'd give me until end of summer. That's six weeks, Haze."

Six weeks.

My mind races. The Fall Classic is in four weeks. Even if we placed well, even if we got attention, we'd need months to rebuild the client base. Months we don't have.

"There has to be another way," I say, but it comes out weaker than I mean it to.

Mae reaches across the desk and covers my hand with hers. Her skin is warm. Papery. She squeezes gently.

"If you've got another solution, honey, I'm listening."

I don't answer.

Because the only solution sitting in my head is the one I can't say out loud.

The silence stretches between us, thick and uncomfortable.

Finally, Mae pulls her hand back and closes the ledger with a soft thump. "I'm sorry. I know this isn't what you wanted to hear."

"It's not your fault," I manage.

"Feels like it is."

I stand, legs unsteady, laptop clutched against my chest like a shield. "I should—I need to tell Eli."

Mae nods. "He'll understand."

Will he?

I turn toward the door, then stop. Look back.

"Mae?"

"Yeah?"

"How close are you? To saying yes to Cole."

She doesn't answer right away. When she does, her voice is so quiet I almost miss it.

"Closer than I want to be."

***

I find Eli in the north pasture, checking fence posts.

He's crouched low, hands working over a section of wire that's come loose, his hat tipped forward against the afternoon sun. His shirt is damp with sweat, dust clinging to his forearms.

He looks up when he hears me coming, squinting against the light.

"Hey," he says, straightening. "Colt looked good this morning. He's really starting to—"

"We can't afford the entry fee."

The words come out flat. Blunt. No buildup.

His expression shifts. Not surprise. Something worse. Like he was already braced for this.

"What do you mean?"

"I mean Mae can't pay it. We're too far behind on everything else. Feed bills, vet bills, repairs—" I swallow hard. "Eight hundred dollars might as well be eight thousand right now."

Eli exhales slowly through his nose. He looks away, jaw working.

The silence stretches between us. Wind rattles through the grass. A horse whinnies in the distance.

Finally, he looks back at me.

"We keep training," he says.

I blink. "What?"

"The colt." His jaw sets, stubborn. "We keep working him. Keep Addie riding. Maybe something changes. Maybe we find the money. Maybe—" He stops. Shakes his head. "I don't know. But we've got four weeks. Giving up now doesn't help anything."

"But if we can't pay—"

"Then we can't pay," he cuts in, voice harder now. "But at least we'll have done the work. At least we'll know we tried everything."

There's something in his tone that makes my chest tight. Not hope exactly. More like refusal to surrender.

"So we just... keep going?" I ask quietly.

"We keep going." He holds my gaze. "Until we can't anymore."

I want to tell him I can fix this. Want to say I have the money. But the words stick.

"Mae said Cole called again," I say instead.

Something flickers across his expression. "When?"

"Yesterday. She didn't tell us." I wrap my arms around myself even though the day is warm. "He gave her six weeks."

Eli goes still. "Six weeks."

"Yeah."

For a long moment, neither of us speaks.

The wind picks up, rattling through the grass, carrying the smell of dust and sun-baked earth. Somewhere in the distance, a horse whinnies.

"Then we've got four weeks to figure this out," Eli says finally. His voice is steady. Controlled. "Four weeks to train. To get Addie ready. To find the money or find another way."

"And if we can't?"

"Then at least Mae will know we tried." He looks at me, something fierce behind the exhaustion in his eyes. "At least she'll know we didn't just hand it over without a fight."

My throat tightens.

"Okay," I manage.

"Okay?"

"Yeah." I nod. "We keep training."

Something eases in his expression. Not relief. Just acknowledgment.

"Four a.m. tomorrow?" he asks.

"I'll be there."

He nods once, sharp and final. Then turns back to the fence.

I stand there for another moment, watching him crouch down again, hands moving over wire with practiced efficiency.

But this time it doesn't feel like dismissal.

It feels like a promise.

We're not giving up.

Not yet.

I turn and walk back toward the house, boots crunching over dry grass, throat tight with everything I can't say.

My room feels too small.

I sit on the edge of the bed, phone in hand, staring at the black screen like it might offer answers.

For a long moment, I don't move. Just sit there with the weight of the afternoon pressing down on my shoulders.

Then I unlock the phone.

Open the banking app.

The numbers load slowly, as if the phone knows what I'm about to do and wants to give me time to reconsider.

Checking Account: $1,043.27

I stare at it.

One thousand forty-three dollars and twenty-seven cents.

That's what's left after five years in Denver. Five years of rent and student loans and trying to build a life that costs more than I make. I'm not broke. But I'm not comfortable either.

Entry fee: $800.

I could do it.

Right now. I could transfer the money. Register us. Tell Mae it's handled. Tell Eli we're going.

My thumb hovers over the screen.

But if I pay it, I'll have $243 left.

Two hundred forty-three dollars.

That's not enough to cover an emergency. Not enough if my car breaks down or I need a bus ticket home—back to Denver, I mean. Not enough if something goes wrong and I need to leave fast.

My chest tightens.

If I use this money, I'm not just paying an entry fee.

I'm betting everything I have that this works.

And if it doesn't—if we compete and nothing changes, if the boarders don't come back, if Mae sells to Cole anyway—I'll be here with nothing. No cushion. No safety net. Just a choice I can't undo.

I close my eyes.

Dad's voice echoes in my head, the way it used to when I was young and couldn't decide something: *Sometimes the scariest choice is the right one, Hazelnut.*

But what if it's not?

What if I bet everything and lose?

I open my eyes and look at the number again.

$1,043.27.

Entry fee: $800.

The math is brutal.

I close the app.

Set the phone down on the bed beside me.

And sit there in the quiet, the weight of it pressing down on my chest until I can barely breathe.

We're still training. Still working toward something that might not happen.

Eli said we keep going until we can't anymore.

I could make it so we can keep going.

Right now.

But not yet.

Not today.

Maybe tomorrow. Maybe the day after. Maybe when the deadline gets close enough that there's no other choice.

Outside, the sun slips lower, painting the room in shades of gold and amber.

Eli said we keep going.

So that's what I'll do.

Even if I don't know yet what it will cost me.

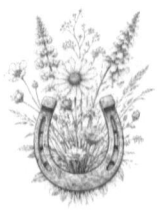

Chapter Twenty-One

Eli

The place is already loud when I get there. Music spills out through the open doors, boots thudding against wood, laughter rising and falling in loose waves. The air smells like beer and dust and something fried that's been sitting too long under heat lamps. Familiar. Easy. The kind of place where nobody expects anything from you except to show up and not spill your drink.

I stand just inside the doorway long enough to take it in. Shae's already laughing with someone near the bar. Addie's halfway through a story, animated and bright. Chace leans in like he's waiting for the punchline.

Hazel's there too, already part of the noise and movement.

She looks lighter. Shoulders looser than I've seen them since she got back. Hair down, dress that catches when she moves, boots I've seen a hundred times that suddenly look different on her. Like she belongs in a room full of people again.

That's the problem.

For a second, I let myself look.

Her dress is short enough to skim the tops of her thighs, showing off legs that are all muscle and smooth skin. The kind of legs I want under my hands, hooked over my hips, locked around my waist. Boots I've seen a hundred times suddenly look dangerous on her—scuffed leather over strong calves, like she could pin me back with just a step forward and I'd let her.

The fabric clings when she moves, tracing the curve of her hips, the line of her waist. It makes me imagine sliding my palm over it, feeling her warmth through the cloth, pushing it higher just to see how far she'd let me go before she told me to stop—or dragged me closer instead.

Her hair is loose down her back, dark against the bare line of her shoulders, brushing over her spine when she turns. I want to gather it in my fist, tilt her head back, see her eyes when I say her name. I want to feel the shiver that runs through her when my mouth finds the place where her neck meets her shoulder.

Heat hits hard and fast, low and insistent. My fingers twitch with the urge to touch her waist, her hips, the inside of her thigh where the dress doesn't quite cover. I want to back her up against a wall, close the space between us until all I can feel is her body pressed into mine, until the rest of the room disappears and there's nothing left but her breath against my mouth.

Fuck. I need to get it together.

It's been two days since we found out we can't afford the entry fee. Two days of working that colt at four a.m., being professional and careful and so goddamn polite it makes my teeth ache. Two days of her talking about plans and possibilities—restoring the ranch, training and boarding, everything that could be again—without ever promising she'll stay to see it through.

I move farther into the room, nodding at a couple of familiar faces. Someone hands me a beer without asking. I take it, more for something to do with my hands than because I want it.

The music shifts, a familiar song pulling a few people toward the floor.

Hazel laughs at something Addie says, her head tipping back just slightly, and the sound hits harder than it should. It always has. There was a time when that laugh felt like a promise. Like something I could count on.

Now it just reminds me how much work it took to stop wanting it.

I keep my distance. Not pointed. Just careful. I don't ignore her. I don't hover either. When our eyes meet, I lift my bottle in brief acknowledgment and look away before the moment can turn into something else.

This is supposed to be light. That was the point of coming. Noise. Distraction. A couple of hours where nothing matters beyond the next song or the next round.

It works. Mostly.

Still, my attention keeps pulling back to Hazel. The way she leans into the table when someone bumps it. The way she doesn't check her phone. The way she fits here without trying.

I tell myself that doesn't mean anything. That people can belong in places they don't intend to stay.

I take a drink and look back toward the dance floor, grounding myself in the noise and the movement and the simple fact that tonight doesn't ask me to decide anything.

Chace finds me near the edge of the room, beer already half gone, grin firmly in place like nothing in the world has ever stuck to him for long. He bumps my shoulder with his.

"You're wound too tight," he says, like he's commenting on the weather.

I don't answer. I don't need to. I just look at him.

Chace takes that in stride. He always does. "I mean it," he adds, lowering his voice just enough to pretend this is private. "She's trying."

My pulse skips. I keep my eyes on the dance floor, on the way Hazel shifts her weight with the music, how she laughs when Shae elbows her too hard.

"Trying isn't the same as staying," I say.

Chace hums, thoughtful in a way that doesn't quite match the grin still tugging at his mouth. "No," he agrees. "But it's also not nothing."

I take a slow drink. The beer tastes flat. I let the silence stretch, let Chace feel it instead of filling it for me. That's always been our balance. Chace talks. I listen. Decide later.

"You don't have to let her back in like that," he says, softer now. "I get why you're guarded. I really do." He tips his head toward Hazel without looking directly at her. "Just saying—keeping your distance might feel safer, but you're not even in the game. And I've never known you to sit on the sidelines. You didn't before. Not with her."

I exhale through my nose.

Friendship—the word doesn't get said, but it's there. The years Hazel and I spent just being that, before it ever got complicated. Before it turned into something... more.

Maybe that's the risk now. Not falling back into love, losing the chance to stand beside her at all.

Can I separate the two?

Chace straightens, decision already made for him. "Anyway," he says, the grin sliding back into place like armor. "I'm not built for brooding."

With that, he drains the rest of his beer, sets the bottle down wherever there's space, and heads for the dance floor without hesitation. He doesn't scan the room. Doesn't second-guess. Just steps into the noise like it belongs to him.

Someone shouts his name. Addie groans when she spots him coming. Chace grins wider, already moving to the beat, boots light, shoulders loose, laughing like tonight is exactly what it's supposed to be.

I watch him go, the ease of it catching in my chest.

Letting go has never been Chace's problem.

I turn my attention back to the room. To Hazel.

She's dancing now. Not carefully. Not for show. Just moving because the music's good and her body remembers how. Her hair swings across her shoulders. Sweat gleams at the back of her neck. She's laughing at something Addie says, breathless and flushed, and I can't look away.

She looks alive. The way I remember from before she left. Before everything got complicated.

And watching her like this—easy in her own skin, fitting back into this life—makes the ache in my chest sharper than it's been in years.

The music shifts. Faster. She spins with Addie, both of them laughing, and I grip my beer harder.

That's when some guy cuts in. Someone I vaguely recognize from town—doesn't matter who. His hand catches her waist, slides lower to her hip, and she laughs, tipping her head back.

It's nothing. Friendly. The kind of thing that happens a hundred times on a dance floor.

She's not mine. Never really was. Won't be in a few weeks when she goes back to Denver.

My jaw locks anyway.

Knowing that doesn't stop the heat that flares when his hand lingers.

I grip my beer hard enough the glass might crack.

Then her eyes find mine across the room.

She goes still. Just for a second. Like she's been caught.

Or like she was looking for me.

Something passes between us. Electric. Unmistakable.

The guy says something. She nods but doesn't look at him. She's watching me watch her, and the air between us feels charged even with twenty feet and a dance floor in the way.

I don't look away.

Neither does she.

My pulse pounds harder than the music warrants.

Then someone pulls her into another spin and the moment breaks.

But when I look back, she's still watching me over her shoulder.

Chace's voice echoes in my head: *You're not in the game. I've never known you to sit on the sidelines.*

Fuck it. He's right.

Five years I've spent convincing myself I'm fine with absence. Fine with the distance. Fine with wanting someone I can't have.

And maybe in a few weeks I'll have to go back to that.

But tonight—

Tonight I'm done pretending.

I set my beer down.

She's on the dance floor, breathless and flushed, laughing. I start across the room.

The crowd shifts. Bodies move between us. But her eyes find mine through the noise.

She goes still.

I don't look away. Don't slow down. Just keep moving toward her.

The music pounds. People brush past. But the space between us narrows with every step.

When I reach the edge of the dance floor, I stop.

She's watching me, chest rising and falling from dancing, waiting.

I hold out my hand.

"Dance with me."

For a second, she doesn't move. Just looks at my hand, then my face. Like she's not sure she heard me right.

Then she smiles.

It's not the careful smile from earlier. Not the one she uses to cover hurt. This one is real, breaking across her face slow and surprised, and something in my chest cracks wide open.

"You sure about that?" she asks, eyes bright. "You're a terrible dancer."

The lightness in her voice makes me want to pull her close right now. Skip the dancing entirely.

"That right?"

"I've seen the evidence." She's grinning now. "Multiple times."

"That was—"

"Three separate occasions," she cuts in. "And you stepped on my boots. Repeatedly."

"You didn't move."

"Because you told me not to."

I huff a laugh. "So is that a no?"

"No." She reaches for my hand, still smiling. "That's a yes."

Her fingers slip into mine, warm and slightly damp from dancing, and the feel of her hand in mine after five years hits harder than it should. I pull her closer, my other hand finding her waist—

"Well, well."

Cole's voice cuts through the moment like a knife.

Hazel's hand tightens in mine before she pulls away. We both turn.

"Hazel," he says, nodding. Then his gaze slides to me, amused. "Dawson. Some habits die hard, huh?"

I step forward. "You should keep moving."

Cole ignores me, attention settling back on Hazel. "Mae give any more thought to my offer?"

The question lands exactly how he means it to. Public. Direct.

Hazel's voice is tight. "When Mae wants to discuss business, she'll call you."

"Of course." Cole shrugs, easy. "Just seems like the kind of decision that shouldn't wait too long. Market being what it is." His smile doesn't reach his eyes. "Hate to see her wait until there's no choice left."

I step closer. "She said no."

Cole finally looks at me, amused. "Did she? Or is that you deciding for her?"

"Back off, Cole."

"I'm having a conversation." Cole's tone stays pleasant. Reasonable. "About business. Which, last I checked, doesn't concern the hired help."

That does it.

The words hit like a slap. *Hired help.* Like I'm nothing. Like five years of holding that ranch together means nothing.

My hands curl into fists. I step forward, anger flashing hot and immediate.

Hazel reaches for my arm but I'm already moving.

Chace is there before I can do something I'll regret.

He wedges himself between us, one hand out, firm but controlled. "Alright," he says, voice steady. "That's enough."

Cole chuckles softly. "Touchy."

"Yeah," Chace says, not looking at him. "And you're done."

He turns to me, lowers his voice. "Not worth it."

My chest is tight, every muscle coiled. I don't look away from Cole.

Chace leans in closer. "Let's call it a night."

The silence stretches.

Cole takes a step back, satisfied. He looks at Hazel one more time. "Offer stands, Hazel. For now."

Then to me, still smiling: "Enjoy the rest of your night, Dawson."

He walks away like he's already won.

My jaw aches from clenching it so hard.

"Come on," Chace says quietly. "Let's get some air."

Outside, the cool night hits my face. The noise from the bar fades behind us, replaced by the sound of gravel crunching under boots.

Shae's already heading for her car, phone out, clearly done with the night. Addie touches Hazel's arm, says something quiet. Hazel nods but doesn't look convinced of whatever Addie just said.

My hands are still fists. The adrenaline hasn't faded. If anything, it's worse out here in the quiet.

Hired help.

Like I don't bleed for that ranch every goddamn day.

Hazel's standing near Shae's car, arms wrapped around herself. Her expression is tight. Angry. But there's something else underneath it. Embarrassment, maybe. Or fear.

Cole just made it public. Made his offer known. Everyone in there heard him talk about Mae's situation, about him trying to buy the ranch. About the fact that Mae might need to sell.

About me being nothing but an employee.

I look at her across the gravel lot.

She looks back.

For a second, neither of us moves.

Then I'm walking toward her.

I stop a few feet away. "Ride with me."

I'm not asking.

She looks at me for a long moment, like she's trying to read something in my face.

Then she nods. "Yeah."

I walk to my truck, open the passenger door, and step back giving her access. She climbs in without another word. I close the door, walk around and get in.

We pull out of the lot in silence.

But it's not empty.

It's full of everything that almost happened back there. Me crossing that room. Her saying yes. The moment Cole stole before her hand could stay in mine.

And underneath it all—the question neither of us has answered.

What the hell are we doing?

I grip the steering wheel and drive.

Chapter Twenty-Two

Hazel

The truck pulls out of the lot in silence. Not the comfortable kind. This one sits between us, tight and charged.

I should have stayed home tonight.

The thought hits somewhere between the bar's fading lights and the first stretch of empty road. Should have known Cole would show up. Should have seen it coming. Should have protected that moment better somehow.

But I didn't.

Eli crossed the room. Asked me to dance. And for one perfect second, his hand was in mine and everything else disappeared.

Then Cole showed up and turned everything sharp and public and humiliating.

And now I'm in Eli's truck instead of Shae's car, and the silence between us is so heavy I can barely breathe through it.

I feel it in the way Eli grips the steering wheel. One hand loose, the other firm. Knuckles pale in the passing glow of the bar lights before the road darkens and the world narrows to headlights and dust.

The music from inside still echoes faintly in my ears. Boots. Laughter. The hum of something that had felt good just minutes ago. Now the night feels different. Thinner. Exposed.

I glance at him from the corner of my eye.

His jaw is set, gaze locked on the road ahead like it might offer instructions. He hasn't said a word since we got in. Not when he opened my door. Not when I buckled in. Not even when the tires crunched over gravel and pulled us away from the noise.

He's holding everything tight. The bar. Cole. Chace stepping in before Eli could throw the first punch.

I shift in my seat, the leather warm against my thighs. The silence stretches. Presses.

This won't ease on its own. I could let it sit. Let the weight of it ride all the way back to the ranch, thick and unresolved.

But I don't want that.

We're maybe five minutes out when I finally speak.

The gravel hums under the tires. Windows cracked just enough to let the night in. Music from the dance still rings in my ears—fiddle and boots and laughter lingering like warmth.

"You know," I say, tipping my head toward him, "I think the town should issue a warning before letting you on the dance floor."

He shoots me a look, one brow lifting. "Oh yeah?"

"Absolutely," I say. "Danger to nearby toes. Severe lack of rhythm. Possible emotional distress."

A corner of his mouth twitches. "That right."

"Mm-hmm. I watched three women flee in fear when you came on the dance floor."

He snorts, then slows the truck. "You got a real imagination."

"I'm generous like that."

He doesn't answer. Just eases the truck onto the shoulder where the road widens, kills the engine, and pops his door open. Before I can ask what he's doing, he's out, circling around to my side. He opens my door and holds out his hand.

"Come on."

I look at his hand, then his face. There's something different in his expression now. Lighter. Almost playful.

"Eli."

"Hazel." He says it back like a challenge, mouth twitching at the corner.

"That tone never ends well for me."

"Trust me." His hand is still out, waiting.

I take his hand. He leads me around back, hops up into the bed of the truck in one easy motion, then turns and offers his hand again. I climb up, laughing when he tugs me closer than necessary.

He leans in, voice low. "Gonna show you exactly how bad I am."

The radio crackles to life, country spilling out into the open night. We stand there, framed by dark fields and a sky thick with stars. He takes my hand, the other settling at my waist, and starts to move.

I laugh. "Eli. You're proving my point."

He rolls his eyes. "You're the one counting steps."

"I'm observing."

"Uh-huh."

He tries a spin. It goes crooked. I step on his boot. We both laugh, the sound loose and easy, the way it used to be.

"Careful," I say. "You'll pull something."

"Worth it," he says, grinning.

The song shifts. Slower. Softer. Something about long roads and coming home.

We're still moving, but the playfulness bleeds away with the tempo. His hand slides from my waist to my hip, more instinct than intention, and he pulls me in.

Closer than before.

The laughter fades. Not gone. Just quieter. Like we both feel the moment changing and don't want to break it with sound.

The night feels closer suddenly. The air warmer.

My pulse picks up.

This. This is what I forgot. Not just the dancing or the closeness. But this specific feeling—being held by him. The way my body remembers his before my mind catches up. How natural it feels to be here, in his arms, like no time passed at all.

Like I never left.

The thought should scare me. It doesn't.

He rests his forehead near my temple, humming the tune under his breath, the sound vibrating low and steady. His thumb moves, a small, absent stroke along my hip, back and forth, back and forth.

I swallow.

We sway. Barely dancing now. Just breathing in time. His chest is solid against mine. The way his hand fits there makes my skin buzz.

I tip my head back to look at him.

His eyes drop to my mouth, then lift again.

The air between us feels electric. Charged. Like one wrong move could break whatever this is.

My hand slides up his chest, stopping just below his collarbone. I feel the beat there. Strong. Certain. Faster than it should be.

He's not breathing steady either.

"Hazel," he says, voice rough. Not a question. Not quite a warning. Just my name, like he's testing it on his tongue.

The space between us thins.

I should step back. Give us both room to think. To remember all the reasons this is complicated.

But I don't want to.

His hand tightens on my hip. Anchoring.

His head dips. Mine tilts.

I can feel his breath against my mouth. Warm. Close.

My eyes start to close—

Headlights flare down the road.

A pickup roars past, engine loud, dust kicking up in its wake. The moment snaps clean in two.

He steps back like he's been burned, breath leaving him in a rush.

"Guess I win," he says. "Not a horrible dancer."

I smile, heat still humming under my skin. "I'll give you... improved."

He hops down, offers his hand again. I take it. When we slide back into the cab, the radio still plays, softer now, like it knows.

We drive the rest of the way in easy quiet. But the space between us feels different.

The truck rolls to a stop in front of the house, headlights washing over the porch rail and the worn steps. Gravel crunches once more as he cuts the engine, the night settling in around us.

He's out before I have time to unbuckle, already moving around the hood. He opens my door and holds out his hand like it's second nature.

I take it.

The ground is cool beneath my boots. We walk towards the steps together, close enough that I can feel the heat of him at my side, close enough that neither of us comments on it. The house looms quiet, porch light glowing soft and familiar.

At the bottom step, he slows.

"I shouldn't have almost lost it back there," he says. His voice is low, scraped raw around the edges. "With Cole."

I turn toward him. Really look at him now. The tension still coiled in his shoulders, restraint holding him together.

"It's okay," I say. "Cole's had it coming for a long time."

That earns a breath of a laugh. Something loosens.

We climb the steps. The porch boards creak beneath our weight, a sound I've known my whole life. He stops near the door, hands sliding into his pockets like he's giving himself something to do with them.

For a second, neither of us moves.

I shift, needing air. "Next time we're out dancing," I say, lighter than I feel, "we're definitely working on those moves."

He nods once, something softening in his expression. "Next time."

He steps back, nods again like that's the end of it, and turns away.

He makes it two steps.

"Fuck it," he mutters to himself.

I barely have time to register the words before he's back—boots thudding against the porch, hands already on me, decisive and sure. He grabs my face, fingers warm and familiar along my jaw, and kisses me hard.

Not careful. Not slow.

The kiss lands with force, all heat and muscle memory, like something that's been held back too long. I gasp into it, my back hitting the door as he presses in, solid and overwhelming. His mouth moves against mine like he remembers exactly how. Like he never forgot.

My hands come up on instinct, clutching his shirt, pulling him closer. The night tilts. My pulse roars in my ears. Everything sharpens—the scrape of his stubble against my skin, the heat of his body, the way his grip tightens like he's anchoring himself.

His kiss deepens, hungry and sure, and for a breathless moment the world narrows to this porch, this body, this familiar gravity snapping back into place.

Then he pulls back.

His forehead rests against mine, breath heavy, hands still framing my face like letting go would be a mistake.

"I just needed to know," he says, voice rough and quiet, "that you're still there."

Then he drops his hands.

Steps back.

Turns and walks off the porch without looking back, boots hitting gravel, the sound fading into the dark.

I don't move.

My lips burn. My heart is pounding hard enough I can feel it everywhere. I stare after him, breath coming uneven, the night suddenly too quiet around me.

I press my palm flat against the door behind me, grounding myself, and swallow.

Chapter Twenty-Three

Eli

I shouldn't have fucking kissed her.

The thought lands the second I wake up, sharp and unwelcome, like it's been waiting for me to open my eyes.

Because I know how this goes.

Five years ago, I let myself touch her. Thought it meant something.

The next morning, she was gone.

I sit up before the memory can dig in deeper, boots already halfway on, because staying still gives it room.

The ranch is quiet in that early-morning way that feels earned. No music. No voices. Just the low creak of boards and the distant shuffle of horses shifting in their stalls. I like it better like this. Before people. Before thoughts.

I head straight for the trailers.

They've been sitting too long. Dust filmed thick over the metal, tires half a breath from flat. The sight of them twists something in my chest I don't have time to examine. We used to haul out all the time. Used to circle dates on the calendar instead of crossing them off.

That was before everything else took priority.

I grab the hose and start checking pressure, crouched low, hands already dirty. The air smells like dust and old leather. Familiar. Solid. This I can fix.

We'll need these soon enough. Fall Classic or something before. Eyes bring interest, and interest brings boarders, and boarders keep the ranch breathing. We screw this up and it's another door quietly closing. Ranch first. Always.

I move through the tack room methodically, laying everything out the way I remember it being done. Saddles, bridles, clean pads—anything frayed gets set aside. Anything questionable gets replaced. No shortcuts.

That's when her voice slips in where it doesn't belong.

Not real—not yet—just memory.

Hazel laughing in the truck. Hazel teasing me about my dancing. Hazel pressed against me on the porch, warm and sure, like nothing had ever ended.

Like five years didn't happen.

My stomach drops.

She didn't say she was staying.

I tighten a cinch strap until my hands ache, then loosen it a notch because too tight breaks things just as fast as too loose. The lesson sticks. Always has.

I don't ask for what won't be offered.

That's the rule now.

The door creaks behind me and I don't look up. I already know who it is. I can feel the shift in the air, the way the space fills without sound.

My hands still on the bridle.

Last night rushes back—her mouth under mine, the way she gasped into the kiss, how her body felt pressed against the door.

But underneath that is older memory. Stronger. The kind that lives in your hands and won't let go.

The weight of her. The sounds she made. The way she fit against me.

I force my hands to keep moving.

"You're up early," Hazel says.

Neutral. Easy. Like last night didn't happen the way it did.

"Plenty to do," I answer, keeping my focus on the tack in front of me.

I still haven't looked at her. Can't. Not yet.

Because if I look at her now, I'll remember too much. And if I remember, I'll want.

I already know how that story ends.

She steps further in. I hear it in the soft scuff of her boots, the pause she takes like she's reading the room. She's good at that. Always was.

"Looks like you're getting ready to haul," she says.

"Just checking gear."

"Making sure it's ready?"

I nod once. Still not looking at her.

Silence stretches. Not awkward. Charged. The kind that presses instead of fades.

"I was going to start working the colt," she says finally. Practical. On task. Like this is just another morning.

"I've got it," I say, too quick.

Her breath changes. Small thing. But I catch it.

"I didn't say you didn't," she replies.

I glance up then. She's standing near the doorway, arms crossed, expression calm but watchful. Not defensive. Not retreating.

The old rhythm hums between us, immediate and dangerous.

"Help me load the tack," I say.

It's not an invitation. It's a decision.

She doesn't hesitate. Just steps forward and grabs the other end of the trunk like she's always known where to stand. We lift together, muscle memory slotting into place like it never left.

That's what scares me.

We work without talking for a few minutes, moving around each other with practiced ease. She brushes past me reaching for a bridle, close enough I catch the scent of her—soap and something else I remember from last night when she was pressed against me.

My jaw tightens.

I step to the side, putting distance between us. Not enough. Never enough in a space this small.

She knows where everything goes. Knows what I'll check twice. Knows which straps I'll trust and which ones I won't.

And I know how her mouth tastes. How her hands feel fisted in my shirt.

I shouldn't know that again. Shouldn't want to know it again.

But I do.

"You think the weather's going to hold?" she asks.

I glance outside. The sky's already starting to bruise at the edges, clouds stacked higher than they should be this early.

"Forecast says it will," I say.

She hums, unconvinced. "It's shifting faster than they said."

I don't respond. I don't want to give the worry more space than it already has.

We finish loading and step back, taking in the trailer together. It looks right. Ready. The sight settles something in me I hadn't realized was off.

A gust of wind hits the barn hard enough to rattle the loose tin along the roof. Somewhere down the line, a gate slams. A horse squeals, sharp and high, followed by the hollow bang of metal.

Hazel turns her head toward the sound at the same time I do.

"That's not good," she says.

I'm already moving. "The pasture gate."

The first drops of rain hit the dirt as we reach the barn doors, big and cold, leaving dark spots that spread fast. The air shifts, heavy and electric.

Then I see him.

The colt. Out in the pasture, head high, already agitated. The gate swings wide behind him, one hinge torn loose, chain dangling.

"Shit," I breathe.

"He's loose," Hazel says, already moving.

The rain doesn't ease in. It comes down hard.

Fat drops turn the dirt slick in seconds, the air cooling fast. Wind whips through the yard, and thunder cracks overhead like a gunshot.

The colt bolts.

He runs the fence line, panicked, whites of his eyes flashing. Another crack of thunder and he spins, hooves sliding in the mud.

"He's going to hurt himself," Hazel shouts over the wind.

"I know."

We break into a run, boots skidding as mud grabs at the soles. Rain slants sideways now, stinging my face, plastering my shirt to my back. The colt is at the far end of the pasture, spinning in tight circles, fear taking over.

"Spread out," I call to Hazel. "We need to corner him toward the gate."

She nods, already angling left. No hesitation. Just moving.

The rain pounds harder. Wind screams. The colt tosses his head, nostrils flaring, trying to decide which way to run.

"Easy," I say, voice low and steady despite the chaos. "Easy, boy."

He doesn't believe me.

He lunges right, toward the fence. I cut him off, arms wide. He spins back toward Hazel.

She stands her ground, calm, hands out. "Hey. I've got you."

The colt dances in place, trapped between us, sides heaving.

"Slow," I say to Hazel. "We move together."

We close in, step by step. The colt's ears flick back and forth, calculating. Thunder cracks again and he rears, forelegs striking air.

"Shit—"

Hazel moves without thinking, closing the distance fast, and grabs for the halter still on his head. The lead rope dangles, soaked and heavy. She catches it.

The colt jerks hard, nearly pulling her off her feet.

I lunge forward, grabbing on beside her, both of us hauling back with everything we've got.

"We need to move," I shout over the wind. "Now."

"The barn's too far," Hazel yells back. "He won't make it."

She's right. The barn is a hundred yards across open ground. He's already panicking. If we try to force him that far in this storm, he'll fight us the whole way. Could hurt himself. Could hurt us.

I scan fast.

The equipment shed. Thirty yards. Enclosed. Solid.

"There," I point. "The shed."

"Can we get him in?"

"We don't have a choice."

The colt surges again, pulling hard against both of us. My boots slide in the mud. Rain pours down, cold and relentless.

"I need you," I say, not looking at her. Not soft. Not emotional. Just fact.

"I'm here," she answers, immediate.

We move together, bodies angled in, both pulling, both fighting to keep control as the colt tries to bolt. Mud sucks at my boots. Rain blinds me. Thunder keeps cracking overhead, each one making the colt jerk harder.

Thirty yards feels like thirty miles.

But we make it.

I yank the shed door open, wind tearing at it, and haul the colt inside with Hazel right there beside me, both of us soaked through, both of us moving on instinct.

The door slams shut behind us, cutting off the worst of the storm.

The space is tight. Close. The air heavy with damp hay and sweat and rain.

The colt finally stills, sides heaving, fear giving way to confusion.

I suck in a breath I didn't realize I was holding.

And then I make the mistake of looking at her.

Hazel's hair is plastered to her neck, her shirt clinging to her shoulders, outlining every curve. Water drips from her jaw. Mud streaks her arms. She's breathing hard, chest rising and falling.

Fuck.

I've seen her like this before. Breathless. Flushed.

My jaw tightens. I look away fast.

Because we're alone. In a space barely big enough for the three of us. Storm raging outside. Adrenaline still pumping from the run, from fighting the colt, from being this close.

"That was close," she says, voice slightly breathless.

I nod, not trusting myself to speak.

The shed creaks around us as the storm keeps throwing itself against the walls, rain rattling the roof. The colt shifts, calmer now, finally registering that he's safe.

But I'm not calm.

Because she's standing three feet away, soaked and muddy and breathing hard, and my hands remember exactly how she feels.

"Eli," she says quietly.

I make the mistake of looking at her again.

Her eyes are on mine. Dark. Searching.

"Yeah," I manage.

"About last night—"

"Don't," I cut her off. Too fast. Too sharp.

Because if we talk about the kiss, we'll have to talk about what comes after.

Her mouth closes. Something flickers across her face.

The air between us feels electric. Charged.

Not from the storm.

From us.

I take a step back, hitting the wall. Putting distance where it should be.

Even though every part of me wants to move forward instead.

"We should wait for the rain to ease," I say, voice rough.

She nods slowly. Doesn't look away.

The shed feels smaller by the second.

The colt lowers his head at last, breath slowing, fear bleeding out of him in uneven huffs.

I wish I could do the same.

The storm doesn't sound like it's letting up anytime soon.

I tell myself we'll wait it out. That this is just weather. Just work. Just another crisis.

That I can stand here three feet from her without wanting to close the distance.

That the kiss was a mistake I won't repeat.

But standing here, boxed in by rain and walls and memory—her soaked clothes clinging to her body, her eyes still on mine—I know I'm lying to myself.

I've already crossed the line I spent five years drawing in the dirt.

And the worst part is—I'd do it again.

I'd kiss her again. Touch her again.

Even knowing exactly how this story ends.

That's how fucked I am.

Chapter Twenty-Four

Hazel

The rain is louder in here.

It hammers the metal roof in uneven bursts, a sharp, hollow sound that fills the space and leaves nowhere for silence to hide. Wind rattles the walls. Something loose bangs once, then again, metal on metal, the rhythm wrong and jarring.

The shed is smaller than it looked from the outside.

Hay bales stack close along one wall, the air thick with damp and dust and the warm, animal smell of the colt pressed between us. He breathes hard, nostrils flaring, every exhale loud in the tight space. I can feel it in my chest, like my own lungs are trying to match his.

I'm suddenly aware of everything.

Mud caked on my jeans. Rain-soaked shirt plastered to my skin, cold now that we've stopped moving. My hair dripping down my back. The burn in my arms from hauling the colt through the storm.

And the way my pulse is beating low and fast—not from the run anymore, but from how close Eli is standing now that we've stopped moving.

Heat pools low in my stomach, having nothing to do with the temperature in here.

Too close.

He hasn't said a word.

That's how I know something's different.

Eli is quiet when he's thinking, but this is something else. This is restraint. His body is still, shoulders tight, like he's holding himself in place by force. I don't look at him right away, but I don't need to. I can feel him there. Solid. Familiar. A presence that fills the space whether I invite it or not.

Five minutes ago, we were moving. Solving. Reacting.

Now we're just... here.

The awareness settles in slow and heavy. This isn't accidental. This isn't the storm's fault. This is what happens when we stop pretending we don't feel it.

My hand tightens on the lead without me meaning to.

And then the memory hits.

The porch. The rough scrape of his stubble against my skin. The way his hands framed my face like he needed to anchor himself there. The kiss wasn't careful. It wasn't curious. It landed hard, like something he'd been holding back too long.

Like something he didn't trust himself with.

My mouth still remembers it. The pressure. The certainty. The way he pulled back just enough to breathe before saying the thing that's been sitting under my skin ever since.

I just needed to know that you're still there.

My throat tightens.

I don't know what scares me more—that he needed to know, or that the answer was yes without me having to think about it.

The colt shifts, bumping my hip lightly, grounding me back in the present. I murmur to him without looking away from the space in front of me, voice low and steady. It's easier to focus on him. On something that needs calm instead of clarity.

Eli shifts his weight beside me.

The smallest movement. Barely anything.

But my pulse jumps anyway.

The air feels charged now, different from the chaos outside. Thicker. Waiting. Like the moment right before something breaks, or changes, or can't be undone.

And we're both standing perfectly still, pretending we don't feel it.

The colt shifts again, hooves scuffing softly against the dirt floor. I keep my hand steady on the lead, rubbing a slow circle at his cheek until his breathing evens out.

"He's settling," I say. "That first panic spike burned off fast."

Eli nods once. "He does that."

Short. Controlled.

The rain keeps pounding the roof, a steady roar that turns the shed into its own small world. Wind rattles the door hard enough to make the hinges groan. I glance toward it, then back to the colt.

"We can't leave him in here all night," I say. "Once the worst of it passes, he should go back to his stall."

"Agreed."

Another nod. Still not looking at me.

I swallow and shift my stance, boots scraping hay. "If the temperature drops like this, he'll be tight tomorrow. We'll need to warm him up longer."

"We'll adjust," Eli says. "No shortcuts."

Of course.

"How long do you think the storm'll last?" I ask.

"Hour. Maybe two."

"And the pasture gate?"

"I'll check it once this lets up."

He glances at the roof instead of at me.

I nod, even though he can't see it. "If the wind keeps up, the west fence might need a walk-through too."

"I know."

Clipped. Efficient. Nothing wasted.

Silence fills the shed again, thick and heavy. The colt lowers his head, finally calm, and I rest my forehead briefly against his neck, breathing him in. Hay. Warmth. Familiar things.

I straighten and risk a look at Eli.

He's turned slightly away from me now, hands on his hips, gaze fixed on the far wall like it's offering answers. He won't look at me for more than a second at a time. When he does, it's quick. Careful. Like eye contact might knock something loose he can't afford to feel.

Five minutes ago, he was hauling a panicked horse through a storm without thinking twice.

Now he won't meet my eyes.

I know why.

This is the Eli who locks everything down because wanting more feels dangerous. The Eli who believes if he keeps moving, keeps planning, keeps his hands busy, the past won't catch up to him.

The Eli who learned, the hard way, what happens when he lets himself want something without guarantees.

I tighten my grip on the lead, grounding myself, and focus back on the colt. On the rain. On the work.

Anything but the memory pressing in from the edges. The morning light years ago. The quiet after. The way leaving felt like the only way to breathe and also like the worst thing I've ever done.

"We should remove his halter," I say, breaking the silence. "He's soaked through."

Eli nods. "Yeah. Good call."

It's the first thing he's said that sounds like agreement instead of control.

The storm rages on outside, rain pounding, wind screaming, time stretching thin. And we stand here, shoulder to shoulder without touching, talking about horses and weather and equipment like none of the rest of it exists.

Like this isn't avoidance.

Like we don't both know exactly what's sitting between us, waiting for one of us to stop pretending.

Eli reaches for the halter at the same time I do, our hands brushing for half a second before he pulls back like he's been burned.

"I've got it," he says.

The words are sharp. Unnecessary.

I still my hand but don't step away. "I wasn't taking it from you."

"I know," he says, already turning away, like that settles it.

Something tightens low in my chest.

"You don't have to shut me out every time we work together," I say. Calm. Measured. "I can handle a halter without everything turning into a standoff."

He stops moving.

Slowly, he turns back to face me.

"That's not what this is," he says.

"Then what is it?" I ask.

The colt shifts between us, sensing the change, and I step closer to his shoulder, narrowing the space without meaning to. Eli mirrors it automatically, muscle memory kicking in, both of us angling in like we always used to.

Too close now.

"Don't," he says quietly.

"Don't what?" I ask, lifting my chin. "Work?"

His jaw tightens. "Don't pretend you don't know."

I feel heat rise in my neck, not embarrassment. Anger. Old and familiar.

"I'm not pretending," I say. "I'm standing here."

"That's the problem," he snaps.

The words crack the air between us.

I blink. "Excuse me?"

"You show up," he says, voice low but tight, "like you never left. Like nothing changed. And you expect me to just—" He cuts himself off, dragging a hand through his wet hair. "You expect me to pretend this is fine."

"I never asked you to pretend," I shoot back.

"No," he says. "You just walked away and let me do it all for you."

The argument ignites all at once, like it's been waiting for oxygen.

"I didn't walk away from you," I say, the words sharp now, too fast to soften. "I walked away from everything."

"You walked away without saying a damn thing," he fires back. "One morning you were there, and the next—" He laughs once, humorless. "Nothing. No explanation. No call. No goodbye."

My chest tightens. "You didn't ask me to stay."

The words land hard.

His eyes flash. "Because I shouldn't have had to."

I take a step closer before I can stop myself. "You don't get to rewrite that. You never said it out loud. You never told me you wanted me to choose you."

My pulse roars in my ears. The shed feels smaller, the walls pressing in as the rain hammers harder overhead.

"You don't know what it felt like," I continue, voice rising despite myself. "To wake up every day and feel like the ground had dropped out from under me. To breathe and still feel like I was suffocating."

He steps closer too now, matching me, the space between us shrinking to inches. "I was there."

"No," I snap. "You were solid. You were rooted. You had direction. I had grief wrapped around my throat and no idea who I was without my dad."

His mouth opens, then closes.

I don't stop.

"Staying felt like choosing one life forever," I say, the words spilling now, sharp and shaking. "And I was twenty-two and drowning. Everything felt permanent and I was breaking. You felt like a cage because you were steady when I wasn't."

The second the word leaves my mouth, I regret it.

His face hardens. Something shutters behind his eyes, like I just confirmed every fear he's been carrying for five years.

"A cage," he repeats quietly. Flatly.

I swallow. "That's not—"

"That's exactly what you meant," he says. "You fucked me and left because staying felt like a trap."

There it is. After all these weeks, he's finally said it. The big issue between us. The thing that broke us apart.

"That is not what happened."

"Then tell me what did," he demands, voice rising now, echoing off the metal walls. "Because from where I was standing, you took everything I had to give and disappeared."

My throat burns.

I remember the morning light through the window. The way his arm had been heavy and warm across my waist. The way panic had crawled up my spine the second I woke up and realized how much that moment meant.

How much it could cost me. How much it changed things.

"I was young," I say, quieter now but no less firm. "And scared. And grieving. And you felt like my forever when I couldn't even survive the day. I wanted you so badly it terrified me."

The silence that follows is thick and volatile.

His eyes close. Just for a second.

When they open, the restraint is gone.

"I'm done pretending," he breathes. "That I still don't want you. That I ever fucking stopped."

He lurches forward, his hand fists in my wet shirt and pulls before I can even think.

His mouth claims mine with force, with memory, with everything he's been holding back since the moment he walked away from me on that porch. I gasp into it, the sound swallowed by him as he presses closer, body solid and unyielding.

It feels like coming home.

And like lighting a match.

My back hits the stacked hay, rough against my shoulders. His hands are on me immediately—one gripping my hip hard enough to bruise, the other sliding up my ribs, dragging my wet shirt with it.

I arch into him without thinking. Need it. Need his hands on my skin, not just through fabric.

He makes a sound low in his throat when I pull at his shirt, yanking it up. My palms find bare skin—stomach, ribs, the hard plane of his chest. Hot despite the rain. Solid. Real.

His mouth leaves mine just long enough to bite out, "Fuck, Hazel—"

Then he's kissing me again, harder, tongue sliding against mine in a rhythm that makes my knees go weak. His thigh pushes between mine, firm pressure exactly where I need it, and I gasp against his mouth.

"Yes," I breathe, not caring how desperate it sounds.

His hand slides higher, thumb brushing the underside of my breast through my bra. Testing. Waiting for me to stop him.

I don't.

I grab his wrist and press his palm flat against me, showing him exactly what I want.

He groans—rough, broken—and his hand tightens, thumb dragging across my nipple through the thin fabric. The friction sends heat straight down my spine, pools liquid and insistent between my thighs.

I rock against his leg, can't help it, and his other hand drops to my ass, pulling me harder against him.

"Hazel." My name is a warning. Or a prayer. Maybe both.

His mouth moves to my jaw, my throat, teeth scraping just enough to make me shiver. My head tips back against the hay, giving him access, and his tongue traces the line of my pulse.

I'm burning. Wet shirt, cold air, and I'm burning alive.

I should stop this.

The thought flashes bright and urgent. I should tell him I can't promise anything. That I'm still deciding. That in a few weeks I might leave and break him all over again.

But I don't want to stop.

I want him. Want this. Even if it's selfish. Even if it makes everything harder.

My hands find his belt. Fumble with the buckle. I need—I don't even know what I need except that it's him, now, here, before either of us can think better of it.

He catches my wrist. Pins it against the hay above my head.

"Wait," he breathes against my collarbone.

"No." I use my free hand to pull his face back to mine, kiss him hard enough to hurt. "Don't wait. Don't think. Just—"

His control snaps.

Both hands are on me now, shoving my shirt higher, baring my stomach, my ribs. His mouth follows the path his hands made, hot and wet and deliberate. He kisses the hollow beneath my ribs. The soft swell above my bra. His teeth catch the edge of the fabric and I stop breathing.

"Eli—"

He looks up at me then, eyes dark and blown, lips swollen, asking the question without words.

I nod.

His hand moves to the clasp at my back. Flicks it open with practiced ease. The straps slide down my shoulders and he pulls the bra away, tosses it somewhere in the hay.

For a second, he just looks. His chest heaves. His hands flex at his sides like he's memorizing this, storing it away.

Then his mouth is on me.

I cry out, can't help it, the sound swallowed by the storm. His tongue circles my nipple, his hand kneading the other breast, and I'm shaking, grinding against his thigh like I can find relief there.

I can't.

"Please," I hear myself say. "Eli, please—"

He kisses his way back up to my mouth, one hand still working my breast, the other sliding down my stomach. His fingers hook into the waistband of my jeans.

"Tell me to stop," he says, voice wrecked.

"Don't you dare."

The button pops free. Zipper slides down. The sound is obscene in the quiet between ragged breaths and rain hammering the roof.

His fingers slip just inside, not far, just enough to trace the edge of my underwear. Just enough to make me whimper. My hips cant forward, begging without words.

"Fuck," he breathes. "You're—"

His hand slides lower, palm cupping me through thin cotton. I'm soaked. Not from the rain.

He feels it. Groans like it costs him something.

"Hazel, we—" He's trying to think. To be reasonable. "We can't—"

"We can," I gasp, reaching for his belt again, getting it open this time. "We are."

His hand moves against me, heel of his palm grinding slow and deliberate. I'm going to come apart. Right here. Like this.

My hand slides into his jeans, finds him —

"ELI!"

Chace's voice cuts through everything, sharp and urgent, like a bucket of cold water.

Eli freezes.

His hand stills against me. His forehead drops to my shoulder. His breath comes in harsh pants against my bare skin.

For half a second, I think he won't stop. That he'll choose this instead. That he'll damn the consequences and take the last step.

"Fuck," he swears against my skin. Low. Broken.

Then he pulls back hard, like ripping free costs him something physical.

His hands leave me. He drags them through his hair, water flying. He won't look at me. Can't.

"Eli!" Chace yells again, closer now. "We've got a problem out here!"

The colt shifts, startled by the raised voices, and I reach for the lead on instinct, trying to ground myself in something solid as my pulse pounds everywhere.

Eli turns toward the door, rain already blowing in around the edges. He pauses with his hand on the latch, shoulders tight, head bowed like he's fighting a war inside himself.

"Stay with him," he says, voice rough. Commanding. Necessary.

Then he's gone.

The door slams open and the storm swallows him whole.

Rain rushes in, cold and sharp, breaking the spell even as my body still hums with it. I stand there shaking, breath uneven, chest bare, jeans unbuttoned, lips burning like a brand.

I fumble for my bra with trembling hands. Pull it on. Button my jeans. Pull my shirt on. Try to breathe.

My body is screaming. Frustrated. Aching. Empty.

I can still feel the ghost of his hand between my thighs. The pressure. The promise of more.

I press my forehead against the colt's neck and swallow the sound that wants to break free.

We were thirty seconds away from—

I don't let myself finish the thought.

Nothing is resolved.

Everything is exposed.

I know, with absolute certainty, that we've crossed a line we can't uncross—and that whatever comes next is going to demand more than either of us is ready to give.

Chapter Twenty-Five

Eli

I didn't sleep.

Couldn't.

Every time I closed my eyes, I was back in that shed. Her back against the hay. Her jeans unbuttoned. My hand on her skin. The sound she made when I touched her.

The way Chace's voice cut through everything.

Thirty more seconds and I would've buried myself in her.

Fuck.

I drain the cup of coffee I'm drinking, black and bitter, boots already on, and head out into the cold.

The ranch is quiet. Too quiet. The kind of stillness that presses in from all sides and makes every thought louder than it should be. Storm damage litters the yard—broken branches, a loose tarp flapping against the equipment shed, mud everywhere. Work that needs doing.

Good.

I grab a rake and start clearing debris, movements sharp and automatic. Muscle memory takes over. Lift. Toss. Repeat. My shoulders burn after the first hour. I don't stop.

Work is the only thing that helps. The only thing that keeps my hands from shaking.

By the time the sun breaks the horizon, I've cleared half the yard. Sweat cools against my back despite the chill. My hands ache. It's not enough.

Nothing is.

Boots crunch on gravel behind me.

I don't turn. I already know who it is.

"Good morning," Hazel says.

Two words. Casual. Like we almost didn't— I grab another branch. "Morning."

She steps closer.

"We need to work the colt," she says. "Fall Classic is four weeks out."

I nod once. Still don't look at her.

"I'll meet you at the pen in ten."

She hesitates. I hear it in the pause, the way her weight shifts on the gravel. Then her footsteps retreat, steady and deliberate, leaving me alone with the mess I'm supposed to be cleaning up.

I exhale slow through my nose and toss the rake aside.

This is going to be a long fucking day.

The colt is wound tight when I get to the pen.

He paces the fence line, head high, ears flicking at every sound. Storm nerves. He remembers yesterday. The chaos. The fear.

I step inside slow, keeping my movements calm, predictable. He watches me but doesn't bolt.

"Easy," I murmur. "We're good today."

Hazel arrives a minute later, lead rope coiled over her shoulder. She doesn't say anything. Just slips through the gate and takes up position on the opposite side of the pen.

The morning sun catches her hair. Her shirt is clean, fitted. She looks like she slept.

I hate her for it.

"Let's start with groundwork," she says, voice steady. Professional.

I nod and clip the lead to the colt's halter.

We've done this a hundred times. Worked horses together since we were teenagers. We know how to move around each other. When to step in. When to give space. When to let the other person lead.

It should be muscle memory.

It's not.

The colt settles after a few minutes, enough that I can start working him through basic movements. Walk. Stop. Back. Turn. Hazel mirrors me on the other side, hands steady, voice low and calm.

But I'm too aware of her.

The way she shifts her weight when the colt moves. The way her hands stay loose on the rope even when he tosses his head. The way she tilts her head slightly, reading his body language.

I force my focus back to the horse.

"He's favoring his left front," Hazel says, stepping closer to examine his gait.

I move in from the other side. We're both crouched low now, watching his feet, close enough that I can smell her—soap and something sweet and the faint trace of hay.

Too close.

She leans in further. Her shoulder brushes mine.

The touch is brief. Accidental.

Heat spikes through me anyway.

I stand up fast. "I'll keep an eye on it."

She straightens too, and I catch the way her breath hitches.

She felt it too.

We keep working. The colt moves between us, responding to our cues, oblivious to the tension crackling in the air.

Hazel reaches across to adjust the halter, and her hand brushes mine on the lead.

This time it's not accidental.

Her pulse jumps under my thumb. She inhales sharp.

I force myself to let go.

"Sorry," I mutter.

"It's fine."

It's not fine.

We circle the pen, working the colt through turns and stops. Every movement requires us to coordinate, to read each other, to move in sync. It's intimate in a way that has nothing to do with touch.

And it's killing me.

Hazel steps in to guide the colt's shoulder, and I move to his hip at the same time. We're sandwiching him now, bodies angled in, working together to shift his weight and balance.

It requires proximity. Trust. Timing.

Her hand lands on his ribcage. Mine lands just below hers.

We're inches apart. Close enough that I can feel the heat of her body. Close enough that when she shifts her weight, her hip brushes my thigh.

The colt settles between us, calm now, trusting.

We don't move.

We should. The exercise is done. But neither of us steps back.

Hazel's breathing has changed. Faster. Shallower. I watch the pulse jump at her throat.

"Eli," she says quietly.

It's not a question. It's not a plea. Just my name, said in a way that makes my chest tighten and my hands ache to reach for her.

I take a step back instead.

The loss of contact feels wrong. Immediate.

"We should run him through it again," I say, voice rougher than I mean it to be.

She nods once, not looking at me. "Yeah."

We reset. Work the colt through the same exercise. Then again.

Each time, we end up too close. Each time, the air gets thicker. Each time, it takes more effort to step back.

By the fourth run-through, sweat dampens my shirt despite the cool morning. My hands shake slightly when I adjust the lead. Not from exertion.

From restraint.

Hazel reaches for the clasp on the halter at the same time I do. Our fingers tangle. This time, neither of us pretends it's an accident.

Her eyes meet mine.

Dark. Wanting. Uncertain.

My hand shifts, fingers threading through hers for half a second.

Her breath catches.

"You're both killing me."

Chace's voice cuts across the pen, loud and unapologetic.

We jerk apart like we've been caught doing something worse than just standing too close.

I turn toward the fence.

Chace is leaning against the rail with Addie and Shae, all three of them watching us like this is entertainment. Addie looks uncomfortable. Shae's expression is carefully neutral.

Chace just grins.

"What?" I snap.

He spreads his hands. "I'm just saying. The sexual tension is so thick out here I can barely breathe. You're making the horse nervous."

Addie elbows him. "Chace—"

"It's true!" He gestures between me and Hazel. "Look at them. They look like they're about to either kill each other or—"

"Chace," Addie warns.

He ignores her, still grinning at us. "Jesus Christ, will you two just fuck already and put us all out of our misery?"

The words land like a bomb.

Silence drops hard and immediate.

Addie closes her eyes. "Oh my god."

Shae just watches, expression unreadable.

Heat crawls up the back of my neck. Not embarrassment. Something sharper. Angrier.

I can feel Hazel standing frozen beside me. Can feel the weight of her stare even though I won't look at her.

The colt shifts nervously between us, picking up on the tension.

"Are you done?" I ask Chace, voice flat.

His grin doesn't falter. "I mean, clearly you're not, which is kind of the whole problem—"

"Chace," Addie hisses. "Shut up."

He raises his hands in surrender. "Alright, alright. I'm just calling it like I see it."

I hand the lead rope to Hazel without a word. Without looking at her.

"I'm done," I say.

Then I walk.

Past the fence. Past Chace with his stupid grin. Past Addie's apologetic expression. Past all of them.

I hear Hazel call my name.

I don't stop.

I can't.

If I turn around now, if I look at her, I won't be able to hold the line I'm barely holding.

I make it to the barn before my hands start shaking.

Not from cold. Not from exhaustion.

From wanting something I can't keep chasing.

I brace my palms against the workbench, head down, breathing slow and controlled like that might settle the chaos under my ribs.

It doesn't work.

I can't keep doing this.

Can't keep standing next to her and pretending I don't want to pull her close. Can't keep working beside her like my body doesn't remember exactly how she felt under my hands. Can't survive another almost.

Another interruption.

Another moment where she looks at me like she wants this but won't say it out loud.

I shove off the bench and pace the length of the barn once, then again, boots thudding against the concrete.

I've loved her my whole life.

That's the problem.

Not that I want her. Not that I need her. But that I've always known exactly what it feels like to have her and lose her, and I'm not strong enough to do it again.

She has to choose.

Not me chasing. Not me reaching. Not me standing in a shed with my hands on her body while she gasps my name and then walks away the second someone interrupts.

She has to come to me.

Or let me go.

The barn is quiet except for the sound of my breathing and the distant shuffle of horses in their stalls.

I wait for footsteps behind me.

For her to follow.

For her to say something—anything—that tells me this isn't just me wanting her in pieces.

The minutes stretch.

No one comes.

The realization settles cold and certain.

She's not coming.

Not now. Maybe not ever.

I grab my keys off the workbench and head for my truck, jaw tight, every step deliberate.

I need space. Distance. Anything but standing here waiting for something that isn't going to happen.

The sun sets slow and red by the time I make it back to Dawson Ranch.

My place is quiet. Empty. Exactly what I don't need right now.

I stand on the porch, keys in hand, staring at the door like crossing the threshold will somehow fix the knot in my chest.

It won't.

But I go inside anyway. Drop my keys. Stand in the kitchen with my hands braced on the counter, breathing like I've run miles instead of driven them.

My resolve is holding.

Barely.

I won't go to her. I won't knock on her door. I won't drive back to Clark Ranch and stand outside her window like some lovesick fool hoping she'll look at me the way she did five years ago.

She has to choose.

But standing here, alone in the dark, knowing she's just miles away across the property line, I'm not sure how much longer I can hold this line.

Because if she comes to me now—if she shows up at my door and says she wants this, even without promises, even without guarantees—I'll break.

I'll take whatever she gives me.

Even knowing it won't be enough.

Even knowing "right now" isn't the same as forever.

Even knowing I'll wake up one day and she'll be gone again, and this time I won't survive it.

I'll take it anyway.

Even if it's temporary. Even if it destroys me later.

And I hate myself for it.

But I can't stop wanting her.

I never could.

And if she walks through that door tonight, I'll give her everything.

Even knowing she'll take it with her when she leaves.

Chapter Twenty-Six

Hazel

The ranch is quiet by late afternoon.

Everyone scattered after training. Chace muttered something about checking the north fence line. Addie disappeared toward her house without a word. And Eli—

Eli walked away.

I've been finding things to do ever since. Mucking stalls. Organizing tack. Sweeping until the concrete shows through years of scuff marks.

Anything to avoid the fact that I watched him leave and didn't follow.

The sun slants low through the barn doors now. My shirt sticks to my back. I've been at this for hours and I still can't settle.

Chace's voice keeps echoing. *Jesus Christ, will you two just fuck already and put us all out of our misery.*

The way Eli's jaw tightened before he walked away without looking back.

The way I let him.

I lean against the stall door, breathing hard even though I haven't done anything that warrants it.

He's done chasing me.

He stepped back in the shed. He walked away today. That wasn't distance. That was a line.

He's waiting for me to choose.

My phone buzzes in my back pocket.

I pull it out, expecting Shae or maybe Mae. Instead, it's a number I don't recognize. Local area code.

The voicemail notification pops up, followed by a text.

Hi Hazel, this is Kara from Red Fern Stables. Heard you might be taking boarders again. Any chance you have openings? Also, are you really showing at Fall Classic? Call me.

I stare at the screen.

Red Fern isn't some backyard operation. They're county-over, professional, the kind of place that has waiting lists and references. If they're asking, it means people are watching.

It means the show isn't just hope anymore.

I hit play on the voicemail.

Kara's voice is bright, businesslike. Three horses. Timelines. Feeding schedules. "We've been hearing good things," she says at the end. "Word's getting around that Clark Ranch is back in business."

The voicemail ends.

I lower the phone and look out at the ranch. The barn. The pasture. The house sitting solid in the afternoon light.

This isn't hypothetical anymore.

My thumb hovers before I type back. *Yes, call me. We're rebuilding capacity now.*

I hit send.

The choice feels small. Practical.

But my body doesn't relax.

I head toward the house. Mae needs to know about this.

I find her in the kitchen, hands wrapped around a mug of coffee that's probably gone cold. She's staring out the window, calculating something in her head.

"Red Fern Stables called," I say from the doorway.

Her gaze snaps to me. "And?"

"They want to board three horses. Asked about Fall Classic too."

She sets the mug down slow. "That's good. That's real good, Haze."

"Yeah."

She studies me. "You don't sound convinced."

"I am. It's just—it's real now. People are watching."

"We will get this done," Mae cuts in. Matter-of-fact. "You and that boy have been working the colt hard. The ranch is coming back together."

I nod. My throat feels tight.

"Cole stopped by yesterday," Mae says after a beat. "While you were in town."

My stomach drops. "What did he want?"

"Same thing he always wants." She picks up the mug again. "Reminded me his offer's still on the table. Said he'd hate to see me wait too long."

"Mae—"

"I know." She holds up a hand. "I'm not taking it. But Hazel, if Red Fern boards here and the show goes well, that changes things. That's proof we can do this."

The weight of it settles between us.

"You're staying, right?" Mae asks. Not accusing. Just asking. "Through Fall Classic at least?"

"Yeah," I say. And mean it.

She nods once, then turns back to the window. "Good. Now go tell Eli about the call. He'll want to know."

I blink. "What?"

"He's been working himself to the bone to help get that colt ready. He deserves to hear it's paying off." Mae glances at me, something knowing in her eyes. "And you've been pacing around here like a caged animal all afternoon. Go."

My face heats.

She's not wrong.

"Okay," I say finally.

Mae just nods and goes back to her coffee.

I walk back outside, the screen door slapping shut behind me. The air feels cooler now, shadows stretching long across the yard.

I head to the barn and rinse my hands under the spigot, staring at the cracked mirror above the basin.

I look tired. Steadier too.

Eli should know about Red Fern. He's been training the colt since before I got here, putting in hours no one asked for because he cares about this place.

But that's not the only reason I need to see him.

He won't come to me again.

He stepped back last night. He walked away today. He's holding himself still on purpose, waiting for me to decide.

I think about that morning five years ago. Waking up next to him. The panic that hit when I realized how permanent it felt.

Standing in the doorway felt safer than stepping back in.

I told myself I needed space.

What I really needed was courage.

I dry my hands on my jeans.

I can't promise I'll never get scared again.

But I can promise tonight. And tomorrow. And every day I choose to show up instead of running.

That's not forever. But it's more than I've given him in five years.

If I want him, I have to stop making him wait for certainty I can't give.

I have to choose him out loud.

Right now.

I grab my keys and walk toward my truck. The sun is lower now, the light going gold across the yard.

My heart pounds as I pull the door open.

I need to tell him about Red Fern.

And I need to stop pretending that's the only reason I'm going.

I slide into the seat, engine turning over. My hands grip the wheel. My chest feels tight.

I pull out of the drive and turn toward Dawson Ranch.

The road between our properties is one I've driven my whole life. I know every dip and turn, the spot where the fence line shifts from Clark wood posts to Dawson steel.

My hands stay tight on the wheel.

The fence line appears on my left. I've ridden this stretch more times than I can count. Run it. Walked it.

It's not far. Never has been.

Just far enough that you have to choose to cross it.

The road curves, and his cabin comes into view through the trees. Small. Tucked back from the main house. His truck sits in the drive.

He's there.

My stomach flips.

I pull in next to his truck and kill the engine. The sudden silence feels too loud.

I sit there, hands still on the wheel, staring at the cabin door.

My hands shake when I reach for the door handle.

Because it's not just about the call.

It's about the shed. The porch. The way he's been holding himself back.

I open the truck door and step out. The evening air is cooler now, carrying the smell of pine and earth. His cabin sits quiet, a light on inside.

He's in there.

And I'm out here.

My heart pounds so hard I feel it in my throat.

This is the choice.

Not someday. Not when I'm sure. Right now.

I cross the gravel toward his door, each step deliberate, and don't let myself slow down.

Chapter Twenty-Seven

Hazel

I don't knock.

The cabin is quiet except for the low hum of the overhead light and water running in the sink. Eli stands with his back to me, sleeves shoved past his elbows, hands braced on the counter.

He goes still.

"Hazel." He doesn't turn around. Just says my name like he's testing whether I'm real.

"I need to talk to you."

He turns slowly. His eyes search my face—guarded but open, wary but wanting. The tension in his jaw could crack teeth.

"Okay," he says.

I step inside and close the door behind me. The click of the latch sounds too loud in the quiet.

"Red Fern Stables called," I say. "They want to board three horses. Asked about Fall Classic."

Something flickers across his face. Not quite relief.

"That's good," he says carefully.

"Yeah." I swallow. "Mae said Cole's still pressuring her. But if we prove the ranch works—if the show goes well—she won't have to sell. Which means I need to stay. Through Fall Classic at least."

He waits. Doesn't move. Doesn't give me anything.

"But that's not why I'm here," I say.

His jaw works. "Why are you here?"

"Because I can't promise you forever right now." The words come out steadier than I feel. "I can't tell you I'll never leave, that I'll never get scared again."

I watch his shoulders tense, watch him brace for the blow he thinks is coming.

"But I can promise you tonight," I continue. "And tomorrow. And every day I wake up and choose to be here. I can't give you certainty about next year. But I can give you all of me, right now, without holding back."

He's so still I can see his pulse jumping at his throat.

"Leaving you was the worst thing I ever did," I say, voice cracking. "And I'm not asking you to forget that. I'm asking you to let me choose you now. Fully. Not halfway. Not one foot out the door."

I take another step closer. My pulse thuds everywhere at once.

"That's all I have, Eli. But it's yours if you want it."

For a long moment, he just stares at me. Then he shakes his head once, sharp.

"That's not enough."

The words land like a physical blow.

"It has to be," I say. "Because it's all I can give."

"You're asking me to take you knowing you might leave again." His voice is rough, controlled, but barely. "You're asking me to survive that twice."

"Yes."

The word hangs between us.

He turns away, runs both hands through his hair, spins back. "Jesus Christ, Hazel."

I don't move. Don't look away.

"I've loved you my whole life," he says finally, the words sounding torn from somewhere deep. Like he's never said them out loud before. Like saying them now might break him. "And you're standing here asking me to risk it again. For what? For right now? For as long as you feel like staying?"

"Yes," I say again, quieter this time.

His hands flex at his sides. "You can't ask me that."

"I know."

"It's not enough."

"I know that too."

Silence fills the cabin.

He's staring at me like he's trying to see the future. Trying to calculate whether "right now" is worth the inevitable ending. Whether he can survive loving me and losing me again.

I watch him make the choice.

See the exact moment his resolve cracks.

He stares at me. Something warring in his eyes—anger and want and a kind of desperation I recognize because I feel it too.

"Fuck," he breathes. Then again, louder, "Fuck."

He crosses the room in three long strides.

His hands are on me before my next breath, fingers firm at my waist, pulling me into him like restraint has finally lost. His mouth crashes into mine—rough and urgent and unapologetic.

I gasp against him. The sound vanishes into his mouth.

The kiss is all teeth and breath and pressure. Years of almost and not yet and what if pouring out in one collision. His hands slide up my back, over every curve, then down again, gripping my hips like he needs to make sure I'm real.

I don't step back.

I cling to him, fisting his shirt, pulling him closer even though there's no space left between us.

He breaks the kiss only to press his forehead to mine, breath ragged. "I'll take it," he says, voice wrecked. "I'll take whatever you give me. Because walking away from you is worse than surviving you leaving again."

Then he's kissing me again—slower this time, deeper, like he's memorizing the taste of me. Heat pools low in my belly, spreading through my thighs, tightening at my core.

My fingers tug at his shirt and he moves backward, pulling me with him. We stumble toward the bed, his hands never leaving my body, and when the backs of my legs hit the mattress I fall and he follows, his weight pressing me into the springs.

His mouth leaves mine to trail along my jaw, down my neck. Each kiss deliberate. Claiming. His breath is hot against my collarbone and he pauses there, like he's grounding himself before he loses control completely.

Then his hands find the hem of my shirt.

He lifts his head just enough to look at me. Not asking permission. Confirming what he already knows.

My shaky exhale answers for him.

He pulls my shirt up and off in one smooth motion, tosses it aside without looking. The cool air hits my skin a second before his hands do. His palms skim up my ribs, over the newly bare skin, calloused and warm, and the sound that escapes me is embarrassingly soft.

He exhales like he's been holding his breath for years.

Then he sits back just enough to strip off his own shirt—quick, efficient, like it's in his way. His chest is broad and solid, muscle earned from years of ranch work. Fencing. Hauling hay. Breaking horses. His arms flex as he tosses the shirt aside and the sight of him above me makes my stomach twist hard.

He leans down again, his mouth finding my shoulder, then lower. When his lips close around my nipple through the thin fabric of my bra, I arch into him with a gasp. His tongue flicks over the sensitive peak and heat courses through me, molten and insistent.

His hands move to my back, finding the clasp of my bra. He unhooks it without fumbling, slides the straps down my arms, and pulls it away. For a second he just looks at me, eyes so dark they're almost black.

"You're beautiful," he says, low and steady.

Then his mouth is on my bare skin. Lips closing around my nipple, tongue working, teeth grazing just enough to make me gasp his name. His hand cups my other breast, thumb brushing over the peak in rhythm with his mouth, and I can't think, can't breathe, can only feel.

My fingers tangle in his hair, holding him there, and he groans against my skin. The vibration of it shoots straight through me.

His hand slides down my stomach, over my hip, to the button of my jeans. He doesn't hesitate. The button pops open, the zipper slides down, and then he's easing the denim over my hips.

I lift to help him and the way he inhales at that—sharp, controlled, almost pained—sends fresh heat through me.

He pulls the jeans off completely, drops them behind him. His hands return immediately, sliding up my calves, my thighs, tracing the lines of me. His touch is sure but there's a tremor beneath it now. A crack in the control.

His mouth grazes my inner thigh, stubble scraping sensitive skin, and I shudder. He places small kisses up, up, until he reaches the edge of my panties. He kisses me there—right over the fabric—teasing, deliberate, his breath hot.

Then he looks up at me with a grin that's pure sin before he hooks his fingers in the waistband and pulls my panties off in one swift movement.

Before I can speak, before I can think, his mouth is on me.

The first touch of his tongue makes my back bow off the bed. My hands fly to his hair, gripping, and he groans against me like this is exactly where he wants to be.

He doesn't rush. His tongue moves in slow, deliberate strokes, learning me, remembering me, taking his time like he has all night. Like he's been waiting years for this and he's going to savor every second.

My thighs tremble. My breath comes in short gasps. Heat builds and builds, coiling tighter with every pass of his tongue, every brush of his lips.

"Eli," I gasp. "Please—"

He responds by sliding one finger inside me, then another, curling them just right while his tongue keeps working and I shatter. Everything blurs as pleasure crashes through me, my whole body tensing and releasing, his name breaking from my lips.

Before I've fully come down he's moving up my body, kissing his way up my stomach, between my breasts, along my throat. I reach for him, hands shaking, and he lets me pull him into a kiss. I can taste myself on his tongue and it makes me want him all over again.

He stands long enough to strip off his jeans and boxers in one motion and when he straightens I get my first real look at him.

Holy shit.

He's thick and hard and ready, and the wanting in his eyes when he sees me looking makes my thighs clench.

He comes back to me, settling between my legs, his weight pressing me into the mattress. Bare skin against bare skin. The heat of him makes my whole body arch instinctively.

His hands move up my sides, over my ribs.

He pauses, forehead resting against mine, breath unsteady.

"You're mine, Hazel," he says, voice rough and absolute. "You always have been. Even if it's temporary. Even if it's just for now. I'll take whatever you give me."

Then his mouth is on mine again and he's right there, pressing against me, and I can feel how much he wants this. How much he's been holding back.

"Please," I whisper against his lips.

He enters me slowly. Inch by devastating inch. The stretch of it makes me cry out, makes my nails dig into his shoulders. He pauses, letting me adjust, his jaw clenched so tight I can see the muscle jumping.

"Okay?" he asks, voice strained.

"Yes. God, yes."

He pushes deeper, filling me completely, and we both groan. For a second he doesn't move, just stays buried inside me, forehead pressed to mine, breathing hard.

Then he starts to move.

Slow at first. Rolling his hips in a steady rhythm that has me gasping. Each thrust deliberate and deep, like he's trying to memorize exactly how I feel around him.

His mouth finds my throat, kissing and sucking the sensitive skin there. One hand grips my hip, holding me in place while he moves. The other slides up to cup my breast, thumb brushing over my nipple in time with his thrusts.

"You feel so good," he breathes against my neck. "So fucking good."

I wrap my legs around his waist, changing the angle, and he groans, thrusting deeper. The new angle has him hitting something inside me that makes stars burst behind my eyelids.

"There," I gasp. "Right there—"

He adjusts, hitting that spot with every thrust now, and I can't think anymore. Can only feel. The stretch of him inside me. The weight of his body. The heat building again, faster this time, sharper.

His rhythm changes. Faster. Harder. The bed frame creaks with every thrust and I don't care. All I care about is this. Him. Us.

My hands slide down his back, feeling his muscles flex under my palms. I dig my nails in and he hisses, hips snapping harder.

"Hazel," he groans. "Fuck, Hazel—"

I pull him down into a kiss, messy and desperate, and he responds by shifting his weight, one hand sliding between us to where we're joined. His thumb finds my clit and I break the kiss with a cry.

"That's it," he says against my mouth. "I want to feel you come around me."

The combination of his thumb circling, his cock driving deep, his voice in my ear—it's too much. The pressure builds to an unbearable peak and then I'm coming again, harder this time, my whole body clenching around him.

"Fuck," he groans, and his rhythm falters. "Hazel, I—"

"Don't stop," I gasp. "Please don't stop."

He doesn't. He keeps moving, keeps thrusting through my orgasm, prolonging it until I'm trembling and gasping beneath him. Then his whole body tenses, his grip on my hip tightening, and with one final deep thrust he comes, his groan muffled against my shoulder.

We stay like that for a long moment. Both of us breathing hard. Both of us trembling. His weight pressing me into the mattress, his face buried in my neck, his heart pounding against mine.

Finally he lifts his head, kisses me once more—slow and soft this time—and carefully pulls out. I feel the loss of him immediately.

He rolls to the side, pulling me with him, tucking me against his chest. One arm comes around my waist, possessive and sure. His other hand finds mine, threading our fingers together.

The world settles slowly.

We're tangled together, sheets twisted around our legs, his arm heavy across my stomach. My cheek rests against his chest, skin cooling. His heart is still working its way back to steady, the thud of it deep beneath my ear.

I should move. I don't.

My fingers trace idle patterns on his ribs—lazy, absent. Not asking. Not promising. Just touching because he's there and I can.

"I can't promise I won't get scared again," I say quietly. The words feel necessary, even now. "Or that I won't wake up one day and panic."

His chest rises under my cheek. Falls.

"But I'm not leaving tonight," I continue. "Or tomorrow. I'm here. And I'm trying."

His hand moves, thumb brushing a quiet line along my ribs.

"That's more than I had yesterday," he says finally.

I lift my head enough to look at him. His eyes are closed, expression softer than I've seen it in days.

"Is it enough?" I ask.

He opens his eyes then. Meets mine without flinching.

"It has to be," he says.

Something tightens in my chest—gratitude and guilt and something more dangerous I won't name yet.

I settle back against him, fitting into the space like muscle memory. He pulls the blanket higher, tucks it around my shoulders, his touch careful in a way that feels dangerous all on its own.

Outside, the ranch is quiet. No urgency. No future pounding at the door yet.

Just this. Just us.

His breath evens out. Mine follows.

I tell myself this is all it is—heat and comfort and a night we won't name.

But my body already knows the truth.

It always has.

Chapter Twenty-Eight

Hazel

Morning comes quietly.

No alarm. No rush. Just soft gray light pressing through the bathroom window and the sound of pipes knocking awake beneath the floorboards.

I stand under the shower, letting the water run hot against my shoulders. My muscles ache in places that have nothing to do with ranch work. My thighs. My hips. The base of my spine where his hands gripped last night.

Three days since I went to his cabin and didn't leave until dawn. Three days of falling into a pattern I'm not ready to name.

Work until sunset. Then night comes, and I'm at his door again.

I wake up tangled in him every morning. Warm. Heavy-limbed. Safe in a way I haven't let myself feel in years.

If Mae's noticed, she hasn't said anything. Just coffee in the pot every morning and questions about fence posts and whether the colt ate his grain.

I shut off the water and step out, steam curling around me. Pull on jeans and a clean shirt, braid my hair while still barefoot.

Today I'm paying the Fall Classic registration fee.

The envelope sits on my dresser. I count the money again even though I already know the number. The last of my savings. Everything I scraped together before I came back here.

Everything I told myself I wouldn't touch unless there was no other choice.

I tuck the envelope into my bag and head downstairs.

The scent of coffee reaches me before the sound of voices. Mae's laugh carries from the kitchen, easy and unguarded, mingling with another voice that makes my steps slow without permission.

When I turn the corner, he's there.

Eli stands at the counter, one hip leaned back against it, mug in hand. Worn t-shirt. Hair still damp. Comfortable in the space like he's always belonged here.

My breath catches.

The memory hits without warning. His hands last night. The way my body arched into them. The sound he pulled from me when I lost control.

Heat rushes my cheeks.

His eyes lift and meet mine.

I stop short in the doorway.

His mouth curves slowly. That smile. The one I haven't seen in far too long. The one that used to be reserved just for me—soft at the edges, dangerous in the middle.

There's relief in it. Desire. Something earned.

And something knowing. He knows exactly what he's doing to me.

His gaze lingers, dark and steady, and I feel it in my body before my brain can catch up. The unspoken truth hums between us. He's thinking the same thing I am. Last night. My hands on his back. His mouth at my ear. The way he made me come apart and held me there while I shook.

And he's enjoying the hell out of it.

I pull my face into what I hope passes for indifference, like I haven't just been caught mid-thought.

"Morning, Eli."

I reach past him for the coffee pot, brushing against his side just enough to be accidental. Just enough to spike my pulse and make my breath hitch. His warmth is immediate, familiar, grounding in the most dangerous way.

"Morning, Hazel," he says simply.

His voice does things to me that should be illegal before caffeine.

Get it together, I tell myself.

I turn quickly, putting space between us before I do something catastrophically stupid. Like kiss him. Like drag him down the hall. Like forget that Mae is standing three feet away and very much awake.

I pour my coffee with hands that absolutely don't shake.

"I'm heading into town today," I say, aiming for casual. "Need to pay the registration fee for Fall Classic."

Mae lights up immediately. "That's fantastic. That colt looks better every day. Addie seems real comfortable on him too."

I nod, taking a careful sip. The coffee's strong. Bitter. Welcome.

Eli speaks then, easy but sure. "You've done good work with him. He's calmer. Listening better. That doesn't happen by accident."

The praise lands warm and unguarded. It shouldn't mean this much. It absolutely does.

"Thanks," I say quietly.

We make small talk after that. Weather. Fence repairs. The way the ground is finally starting to dry out. Normal things. Necessary things. All of it threaded with something charged and unspoken that makes every second stretch.

Eli finishes his coffee and sets the mug in the sink. "I'm gonna head out and get started. When you're back, I could use your help in the east pasture."

"Okay," I say. Too quickly.

He nods once, eyes flicking to mine like a promise, then he's gone.

The door closes behind him and I let out a breath I didn't realize I was holding.

I grab my bag and cross the kitchen, kissing Mae on the cheek. "I'll be back later."

She hums. "Drive safe."

I'm halfway out the door when her voice follows me.

"Oh, and Hazel?"

I pause.

"If you're going to keep sneaking in early in the mornings, it'd be nice if you could start the coffee for me."

I turn just in time to see her wink.

Then she disappears down the hall before I can say a word.

Oh my god.

She knows.

I want to crawl into the earth and never come out.

I make it to my truck in a daze, start the engine, hands still warm on the steering wheel. As I pull out, I catch sight of Eli riding toward the east pasture, easy in the saddle, familiar as breath.

Something shifts in me, watching him.

What have I gotten myself into again?

The drive into town passes quickly, windows down, radio low.

The fair office is smaller than I remember. Or maybe I'm just bigger now. Older. Less willing to be impressed by chipped counters and faded flyers taped crooked to corkboards. The kind of place that used to feel official and important when I was a kid, where ribbons and entry numbers meant something bigger than they do now.

The woman behind the desk looks up as I step inside. Her eyes flick over me, hesitate, then sharpen with recognition.

"Well, I'll be," she says, her mouth curving slowly. "Hazel Clark."

I smile back, polite, contained. "Hi."

She comes around the counter without thinking, hands braced on her hips as she studies me. Not rude. Just curious in that small-town way that never quite goes away.

"Been a while," she says. "You're looking good."

"Thanks."

She asks about Mae. The ranch. Whether I'm staying long this time.

"We'll see," I say. "I'm helping Mae for now."

She nods like she understands something I haven't said.

I pull the envelope from my bag and slide it across the counter. My fingers linger on the edge for half a second longer than necessary before letting go.

She opens it, counts quickly, then looks back up at me. "You're entered. Fall Classic is three weeks out. You and Addie Dawson on the colt showcase, right?"

"Yes."

She makes a note and hands me a receipt.

I stare at it. Just like that, the money's gone. The last of it. Years of saving reduced to a slip of paper and a checkmark on a list.

No safety net. No backup plan. Everything on this colt and this show.

I should feel terrified.

Instead, I feel lighter and heavier all at once.

Committed.

As I turn to go, she clears her throat.

"You know," she says, softer now, "you're taking right after your daddy."

I pause.

"He was a good man," she adds. "Did right by folks. Took care of his horses. Took care of people too."

The words land hard and sudden, pressing against something tender I didn't know was exposed.

"He'd be proud to see you back here," she says. "Proud you're doing this."

I manage a nod. Manage not to let my voice crack when I say thank you.

Outside, the sun feels brighter. Sharper. Like it shifted while I was inside.

I make it to my truck and sit for a moment, hands on the wheel, the receipt still clutched in my fingers.

He'd be proud.

I hope so.

I'm pulling back onto ranch property when my phone buzzes in the cupholder.

Unknown number.

I answer, putting it on speaker. "Hello?"

"Hazel Clark?" The voice is professional, confident. "This is Renee Whitman. Kara from Red Fern gave me your number. I heard you might be taking on boarders."

Red Fern recommended us. My pulse kicks.

"We are," I say carefully.

"I'd like to come see your operation," Renee continues. "Watch you work, meet your crew. I'm looking for quality care and consistent training, and Kara spoke highly of what you're building."

My hands tighten on the wheel. "When were you thinking?"

"Tomorrow morning, if that works? Early. I know it's short notice."

Tomorrow.

We're not ready. Or maybe we are. Maybe this is exactly what we need.

"Tomorrow works," I say, surprised by how steady my voice sounds.

"Perfect. I'll be there at nine."

She hangs up.

I sit in my truck for a long moment, engine idling, phone silent in my lap. An investor. Coming tomorrow to see if we're worth the risk.

This is real.

I need to tell Mae. And Eli.

Something uncertain settles in my stomach—hope and terror in equal measure.

I grab my bag and head for the house.

Chapter Twenty-Nine

Hazel

The investor is early.

That's the first problem.

I see the truck before I even pull all the way into the drive—dark, polished, definitely not from around here. It's parked too neatly near the barn, angled like someone who's used to being impressed on purpose.

My stomach drops.

I cut the engine and sit there for a second longer than necessary, hands still on the wheel. Mae's words from this morning replay in my head whether I want them to or not.

This has to work, Hazel. We don't get another shot like this.

I grab Eli's hat from the seat beside me and shove the door open.

By the time I reach the barn, Addie's already mounted, the colt sidestepping with restless energy beneath her. Eli's checking a cinch, calm as ever, like the entire future of the ranch isn't balanced on how today goes.

The woman by the rail turns when she hears my boots on the gravel. Late forties, maybe. Crisp jeans. Clean boots that haven't seen much dirt. Sharp eyes that miss nothing.

"You must be Hazel Clark," she says, offering her hand. "I'm Renee Whitman."

I shake it, keeping my grip firm. "Glad you made it out. Sorry I wasn't here when you arrived."

"Don't apologize. Your aunt has been wonderful." She gestures toward the pen where Addie's warming up the colt. "And your crew was kind enough to get started without you."

Crew. Like we're a real operation with staff and structure and not held together by hope and early mornings.

"We try to stay efficient," I say, which is true enough.

Renee's gaze drifts past me—to the pen, to the colt, to Eli standing at the rail with his arms crossed. Watching. Assessing.

"I've heard good things," she says. "Enough to drive out early. Red Fern mentioned you might have capacity opening up."

"We do," I say carefully. "We're rebuilding slowly. Making sure we can offer the level of care people expect."

"Smart." Renee turns back to the pen. "Show me what you've got."

Addie swings the colt into motion and everything in me narrows to the rhythm of it. The way the horse listens. The way Addie rides like she belongs there, confident and light. The way Eli watches without interfering, only stepping in when necessary with a word or a gesture.

The colt moves clean. No hesitation. No rough edges.

Three weeks of work showing in every stride.

Renee asks questions. Smart ones. About training timelines. Feeding protocols. Turnout schedules. Insurance. Vet access.

About stability.

I answer carefully. Honestly. I talk about training philosophy, about long-term care, about building something sustainable instead of flashy. I don't mention how close we are to the edge. I don't mention how badly we need her to say yes.

At one point, she glances at Eli.

"You work closely together?" she asks.

The question lands heavier than it should.

"Every day," I say, maybe a beat too quickly. "He's been training with us since before I got here. Knows the operation inside and out."

Eli looks at me then. Just a glance. But something in his expression shifts, like he understands the weight behind her question. The implication that stability means more than just good horses and clean stalls.

It means people who stay.

Renee watches Addie bring the colt through a tight turn, then nods slowly. "Impressive. Really impressive."

My chest loosens slightly.

"I'd like to think on it," she continues. "I'll be in touch by end of week."

Relief hits me. Not a yes, but not a no either.

"That works," I say. "Take whatever time you need."

She smiles, more genuine this time. "I appreciate that. You'll hear from me soon."

We shake hands again and I walk her back to her car, making small talk about the drive and the weather and Fall Classic. She asks about the show, about Addie's experience, about whether we'll be taking on more riders after.

I give her optimistic answers. Careful ones.

When her truck finally pulls away, dust settling in its wake, the ranch exhales.

Addie whoops from the pen, sliding off the colt and throwing her arms around my neck before I can brace for it. "Did you see her face? She was sold. Completely sold."

"Not yet," I say, laughing despite myself. "But we're close."

"Close enough." Addie grins. "Mae's going to lose her mind."

Eli meets my eyes over Addie's shoulder. Something unspoken passes between us.

This matters.

Everything matters.

Addie heads toward the barn to cool the colt, still buzzing with energy, and the pen goes quiet. The sun sits low now, casting everything gold. My pulse is still too fast, adrenaline not quite settled.

I turn to face him, leaning back against the fence. The movement puts me right in front of him and he doesn't step back. Just looks down at me, that barely-there smirk still playing at his mouth.

"Something you want to say?" I ask.

"Not particularly."

"Then why are you standing so close?"

"Am I?" He shifts even closer, one hand coming up to rest on the fence rail beside my head. Not touching me. Just boxing me in. "Hadn't noticed."

My pulse kicks up. "Liar."

"Prove it."

The challenge hangs between us. Addie's voice carries across the pen, talking to the colt, oblivious. The sun slants through the trees. Everything smells like dust and hay and the faint edge of his soap.

I reach up and push the brim back just enough to see him clearly.

"You're trying to distract me," I say.

"Is it working?"

"Maybe."

His eyes drop to my mouth. Stay there. "Good."

Then he's kissing me—not rushed, not desperate like those first nights, but slow and sure. Like he knows exactly what he's doing. Like he's got all the time in the world and plans to use it.

I kiss him back, hands sliding up his chest to his shoulders, and he makes this low sound in his throat that sends heat straight through me.

His free hand finds my waist, thumb brushing the bare skin where my shirt's ridden up, and I arch into him without thinking. He responds by pressing closer, his hips pinning me against the fence, and suddenly I'm very aware of every point where our bodies touch.

He breaks the kiss, but only just. His forehead rests against mine, breath uneven.

"We should stop," he says.

"Probably."

Neither of us moves.

His hand slides from my waist to my hip, fingers curling around the belt loop of my jeans. Not pulling. Just holding. Like he's considering his options.

"Addie's right there," I point out.

"I know."

"And Chace is probably around somewhere."

"Don't care."

I laugh against his mouth and he kisses me again, deeper this time, his tongue sliding against mine in a way that makes my knees weak. His other hand comes down from the fence to cup my jaw, tilting my head exactly where he wants it, and I let him because this—us—is still new enough to feel like stolen time.

Like something I might wake up from.

His mouth moves to my jaw, then my neck, finding that spot just below my ear that makes me gasp. He knows it now. Learned it over the past two weeks. Memorized it.

"Eli," I breathe.

"Hmm?"

"We really should stop."

"You keep saying that." His teeth graze my neck and I shudder. "Not very convincing."

My hands slide into his hair, holding him there even as I'm telling him to stop. "Someone's going to see."

"Let them."

He kisses me again, hard and claiming, and for a second I forget why stopping was important. Forget everything except the heat of his mouth and the solid weight of him against me and the way his hands feel on my body.

Then Chace's voice cuts across the pen.

"Jesus Christ, can you two not do that where I have to witness it?"

Eli pulls back with a sigh, but he doesn't step away. Just turns his head enough to look over his shoulder.

"Little busy here, Chace."

"Yeah, I can see that. It's traumatizing."

I duck my head, laughing into Eli's chest, and feel the rumble of his answering chuckle.

"Go away," Eli calls back.

"I'm trying to work."

"And now you're leaving."

Chace mutters something I don't catch, but I hear his boots retreating across the packed dirt. Addie's laugh follows him, bright and clear.

Eli looks back down at me, eyes warm, mouth curved.

"Where were we?" he asks.

I push at his chest, still grinning. "We were stopping."

"That doesn't sound right."

"It's not. But we should anyway." I reach up and tip his old hat back into place. "For now."

Something flickers in his expression. Heat. Promise.

"For now," he agrees.

Then he leans in close, mouth brushing my ear. "But tonight, that hat stays on."

My breath catches. "Yeah?"

"Yeah."

He steps back, finally giving me space, and the loss of his warmth feels like a shock. He looks at me for a long moment—taking in his hat, the flush I know is in my cheeks, the way I'm still leaning against the fence like my legs might not hold me.

"See you tonight, Clark," he says.

Then he's walking away, back straight, hands in his pockets, looking for all the world like he didn't just promise me something that's going to make the rest of this day feel about ten hours too long.

I watch him go, heart pounding, and shake my head.

***

I text him after dinner.

Me: You still expecting me tonight?

The response is immediate.

Eli: Yeah. You coming?

Me: Depends. You still want the hat?

Eli: Definitely want the hat.

I grin at my phone, heat already pooling low in my stomach.

Me: Give me twenty minutes.

His cabin is dark when I pull up except for the light over the door. I grab my hat from the passenger seat—I'd left it in the truck on purpose—and head inside without knocking.

He's waiting.

Leaning against the kitchen counter in jeans and nothing else, bare feet, hair still damp from the shower. He straightens when he sees me, eyes tracking down my body and back up, lingering on the hat.

"You wore it," he says.

"You asked me to."

"I did." He pushes off the counter and crosses to me. Slow. Deliberate. "Wasn't sure you would."

"When have I ever not done what you asked?"

His mouth curves. "Want me to make a list?"

I laugh and he catches me around the waist, pulling me flush against him. His skin is warm, still smelling like soap, and I slide my hands up his chest just to feel the solid muscle under my palms.

"Hi," I murmur.

"Hi."

He kisses me. Not gentle. Not hesitant. Just claiming, like he's been waiting all day for this and now that I'm here, he's not wasting time.

I kiss him back, fingers curling into his shoulders, and he walks me backward toward the bedroom without breaking contact. My legs hit the edge of the bed and I sink down, pulling him with me.

He follows, bracing himself above me, and reaches up to tip my hat back so he can see my face.

"Leave it on," he says.

"That was the deal."

"Good." His mouth finds my neck, teeth grazing the sensitive spot below my ear, and I arch into him. "Because I've been thinking about this all day."

"Yeah?"

"Yeah." His hands slide under my shirt, palms warm against my ribs. "You in this hat. In my bed. Exactly like this."

Heat floods through me. I reach for his belt, and he helps me, clothes disappearing in a tangle of limbs and breathless laughter.

The hat stays on.

***

After, we're both breathing hard, tangled together, the hat somehow still miraculously on my head though listing dramatically to one side.

Eli reaches up and straightens it, grinning. "Told you it should stay on."

I laugh and shove at his chest weakly. "You're ridiculous."

"You love it."

I do. God help me, I do.

He rolls to the side, pulling me with him so I'm tucked against his chest, his arm solid around my waist. My hat finally falls off, tumbling to the floor, and neither of us bothers to retrieve it.

For a while, we just lie there. Breathing. Existing.

His hand traces lazy patterns on my back. My fingers draw circles on his chest.

"You think Renee's going to say yes?" I ask eventually.

"Yeah. I do."

"You sound sure."

"I am. She saw what we're building here. She saw you with that colt. She's smart enough to recognize something good."

I tilt my head to look up at him. "And if she doesn't?"

"Then we find someone else. We keep going." His hand tightens on my waist. "We're not stopping, Hazel. Whatever it takes."

Whatever it takes.

The words settle warm in my chest, and I press my face back into his shoulder, breathing him in.

This. This is what I want.

Not just him, but this. The work. The ranch. The feeling of building something that matters.

I just don't know yet if I'm brave enough to keep it.

Chapter Thirty

Hazel

The alarm goes off at three-thirty and I'm already awake.

Eli's arm is heavy across my waist, his chest warm against my back, breath even and slow in the dark. We're in his cabin again. It's become easier to just stay.

I slip out of bed carefully, trying not to wake him, but his hand catches my wrist before I make it two steps.

"Where you going?" His voice is rough with sleep.

"Training. Four a.m., remember?"

"It's three-thirty."

"I need to grab clean clothes from Mae's first."

He tugs gently and I let him pull me back down, sitting on the edge of the bed. His thumb traces circles on the inside of my wrist.

"You could just keep clothes here," he says.

The offer hangs between us. Casual. Not casual at all.

"That would be convenient," I admit.

"Very convenient."

I lean down and kiss him. "I'll think about it."

A week ago, my boss gave me one final extension on my leave. One more week to "get things settled with family." That time is almost up now. Fall Classic is a week and a half away, and Lauren is expecting me back.

I haven't told anyone I'm even thinking about staying. Not Denver. Not Eli. Not Mae.

I don't know how to say it out loud when I'm still not sure what the answer is.

Eli releases my wrist and stretches, muscles shifting under skin in the dim light from the window. "I'll put coffee on."

By the time I'm dressed and in the kitchen, he's already there. Jeans low on his hips, no shirt yet, hair sticking up in about five different directions. He hands me a mug without a word and I take it, letting the warmth seep into my palms.

I lean against the counter, taking that first sip, and he moves behind me. His arms come around my waist, pulling me back against his chest, chin resting on my shoulder.

"Morning," he murmurs against my neck.

"You already said that."

"Felt like saying it again."

I smile into my coffee, letting myself lean into him. His skin is warm, solid, and I can feel his heartbeat against my back. Slow and steady.

This. This is what I didn't know I was missing.

His arms around me while the sun comes up. The easy silence that doesn't need filling.

We stand like that for a long moment, just breathing together, and I let myself pretend this could be every morning.

"We should go," I say eventually.

"We should." Neither of us moves. His arms tighten slightly, and he presses a kiss to my temple before letting me go.

The drive to Clark Ranch is quiet, his truck rumbling through the pre-dawn dark, my hand on his thigh. When we pull up to the barn, Mae's kitchen light is already on, same as every morning.

The colt nickers when he hears us approaching his stall. Two weeks of consistent work and he's starting to anticipate the routine. Look forward to it, even.

Eli grabs the halter and I follow him in, running my hand down the colt's neck while Eli clips the lead.

"He feels good," I say.

"He does."

We lead him out to the round pen and fall into the rhythm we've built. Eli warms him up on the lunge line while I watch, checking his movement, looking for any sign of soreness or resistance.

There's none.

Just smooth, powerful strides. Confidence in every step.

Addie shows up at four-thirty, right on schedule, already talking about the pattern she wants to work on. She rides for an hour while Eli and I watch, making small adjustments, calling out encouragement.

The colt is ready. Really ready. You can see it in the way he moves—listening, trusting, confident. Addie sits him like she was born to it.

Renee's two horses are arriving next week, right after the Classic. Two more inquiries came in yesterday. Mae's started talking about hiring help for mucking stalls.

Everything is working.

Everything.

By the time we cool the colt down and turn him out, the sun's fully up, painting everything gold.

"Same time tomorrow?" Addie asks, already heading toward her truck.

"Same time," I confirm.

She waves and drives off, and it's just me and Eli standing in the barn aisle.

He steps closer, hand finding my hip. "You got plans today?"

"Besides the usual? Not really."

"Good." His mouth curves. "Because I'm taking you somewhere."

"Where?"

"It's a surprise."

I raise an eyebrow. "A surprise."

"Yeah. And before you start listing all the things that need doing—the fence line can wait. The hay delivery's not until tomorrow. Mae's got the afternoon covered." He tips my chin up. "One day, Hazel. Just us."

Something warm unfurls in my chest. "Okay."

"Yeah?"

"Yeah."

His smile is slow and devastating. "Go get changed. Something comfortable. I'll pick you up in an hour."

An hour later, I'm standing on Mae's porch when his truck pulls up.

I've changed into jeans and a soft flannel shirt, boots that have seen better days, hair pulled back in a loose braid. Mae watched me get ready with a knowing look but didn't ask questions.

Eli gets out, and I notice the bed of his truck is loaded with something covered by a tarp.

"What's all that?" I ask, climbing in.

"You'll see."

We drive out past the main pastures, past the fence lines I know by heart, toward the back corner of Dawson property where the land starts to roll and the trees get thicker. I haven't been out here in years—not since we were teenagers and used to ride out to explore.

"Where are we going?" I ask.

"You'll recognize it when we get there."

The road narrows to a dirt track, then disappears altogether. He pulls off near a stand of pines and kills the engine.

When I step out, I can see the ridge through the trees. The spot where the property overlooks the valley, where you can see for miles on a clear day.

My breath catches. "Eli."

"Come on."

He grabs a basket from the truck bed, along with a blanket, and leads me through the trees. The ground slopes up gently, pine needles soft under our boots, the air smelling like sun-warmed sap and wild grass.

When we break through the tree line, the view opens up.

Rolling hills. The valley spreading out below us, green and gold and endless. Mountains in the distance, still capped with snow. The sky so blue it almost hurts to look at.

"I forgot how beautiful this is," I say quietly.

"I know." He sets the basket down and spreads the blanket in the shade of a massive pine. "Used to come out here when I needed to think. After you left."

Something tightens in my chest.

He unpacks the basket—sandwiches, fruit, cold drinks, cookies that look suspiciously like Mae's recipe.

"Did Mae know about this?" I ask.

"She might've helped with the food." He grins. "And she might've told me I was an idiot if I didn't bring you out here."

I laugh and settle onto the blanket beside him. "Mae's a romantic."

"Mae's smart."

We eat slowly, talking about nothing important. The weather. The colt. Addie's nerves about the Classic. He tells me about Chace getting into an argument with a fence post that the fence post definitely won. I tell him about the woman from the next county who wants to board three horses if we have space.

"We might need to expand the barn," I say, reaching for another cookie.

"We could. There's room on the north side. Wouldn't be hard to add six stalls."

We.

The word hangs between us.

I don't correct it.

After we eat, I lie back on the blanket, looking up through the pine branches at the sky. Eli settles beside me, propped on one elbow, looking down at me.

"What?" I ask.

"Nothing. Just—" He reaches out, tucking a strand of hair behind my ear. "You look happy."

"I am happy."

"Good." His hand lingers, thumb brushing my cheekbone. "You deserve to be."

My throat tightens. "Eli—"

He leans down and kisses me. Soft. Sweet. Not urgent or desperate like it's been lately. Just tender.

I kiss him back, hands sliding up to his shoulders, pulling him closer. He settles over me, careful not to put his full weight on me, one hand cradling my face.

The kiss deepens. His tongue slides against mine and I make a soft sound, fingers curling into his shirt. He responds by pressing closer, his body warm and solid against mine.

His mouth leaves mine to trail along my jaw, down my neck, finding that spot below my ear that makes me gasp. His hand slides under my shirt, palm warm against my ribs.

"Eli," I breathe.

"Hmm?"

"Someone could—"

"No one comes out here." His mouth curves against my skin. "Just us."

His hand moves higher, thumb brushing the underside of my breast through my bra, and heat floods through me. I arch into him and he groans, low and rough.

"Hazel."

My name sounds like a prayer.

I pull him back down into a kiss, hands sliding up his back, and he responds by settling more fully against me. I can feel him, hard against my hip, and the wanting is sudden and overwhelming.

"Yeah?" he asks, voice rough, eyes dark.

"Yeah."

After, we lie tangled together on the blanket, the sun warm on our skin, the breeze carrying the scent of pine and wild grass. His arm is solid around my waist, my head on his chest, our breathing slowly evening out.

"This was a good idea," I murmur.

I feel his chest rumble with quiet laughter. "Told you."

"You're very smug about it."

"I earned it."

I laugh and swat at him weakly. He catches my hand, threading our fingers together, and brings them to his lips.

For a long time, we just lie there. Breathing. Existing. The world quiet except for the wind in the pines and the distant call of a hawk.

"Fall Classic's coming up fast," he says eventually.

"Ten days."

"You nervous?"

"A little. More for Addie than anything. She's ready, but it's still a lot of pressure."

"She'll be fine. She's got you." He pauses. "We've got a good thing going here, Hazel."

The words settle heavy in my chest.

"Yeah," I say quietly. "We do."

He's quiet for a moment, his hand still tracing patterns on my back. "After the Classic, with Renee's horses coming, and those other inquiries—we're going to need help. Real help. Maybe someone full-time to manage the cattle."

We.

There it is again.

"That makes sense," I manage.

"Mae mentioned you've been keeping track of everything. Schedules, clients, feed orders. Said you're good at it."

"It's just organization."

"It's more than that." He shifts so he can look at me. "You're building something here. We are."

My throat feels tight. "Eli—"

"I'm not asking for anything," he says quietly. "I'm just saying—whatever happens, whatever you decide—this place is better with you in it. I'm better with you in it."

The words land like stones in still water, rippling outward, impossible to ignore.

I want to tell him. Want to say that I'm thinking about staying, that I haven't told Denver yet, that I have six days to make a choice that feels impossible.

But the words stick in my throat.

Because what if I choose wrong? What if I stay and can't make it work? What if I leave and regret it for the rest of my life?

"Come on," he says, sitting up and pulling me with him. "We should head back before Mae sends a search party."

We pack up the blanket and basket, our movements slow and easy, and I try to memorize this. The view. The way the light falls through the trees. The way his hand feels in mine.

The way it feels to be happy.

That night, I'm alone in my room at Mae's, staring at my phone.

Email notification from Lauren. Subject: **Final Decision - Need Confirmation by Wednesday**

Wednesday.

Six days from now.

The day after Fall Classic.

I open it.

Hazel,

I need your final answer by end of business Wednesday. If you're staying in Montana, I need to know so I can move forward with other candidates for your position. If you're coming back, I need a return date.

This is the last extension. I need to hear from you.

- Lauren

I set the phone down and stare at the ceiling.

Everything is working. The ranch. The colt. The boarders. Eli.

Everything is finally, impossibly working.

And in six days, I have to choose.

Stay here and build something real. Or go back to the life I spent five years creating.

I don't know how to choose between two futures when both feel like losing something I can't afford to lose.

The worst part is, I still haven't told Eli. Haven't told Mae. Haven't told anyone that this choice is even in front of me.

Because saying it out loud makes it real.

And I'm not ready for it to be real yet.

Chapter Thirty-One

Eli

Four days since our picnic.

Four days since I took her out to the ridge and let myself believe this could last. Since then, it's been more of the same—waking up with her tangled in sheets that have smelled like her for weeks now. Driving to the ranch together in the pre-dawn dark, her hand on my thigh, coffee in the cupholder, comfortable silence that doesn't need filling.

It's become routine. Expected.

She hasn't gone back to Mae's since the night we started this. Keeps a toothbrush in my bathroom now. Leaves hair ties on my nightstand. Her boots by the door next to mine.

I should probably feel like it's moving too fast.

I don't.

This is what I've wanted my whole life. Her. Here. Choosing to stay.

There's just this one thing. Small. Barely worth mentioning.

Her phone's been buzzing more. She checks it, face going careful, then puts it away without saying anything. When I ask if everything's okay, she smiles and says "Yeah, fine," and kisses me until I stop asking.

I tell myself it's nothing.

My phone vibrates while I'm in the shower. Chace.

Chace: Lake tonight- Don't forget. Everyone's going. Bring beer.

I stare at the message for a second, water running down my back, then type back.

Me: Yeah, I'll be there.

Chace: Bring your girl.

The text comes with three emojis—winky face, chili pepper, eggplant—because Chace is nothing if not subtle.

I don't respond to that. Just finish rinsing off and get out, towel around my waist.

I'm pulling on a clean shirt when Hazel emerges from the bedroom, still buttoning her cutoff shorts. She's wearing one of my flannels over a tank top, tucked in on one side, left loose on the other. Her hair's down, falling past her shoulders in waves.

She crosses to the door where her boots are waiting next to mine and pulls them on.

I watch her pull them on, those long legs on full display, shorts sitting high on her thighs, and something twists low in my gut.

"What?" she asks, catching me staring.

"Nothing."

"Liar."

She grins and grabs her jacket, and I'm still standing there wondering if I'll ever stop wanting her this intensely. If this need will ever settle into something manageable instead of constant.

Probably not.

"Come on," she says. "We're gonna be late."

"Yeah. Let's go."

***

The drive to the lake is quiet in the best way.

Her hand lands on my thigh automatically. The way it always does now. I thread our fingers together and she leans back with that soft sigh I've learned means she's content.

"Shae's been harassing me about tonight," she says.

"She give you the 'people will forget you exist' speech?"

"How'd you know?"

"She gave it to me too."

Hazel laughs. "We really are terrible at being social."

"Maybe we're not regular people."

"Maybe not."

The clearing comes into view a few minutes later. Trucks everywhere, parked at angles, headlights cutting through the growing dark. Music thumps loud enough to feel in my chest even with the windows up. Firelight flickers through the trees, orange and gold against the night.

I find a spot near the edge and park. For a second, we just sit there, engine ticking as it cools.

"You good?" she asks.

"Yeah. You?"

"Yeah."

She reaches for the door handle and I catch her wrist, pulling her back for a quick kiss. She smiles against my mouth.

"What was that for?" she asks.

"Nothing. Just wanted to."

Her eyes soften. "Come on. Before Chace sends a search party."

We grab beer from the back and head toward the noise. The heat from the fire hits as soon as we clear the trees. People everywhere—faces we've known our whole lives, voices layered over each other until they blur into one continuous hum.

Chace spots us immediately and grins. "Well, well. Look who showed."

"Don't start," I warn.

"I'm not starting anything." His grin widens. "Just observing."

Shae appears, barefoot, cup in hand. She takes one look at us and smirks. "Oh good. I was starting to think I'd have to drag you both here myself."

"You're very dramatic," Hazel says.

"It's part of my charm."

The group pulls us in. Someone hands me a beer. Someone else launches into a story. The fire crackles and spits, heat rolling off it in waves.

I end up standing next to Hazel, close enough that our arms brush. She leans into me slightly, and I slide my hand to her lower back without thinking. Just resting there.

She glances up at me, something soft in her eyes.

"You two want a chair?" Chace asks, gesturing to the empty spots near the fire.

"We're good," I say.

Hazel shifts closer, her hip against mine, and I keep my hand where it is.

I stand there with my arm around her waist, beer in hand, listening to Chace tell some story about a date that went sideways, and I realize I'm happy.

Not just content. Happy.

This is what I wanted. Her. Here. Part of things. Part of my life. Not hiding. Not temporary.

Or at least, it doesn't feel temporary.

She leans into me, laughing at something Shae said, and I press a kiss to her temple without thinking.

Chace sees it and grins. "You two are disgusting."

"Jealous," I shoot back.

"Extremely."

Hazel looks up at me, smiling, and something in my chest settles.

This is right.

This is—

Her phone buzzes.

She pulls it out, glances at the screen, and goes still.

I feel it immediately. The way her body tenses against mine. The way her smile disappears. The way she takes a half-step away, breaking contact.

"I'll be right back," she says.

"You good?" Shae asks.

"Yeah. Just need to take this."

She's already walking away, phone pressed to her ear.

I watch her go, that happy certainty from thirty seconds ago evaporating.

My hand tightens on my beer.

The conversation flows around me. Someone mentions Fall Classic—only a week out now. Addie lights up, talking about the colt, how confident she feels, how ready they are.

"Hazel's amazing with him," Addie says, grinning. "Seriously. He listens to her better than anyone."

"That's all you," I say automatically. "You're the one riding him."

But I'm not really listening. My attention tracks Hazel, standing alone by the water, her free hand gesturing as she talks.

She's gone maybe five minutes. When she comes back, the ease from before is gone. She takes her place beside me, but there's distance now. She's composed. Guarded. I put my arm back around her waist.

"Everything okay?" Shae asks.

"Yeah. Just—that was my boss. In Denver."

The fire crackles in the sudden silence.

My arm is still around her waist. I don't move it. Don't pull away.

But something inside me goes cold.

"Denver?" Chace asks carefully. "Thought maybe you'd stick around after the Classic."

"I don't know yet." Hazel's voice is careful now. Defensive. "My leave already ended. They've been calling all week. I'm just—I'm keeping my options open. I mean, I'm here now. I'm helping with the ranch. But I don't know what happens after Fall Classic. I'm just taking it day by day."

Taking it day by day.

Keeping her options open.

Her leave already ended.

The words land like physical blows.

"Makes sense," Chace says quietly. "Don't want to burn bridges, right?"

"Right," Hazel says.

Shae changes the subject, steering the conversation toward Fall Classic prep, toward safer ground.

But I'm not listening anymore.

Five minutes ago I was standing here thinking about how right this felt. How settled. How happy.

I thought—

I don't know what I thought.

That maybe she'd decided without saying it. That staying at my place every night was a choice that mattered. That this routine we'd built meant something.

But she's keeping her options open.

Taking it day by day.

Like the last few weeks were just borrowed time.

The fire gets quieter. People start drifting toward the water. The group thins out.

I stay where I am, Hazel still against my side, but the ease from before is gone.

After a while, I lean down close to her ear. "Want another beer?"

She nods, and we drift away from the group toward my truck.

The tailgate's down already—Chace must've grabbed beer earlier. I hop up, reaching into the cooler, and Hazel follows, settling on the edge, legs dangling.

It's quieter here. Still close enough to hear the music and laughter, but far enough that we're not in the middle of it.

I hand her a beer and she takes it, our fingers brushing. She takes a sip, then looks up at the stars starting to appear overhead.

"It's nice," she says softly. "Being here. With everyone."

"Yeah?"

"Yeah." She glances at me. "I forgot what this felt like. Just... being part of things again."

I set my beer down and step closer, moving between her legs. Her breath catches.

"You are part of things," I say quietly. Because I need her to believe it as much as I do.

"I know. It just took me a while to remember that."

My hands find her thighs, warm and bare under my palms. She goes still, watching me.

"This," I say, running my hands up slowly. "Been thinking about this since you put those shorts on."

Her breath catches. "Yeah?"

"Yeah." My thumbs brush the inside of her thighs and she leans forward, her hands sliding to my chest.

"Eli—"

I kiss her. Hard. Her hands fist in my shirt and I pull her closer, needing her against me, needing—

"GET A ROOM!"

Chace's voice carries from across the clearing, followed by laughter.

Hazel pulls back, breathless, and laughs. "Jesus."

I grin, forehead resting against hers. "Subtle."

"Very." She's still smiling, cheeks flushed, and she doesn't move away. Just stays close, her hand on my chest, my hands still on her thighs.

"Should we go back?" she asks.

"Probably."

But neither of us moves right away.

Eventually, we head back toward the fire, her hand in mine. A few people glance over and grin, but nobody makes a big deal out of it.

We settle back into the group. Hazel leans against my side, and I keep my arm around her waist, not hiding, not careful.

Just us.

The conversation shifts to Shae's vet work. She mentions finishing her certification last week—three years of night classes finally done.

"That's amazing," Hazel says. "You must be relieved."

"You have no idea." Shae grins. "Dr. Morris wants me to take on more responsibility now. Better pay, better hours. And I've been thinking about mobile work eventually. Going ranch to ranch instead of waiting for emergencies."

"You'd be good at that," Hazel says.

"You think?"

"Yeah. You're bossy enough."

Shae laughs and flips her off.

The fire crackles. People talk and laugh.

But the tightness in my chest doesn't ease.

Hazel shifts, looking up at me. "You okay?"

"Yeah."

"You got quiet."

"Just tired."

She studies me for a second, then nods. "Yeah. Me too. Should we head out?"

"Yeah."

We say our goodbyes. Walk back to the truck together. She climbs in, and I follow, starting the engine and pulling out onto the dark road.

She's quiet for the first few minutes. Then she shifts in her seat, hand landing on my thigh again.

"Tonight was nice," she says.

"Yeah."

"I'm glad we went."

"Me too."

She's quiet for another beat. Her hand moves slightly, like she wants to say something but doesn't know how.

"You sure you're okay?"

"I'm fine, Hazel."

The words come out flatter than I mean them to. She pulls her hand back. Just an inch. But I feel it.

She doesn't push. Just settles back in her seat, arms crossed now.

The silence isn't comfortable anymore.

When we reach my cabin, I expect her to say something. To acknowledge the distance opening between us.

She doesn't.

Just follows me inside, and the second the door closes behind us, she's on me.

Kissing me hard. Desperate. Her hands already tugging at my shirt.

I kiss her back, hands finding her hips, pulling her against me. Part of me knows this is avoidance. That we should talk about what she said at the lake.

But I don't want to talk.

I want this. Her hands on me. Her body against mine. Proof that she's still here, still mine, even if it's just right now.

Clothes come off and we fall into bed, and for a while nothing else matters.

***

After, she's curled against my side, her head on my chest, breathing soft and even. Asleep, maybe. Or close to it.

I stare at the ceiling, my hand running slow circles on her bare shoulder.

This morning I woke up thinking I had everything I wanted.

Her here. With me. Every morning. Every night.

I thought it meant something.

This is enough, I tell myself now. Right now. This moment. Her here with me.

This is enough.

But it's not.

Because I heard what she said tonight. Keeping her options open. Taking it day by day. Her leave already ended, and she still doesn't know if she's staying.

She's here. But she's not mine. Not really.

Not the way I need her to be.

I pull her closer, pressing my face into her hair, and tell myself it doesn't matter.

This is enough. It has to be.

But the tightness in my chest doesn't ease.

And I know—I know—it's not.

Chapter Thirty-Two

Hazel

I wake to the sound of the shower running and Eli's side of the bed already cold. Not just cool. Cold like he's been up for a while.

Gray pre-dawn light filters through the curtains. His cabin bedroom. I've woken up here enough times now that it should feel familiar.

Today it doesn't.

My body aches in that good way. Last night—after the party—we couldn't keep our hands off each other. That feels like a week ago suddenly.

The shower cuts off.

I sit up, reaching for my shirt from the floor. By the time I've pulled it on, he's coming out of the bathroom, towel around his waist, hair dripping.

"Morning," I say.

"Morning." He doesn't look at me. Just crosses to the dresser and pulls out clothes.

I watch him dress. Jeans. T-shirt. Boots. Efficient movements. No lingering. No glance over his shoulder to catch my eye.

"You're up early," I try.

"Four a.m.'s in twenty minutes."

"I know. I just meant—" I stop. He's already heading for the door. "Eli."

He pauses, hand on the doorframe. Looks at me.

His expression gives me nothing.

"Nothing," I say. "I'll be out in a minute."

He nods once and disappears down the hall.

I sit there staring at the empty doorway. The unease from last night hasn't gone anywhere. It's settled in my chest like a stone.

He's just tired. We stayed late at the lake. Drank too much. That's all.

Except it doesn't feel like that's all.

I push off the bed and get dressed fast. Pull on yesterday's jeans, find my boots by the door, run my fingers through my hair without bothering with a mirror.

By the time I make it to the kitchen, he's already got coffee going. He hands me a mug without a word, our fingers not quite touching.

"Thanks."

"Mm."

We drink in silence. Not the comfortable kind we've built over these past weeks. The kind where we don't need words because everything's already said.

This is different. This sits heavy.

I watch him over the rim of my mug. He's staring out the window at the dark yard, jaw tight, shoulders set like he's bracing for something.

"You sure you're good?" I try.

"Yeah." He doesn't look at me. "Just a long day ahead."

That's not what this is, but I don't push. Don't know how.

"Addie's going to want to work on transitions today. I was thinking we could set up cones for the pattern, maybe—"

"Whatever you think is best."

The words are fine. His tone is fine.

But he's looking out the window when he says it. Not at me.

"Okay." I set my mug down. "We should go."

He drains his coffee and sets the mug in the sink. "Yeah."

He's out the door before I can say anything else.

I follow, chest tight, and climb into his truck without a word.

The drive to Clark Ranch is quiet.

Usually his hand finds my thigh within the first mile. Usually I lean into him, or he makes some comment about how I look half-asleep, or we talk about the day ahead. Small things. Easy things.

Today his hands stay on the wheel, ten and two, eyes on the road.

I sit with my coffee, watching the dark landscape pass through the window, and don't know how to bridge whatever gap opened up overnight.

The fence line between properties appears on the left. Dawson land ending, Clark land beginning. I've crossed this line a hundred times in the past few weeks until I stopped noticing where one ended and the other started.

Today I notice.

When we pull up to the barn, his truck barely stops before he's out, heading for the tack room without waiting for me.

I sit there for a second, hands wrapped around my mug, the engine ticking as it cools.

Something's wrong.

The words sit in my throat. I swallow them.

I get out and follow him inside.

The barn smells like hay and leather and horses settling into morning routines. The colt nickers when he hears us approaching his stall, head over the door, ears pricked forward.

Eli's already got the halter and lead in hand, movements efficient as he opens the stall door.

I step in beside him, reaching to run my hand down the colt's neck. "Hey, buddy. Ready to work?"

The colt leans into my touch, warm and solid. Eli clips the lead without looking at me.

"I'll take him out," he says.

"I can help—"

"I've got it."

Not sharp. Not mean.

Just final.

I step back and watch him lead the colt out into the aisle, then toward the round pen in the growing dawn light.

Addie's truck pulls up just as they disappear through the gate. She hops out, bright-eyed despite the early hour, her energy a sharp contrast to the weight sitting on my chest.

"Morning!" She grabs her helmet from the truck bed. "How's he looking today?"

"Good." I force a smile. "Eli's getting him warmed up now."

We walk to the pen together. The sky's starting to lighten, streaks of pink and orange cutting through the gray. It's going to be a clear day. Hot by afternoon.

Good riding weather.

Eli's already moving the colt through groundwork when we reach the rail. Lunging him at a walk, then a trot, his focus absolute. Every cue precise. Every movement intentional.

Nothing wasted.

Not even a glance in my direction.

Addie starts talking about her plan for today's ride—working on lead changes, tightening up the pattern for Fall Classic, making sure the colt's responsive to subtle cues. I nod along, answering when she asks questions, but my attention keeps drifting to Eli.

To the way he's standing with his back to us.

To the way he hasn't looked at me once since we got here.

"Hazel?"

I blink. "Sorry, what?"

Her eyes narrow slightly. "I asked if you think we should add barrels to the pattern today or wait until tomorrow."

"Oh. Uh—" I refocus. "Tomorrow. Let's make sure the colt's solid on the basics first."

"Okay. Cool." She adjusts her helmet and turns back to watch Eli work.

He brings the colt over a few minutes later, handing the lead to Addie without ceremony. "He's ready for you."

"Thanks." Addie takes the lead and moves to mount up.

I step closer to Eli. Close enough that our arms almost brush. "You want to work him from the center or the rail?"

"Rail's fine."

"Okay."

I wait for him to look at me. To give me anything that feels like us.

He doesn't.

Just moves to the far side of the pen, positioning himself where he can watch Addie work.

I stay where I am for a second, throat tight, then move to the opposite rail.

We work like that for the next hour. Calling out instructions to Addie. Adjusting her position. Praising the colt's responses. Both of us professional. Efficient.

And with the entire pen between us.

The colt moves beautifully. Responsive to every cue, confident in his stride, trusting Addie in a way that makes my chest tight with something like pride. Three weeks ago he was green and uncertain. Now he's ready for competition.

We did this.

Me and Eli and Addie and everyone who's put work into this ranch.

But standing here, watching Addie ride while Eli stays on the opposite side of the pen, it doesn't feel like victory.

When Addie finally dismounts, grinning and breathless, she doesn't seem to notice the tension radiating between me and Eli.

"He felt amazing today," she says. "Like, really amazing. I think we're ready."

"He looked good," Eli says.

"Really good," I add, forcing warmth into my voice. "You're both ready."

Addie beams and leads the colt toward the barn to cool him down, already talking to him in that soft voice she uses when she's pleased.

Leaving me and Eli alone in the pen.

I turn to face him. He's already heading for the gate.

"Eli."

He stops. Doesn't turn around.

"Are we okay?" The words come out quieter than I meant them to.

For a long moment, he doesn't answer. Just stands there, shoulders tight, hands flexing at his sides.

Then he turns. Meets my eyes.

And there's something in his expression that makes my stomach drop.

Not anger. Not coldness.

Resignation.

"We're fine," he says.

The word lands wrong.

He walks away before I can respond.

I stand there in the empty pen, dust settling around my boots, and feel the distance between us stretch into something I can't cross.

By noon, we're in the east pasture repairing fence.

The work is mindless in the best way. Physical. Pull wire. Hammer staples. Move to the next post. The sun beats down, sweat soaking through my shirt within the first twenty minutes, and I focus on the rhythm of it.

Anything but the distance between us.

Eli works ten feet away, methodical and silent. We've repaired fences together a hundred times over the years. Knew how to do it as teenagers. We know the rhythm. Who moves where. When to hand off tools. When to step back so the other person has room to work.

Today it feels choreographed. Careful.

I yank wire tight and hammer a staple into place, the impact jarring up my arm. Move to the next post. Repeat.

My phone buzzes in my back pocket.

I ignore it.

It buzzes again. Then a third time in quick succession.

Eli glances over. Doesn't say anything. Just looks.

I pull the phone out, chest already tight.

Caller ID: **Lauren - Manager**

My boss.

My stomach drops.

I stare at the screen, thumb hovering over the decline button. It rings once more, the vibration insistent against my palm.

Eli's watching now. Not obviously. But I feel his attention shift. Feel the weight of his gaze even though he's pretending to focus on the fence.

"I need to take this," I say, hating how my voice sounds. Apologetic. Guilty.

He nods once and goes back to hammering.

I walk away, boots crunching on dry grass, putting distance between us until I'm far enough that he won't hear.

I answer on the fifth ring.

"Lauren. Hi."

"Hazel! Finally. I've been trying to reach you all morning." Her voice is bright, energetic. The way it always is when she wants something. "You got a minute?"

I glance back at Eli. He's hammering a staple, shoulders tense, focused on the work.

"Yeah. What's up?"

"I'll cut to the chase. We want you back. Not just back—we want to promote you. Senior analyst. Your own team. Twenty percent raise. Full benefits package. Corner office if you want it."

The words hit like punches.

"Lauren—"

"I know what you're going to say. You're helping your aunt. Family stuff. I get it. But Hazel, this is a huge opportunity. We've got projects lined up that need someone with your skill set, and honestly? You're the only one I trust to handle them."

My throat feels tight. "That's—that's really generous. I just—"

"There's more." She's talking fast now, the way she does when she's closing a deal. "We're partnering with three new firms next quarter. International clients. The kind of portfolio that could set you up for VP track in two years. Two years, Hazel. You'd be one of the youngest VPs in the company."

VP track.

The thing I used to daydream about. The goal that kept me working late nights and weekends. The reason I convinced myself leaving here five years ago was the right choice.

"When would you need an answer?" I ask, hating how weak my voice sounds.

"That's the thing." She pauses, and I hear papers shuffling on her end. "I need to know by end of week. Thursday night at the latest. We're restructuring the whole department, and if you're not coming back, I need to move forward without you. It's not personal—it's just logistics. I have to fill the position one way or another."

Thursday.

Three days from now.

Two days before Fall Classic.

"I need to think about it," I say.

"Of course. Take your time. Well—three days." She laughs like it's a joke. "But seriously, Hazel. This is real. This is the kind of position people wait years for. The kind that doesn't come around twice. Don't let it slip away because you're stuck mucking stalls in Montana."

Something sharp twists in my chest. The way she says "mucking stalls"—like I'm wasting time. Like none of this matters.

"I'll call you by Thursday," I say, keeping my voice level.

"Perfect. I'll send over the formal offer letter this afternoon. Salary breakdown, benefits package, start date—the whole nine yards. Look it over and let me know if you have questions."

"Okay."

"Great. Talk soon. And Hazel?" Her tone shifts, more serious now. "I really hope you say yes. You're too talented to waste it."

She hangs up.

I stand there, phone still pressed to my ear, hands shaking.

Senior analyst. My own team. VP track.

Everything I worked for before I came back here.

Everything I told myself I wanted.

The sun beats down on my shoulders. Sweat drips down my spine. In the distance, I can hear the rhythmic sound of Eli hammering staples into fence posts.

My chest feels too tight.

I force myself to turn around. To walk back to the fence line. To pretend my hands aren't trembling.

Eli's moved to the next post. Still working. Still not looking at me.

I pick up the wire cutters and get back to work, my movements mechanical.

"Everything okay?" he asks after a minute. His voice is careful. Neutral.

"Yeah. Just work stuff."

He nods. Doesn't ask what kind of work stuff. Doesn't ask if it's important. Doesn't ask if I'm okay.

Just nods and goes back to the fence.

We finish the section in silence, the sun climbing higher, the temperature rising until the heat feels oppressive.

We head back to the barn.

The afternoon work needs doing. Feed. Water. Stalls. Normal things.

Eli's in the feed room when I walk past. I see him through the door—back to me, scooping grain—and I keep walking. Head to the tack room instead. Find something that needs organizing.

When I come out ten minutes later, he's gone.

I check my phone. Nothing. No messages from him.

I should go to the house.

Instead I stand in the barn aisle, breathing in hay and leather and the faint smell of horses, and try to remember what it felt like yesterday when everything was easy.

By late afternoon, I'm helping Mae in the garden when I see Eli's truck pull out of the drive.

He doesn't come say goodbye. Doesn't stop at the house.

Just leaves.

Mae notices. "That boy left without a word."

"He's probably tired."

"Probably." She doesn't look at me, just keeps pulling weeds. "You two fighting?"

"No."

"Feels like it."

I don't respond. Don't trust my voice.

"Reminds me of when you two were younger," Mae says after a minute. "How you'd tiptoe around each other after some petty argument. Both too stubborn to just say what you meant."

My chest tightens. "It's not like that."

"Isn't it?"

I meet her eyes. She's not accusing. Just observing. Waiting.

"I don't know," I admit quietly.

She nods, satisfied. "Well. You'll figure it out or you won't. But don't wait too long. That kind of careful turns into distance real quick."

She goes back to the garden, leaving me sitting there with dirt on my hands and doubt in my chest.

By evening, I'm alone in my room, staring at my phone.

Email notification from Lauren. **Subject: Time Sensitive - Need Response**

I open it.

Hazel, just checking in. Thursday deadline still stands. This is a great opportunity but I need to move forward either way. Let me know.

Thursday.

Three days from now.

I close the email and set the phone on the nightstand.

Then pick it up again.

Open my texts with Eli.

The last message is from yesterday morning. Him asking if I wanted coffee before we left. Me saying yes.

Normal. Easy.

Before everything shifted.

I type: **Can we talk?**

Stare at it. Delete it.

Type: **I'm sorry.**

Delete that too.

I set the phone down and stare at the ceiling.

Senior analyst. My own team. VP track. Everything I spent five years building.

But all I can see is Eli's face this morning. The careful distance. The resignation in his eyes when he said "We're fine."

We're not fine.

And I can't keep pretending we are.

I can't keep avoiding this conversation just because I don't have the right answer yet.

I grab my keys and head out.

The drive to his cabin is short. Too short.

My hands shake on the wheel. I don't know what I'm going to say when he opens the door. Don't know if I have an answer yet.

But I can't keep running from this.

Can't keep letting him think I've already decided to leave.

His truck is there when I pull up. Lights on inside.

I sit for a long moment, engine ticking as it cools, trying to find the words.

I don't have them.

But I get out anyway.

And knock.

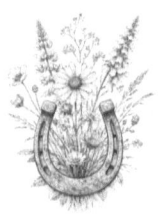

CHAPTER THIRTY-THREE

Hazel

The door opens.

Eli's there, filling the frame, and for a second we just look at each other.

"Hey," he says.

"Hey." My voice comes out steadier than I expected.

He steps back to let me in, and I walk past him into the cabin. The smell hits me immediately—coffee and sawdust and something warm I can't name. Home-adjacent.

He closes the door behind us, and the click of the latch feels final.

I turn to face him. "Can we talk?"

Something shifts in his expression. Not surprise. More like resignation. Like he already knows this conversation isn't going to be easy.

"Yeah," he says. "Of course."

He leans against the counter, arms crossed loosely, waiting.

And I realize I still don't know how to say this.

"I got a call from work," I start. "About a job offer."

His expression doesn't change. No flinch. No tightening. Just attention.

"Okay," he says.

"They're pushing harder about returning," I continue, keeping my voice even. "There's an offer on the table. A promotion. Better pay. More responsibility. The kind of thing you don't usually get offered twice."

I hate the way it sounds when I say it out loud. Bigger. Heavier. More real.

He takes a slow breath, eyes on me. Waiting.

"I wanted to tell you because I didn't want it to feel like I was hiding anything." That's true. Mostly. "This isn't me saying I'm going. It's just—information. Something I have to think through."

"When do they need to know?" he asks.

My stomach twists. "Thursday."

He nods once. The silence stretches.

"I haven't decided yet," I say. The words come out softer than I expect. Careful.

He looks at me for a long second, his face going still in a way I don't recognize right away.

Not angry. Not hurt.

Closed.

"You're leaving," he says.

It's not a question.

It lands between us like something already decided, and for a split second I just stare at him, trying to figure out how we got there so fast.

"That's not what I said." I keep my voice steady, even when my chest tightens. "I said I haven't decided."

He doesn't move. Not closer. Not away. Just still. Arms folded now, weight shifted back onto his heels, like he's bracing for something he already sees coming.

"You're still deciding," he says quietly. "That tells me everything I need to know."

My stomach drops.

I shake my head. "I'm here. Standing right in front of you. I've been here. The ranch is working. *We're* working."

He doesn't argue. Doesn't move. Just looks at me like the conclusion's already drawn.

"I'm not doing this," he says.

"Doing what?"

"Negotiating my own ending."

The words hit like a slap.

"That's not—" I step toward him. "You're making it sound like I'm already gone."

"Aren't you?" He shifts his weight back. Creating space. "You're standing here telling me you haven't decided. That's the same thing."

"No, it's not. I just need—"

"Time." His jaw tightens. "I know."

"What's wrong with that?" My voice climbs despite myself. "I'm allowed to think things through."

"Think about what?" He's not yelling. But something sharp edges into his tone. "Whether I'm worth it?"

"That's not what this is."

"Then what is it?"

"It's about not making a mistake!" The words tumble out too fast. "About not waking up in five years regretting giving up everything I worked for because I was scared or—"

"Or scared of being in love with me?"

I freeze.

He exhales slowly, and when he speaks again his voice is quieter. Harder. "That's what you're afraid of. That choosing me means choosing wrong."

"No. You're twisting—"

"No, I'm listening. Loud and clear, Hazel."

"You're not!" Frustration claws up my throat. "You're acting like I've already chosen against you."

"You haven't chosen." He crosses his arms. "That's the problem."

"I'm not ready yet," I say, and I hate how my voice cracks on the word. "Why can't that be enough for now?"

Something flickers through his expression.

"Because 'for now' is how you left last time."

The room goes still.

My chest tightens. "This isn't the same."

"Isn't it?"

"Mae's fine now. The ranch is stable. You've got Chace, you've got work—you'll be fine."

His expression shifts. Goes cold.

"And we could still see each other," I add quickly, desperately. "Denver's only a few hours away. I could come back on weekends—"

"No."

The word cuts clean through.

"People do long distance—"

"I won't be someone you visit on weekends." His voice stays level but there's steel in it now. "I won't be the thing you keep in Montana while you build your real life somewhere else."

"That's not—"

"You're either here or you're not." He holds my gaze. "There's no in-between."

Panic crawls up my spine. "So this is an ultimatum?"

"It's a boundary."

"It's the same thing!"

"No." He's not yelling. But the word lands hard. "It's me telling you what I can survive. And weekends aren't it."

My hands shake. I press them against my thighs.

"You said you'd take whatever I could give," I say, hearing the desperation now. "You said that."

Pain flickers across his face. Brief. Gone.

"I was wrong." He meets my eyes. "I thought I could. I can't."

Silence stretches.

The words are right there. *I'll stay. I'm choosing you.*

But they won't come.

"I just—" My voice sounds small. "I need a little more time."

Something in him breaks.

"You think I'll be fine." Not a question. An accusation. "You keep talking like the worst thing that happens is things being hard for a while."

"What else—"

"I'll never be fine without you." His voice goes rough. Raw. "I wasn't fine the first time. I learned how to *pretend*." He drags a hand through his hair and I see it shake. "There's a difference."

A tear escapes before I can stop it.

"When you came back," he continues, " For awhile I thought—" He stops. Starts again. "It felt like everything made sense. Like I hadn't been stupid to hope." His voice cracks. "Losing you once almost broke me. Watching you decide to leave again?" He shakes his head. "That's worse."

The words land like physical blows.

My throat closes. Tears burn hot behind my eyes and I can't stop them anymore. One escapes, then another, tracking down my cheeks.

"I'm sorry," I whisper.

It's all I have left. The only truth that matters and it changes nothing.

"I know."

The gentleness in those two words makes it worse somehow. Like he's already letting me go.

I see it now—too late, always too late—how every careful word has been a knife. How "I haven't decided" translates to "you're not enough." How asking for time means I'm already halfway gone.

I thought I was protecting us both.

I was just breaking him slowly instead of all at once.

"I'm not trying to hurt you," I say, but my voice cracks on the words.

"I know," he says again.

The silence that follows feels final.

Then he takes a breath, and I know—I *know*—what's coming before he says it.

"I won't do this again, Hazel."

Not angry. Not pleading. Just absolutely certain.

"I survived you leaving once. I'm not doing it twice."

It's not a plea for me to stay.

It's him protecting himself from me.

The room tilts. My chest feels too tight, like I can't get enough air. I want to say something—anything—that will undo this. That will rewind five minutes and let me walk in here with a different answer.

But I don't have a different answer.

I stand there, waiting. For him to soften. To reach for me. To ask me to stay even though we both know I can't promise I will.

He doesn't.

His expression is closed now. Guarded. The same way it was when I first came back and he didn't trust me yet.

I did this. I put those walls back up.

So I turn toward the door.

My legs don't feel steady. Each step away from him is harder than the last, like I'm walking through water. Or maybe quicksand. Something that's pulling me under.

My hand finds the door handle and I stop.

I don't know what I'm waiting for. Some last word. Some sign that this isn't really happening.

"This wasn't how I wanted it to go," I manage without turning around.

My voice sounds hollow even to my own ears.

"Neither did I, Hazel," he says.

I open the door. The night air hits my face, cold and sharp, and I suck in a breath that doesn't quite fill my lungs.

I don't look back.

I can't.

Because if I see his face right now—if I see what I'm doing to him—I'll break completely. And I need to make it to my truck first.

The gravel crunches under my boots. Each step echoing too loud in the quiet.

I climb in. Pull the door shut. The click of the latch sounds final.

My hands shake so hard I can barely get the key in the ignition.

The engine turns over, too loud, and I force myself to put the truck in reverse. To back out of his driveway. To leave.

I make it to the end of his road before the tears come for real.

Then I can't see anything through them.

I pull over onto the shoulder and just sit there, gripping the steering wheel, trying to breathe through the pressure in my chest.

I just lost the only thing that made staying feel possible.

No—that's not true.

I didn't lose it.

I walked away from it.

Because even now, even sitting here shaking and crying and feeling like my chest is caving in, I still can't say the words he needs to hear.

I'll stay. I choose you. I'm not leaving.

The words are right there.

And I still can't promise them.

What does that make me?

I don't know.

I just know I can't breathe. Can't think. Can't do anything but sit here in the dark and feel everything I just broke.

Chapter Thirty-Four

Eli

Morning comes and I don't move.

The light creeps in through the thin gap between the curtains, pale and gray, cutting across the ceiling above my bed. I've been awake for hours. Long enough to hear the birds start up outside. Long enough to know exactly what time it is without checking.

Training started ten minutes ago.

I stare at the ceiling and let the moment pass.

I'm already dressed. Jeans. T-shirt. Boots laced tight. I did that before the sky even started to lighten, like if I got myself ready it would make the decision easier.

It didn't.

If I show up, I'll break.

The thought lands heavy and certain. Not dramatic. Just true.

I push my palms into the mattress and sit up, elbows braced on my knees. My chest feels tight. Like there's not enough air in the cabin.

I picture the barn anyway. The way the colt will pace when he hears footsteps. Addie checking her watch. Hazel stepping into the pen, scanning for me without realizing she's doing it.

I can't.

Not because I'm angry. Because if I look at her—really look at her—I'll pretend everything's fine just to keep her there another day. Another week. Another maybe.

Last night replays whether I want it to or not. The way she stood in front of me, eyes bright and terrified. The careful way she chose her words. The way she kept saying *time* like it didn't already have teeth.

I meant what I said.

I can't survive hoping again.

I stand and cross to the window. From here I can see the edge of the pasture, dew still clinging to the grass, fence line stretching toward the trees.

The world doesn't pause just because something broke.

I check my phone. No messages. No missed calls.

Good.

I grab my jacket off the chair and shrug it on. The fabric smells faintly like hay and her shampoo. My stomach turns but I don't take it off.

I step out onto the porch. The cool air bites, sharp enough to ground me.

I lock the door behind me and walk toward my truck, boots crunching against the gravel.

I don't know what happens next.

I just know I can't stand in that barn and act like maybe is enough.

I'm halfway to the truck when I hear boots on gravel behind me.

"Thought that might be you."

I stop but don't turn right away. I know that voice. Easy. Unhurried. Chace comes up beside me, hands shoved into the pockets of his hoodie, and glances past me toward the barn like he's just out here taking in the morning.

"You missed training?" I knew someone would come here looking for me.

"Didn't miss it," I say. "I know exactly what time it is."

He huffs out a quiet breath. "Addie noticed. Hazel did too." He pauses, toeing at the gravel. "Asked where you were."

My chest tightens. "What'd you tell her?"

"Nothing. Figured that was your call." He studies me sideways, not pushing, just taking stock the way he does. "Something happened."

I lean back against the hood of the truck and let out a slow breath. "We talked."

"That bad, huh."

I don't correct him.

Chace shifts his weight, giving me room without going anywhere. That's always been his way — close enough that you know he's not leaving, far enough that you don't feel cornered. He lets the silence sit between us until I'm ready to fill it.

"She asked for more time," I say finally.

He nods slowly, like he already knew. Maybe he did. "And you said no."

"I said no."

"Eli—"

"I can't live in maybe, Chace." My voice comes out rougher than I intend. "I've been living in maybe for five years. I'm done."

He's quiet for a moment. When he speaks, his voice is careful. "She's still here."

"She hasn't decided to stay."

"That's not the same thing as leaving."

The words land harder than I expect. I push off the truck and pace a few steps, jaw tight, hand scrubbing the back of my neck. Chace watches me without comment, letting me work through it.

"You know what kills me?" I say, stopping. "It's not even the leaving. It's the not knowing. Standing here every day not knowing if I'm building something or just — filling time until she figures out she doesn't want it."

Chace is quiet for a beat. "That's fair," he says finally. "It is. But Eli—" He hesitates, and I can see him choosing his words carefully, caught between us the way he always is. "She came back. And she didn't have to."

"I know that."

"And she's still here. Working the ranch, working that colt, working to earn something back with you." He pauses. "I'm not saying you're wrong to need more than maybe. You're not. But I don't think she's as far from a decision as you think."

Something tightens in my chest. "You don't know that."

"No," he admits. "I don't." He steps closer and claps a hand on my shoulder, solid and familiar. "What I know is that you skipping training this morning hurt her. And I think you know that too."

I don't answer.

He gives my shoulder a squeeze before letting go. "For what it's worth — you're not wrong to want more than maybe. You never were."

He turns back toward the barn, boots slow on the gravel. Then he pauses without looking back.

"Tomorrow?" he asks quietly.

I stare out at the pasture. "I don't know."

"That's fine," he says. "One day at a time."

He walks away and leaves me standing there alone with the quiet.

This isn't anger.

This is me choosing not to bleed out slowly.

***

By the time Chace heads back, the sun's higher and the morning's half gone.

I stand there another minute. Let the choice finish forming instead of backing out of it.

Then I go looking for Addie.

She's at the rail of the round pen, helmet on, colt walking slow circles. Hazel's not with her. That shouldn't matter. It does.

I don't step inside the pen. Just lean against the fence and wait until Addie notices me.

"Oh—hey." She slows the colt to a stop. "You coming in?"

"No." I clear my throat. "I'm heading out."

She frowns. "Out like… for the day?"

"Yeah." I pause. "For a while actually."

Her frown deepens. "How long's a while?"

"Through the show. I'll be there Saturday, but I'm done training."

She goes still. "What?"

"I'll handle logistics," I say quickly. "Hauling. Paperwork. Whatever you need. But training—Hazel's got it."

"The show's Saturday," Addie says. "You're bailing five days out?"

"I'm not bailing—"

"You're not going to be there." She gestures at the colt. "We've been working toward this for weeks. You, me, Hazel. And now you're just... what? Done?"

"It's not about the colt."

"Then what's it about?"

I hold her gaze. "It's about me needing space."

She studies me, and I watch her piece it together. The missing training this morning. The careful way I'm holding myself. The fact that I won't look toward the barn.

"Oh," she says quietly. Then: "Shit."

"Hazel's a better trainer than I am anyway," I say. "You'll be fine."

"That's not—" She stops. Regroups. "You're really not going to keep working the colt with us?"

"I'll be there Saturday," I remind her. "For hauling, setup, whatever you need. I just won't be training."

She nods slowly. Doesn't push. But I can see it in her face—the disappointment, the confusion, the concern.

"Okay," she says finally. "If that's what you need."

"It is."

I push off the fence and turn before she can ask anything else.

I'm halfway to the truck when movement catches my eye.

Hazel.

Coming out of the barn, scanning the drive like she's looking for someone.

For me.

She hasn't seen me yet. Hasn't looked this direction.

I could call out. Walk over. Pretend yesterday didn't happen.

Every instinct I have pulls toward that sound. Toward her. My hand tightens on the truck door.

I could turn around. Walk back. Take whatever she's willing to give me for however long she's willing to stay.

I could.

The door opens with a metallic click that sounds too loud in the quiet.

I get in.

I don't look back.

I just put space between myself and the place where I'd start bending again.

By the time I reach the far fence line, the sun's high enough to burn the last of the morning chill off my skin. I park, get out, and walk the line alone, checking posts that don't need fixing, tightening wire that's already fine.

It's physical. Mindless. Exactly what I need.

By the time my hands ache and sweat soaks through my shirt, the ache in my chest dulls to something manageable.

Not gone. Just quieter.

I lean against a fence post, breathing hard, staring at nothing.

This isn't me giving up.

It's me stepping back before there's nothing left of me to save.

I tell myself I made the right choice.

I almost believe it.

Chapter Thirty-Five

Hazel

The barn is awake before the sun is.

It's been four days since Eli told me he won't do this again. Four mornings of walking into this barn alone. And today is the day I have to give Denver my answer—accept the promotion or walk away for good.

The colt nickers when he hears my boots on the packed dirt, ears pricked forward, expecting the routine we've built together. Expecting both of us. I check my phone. 3:58am. No messages. Eli would already be here. Four days ago, he would've been leaning against the rail with coffee in hand, that quiet half-smile like we're sharing some private joke.

Now I'm alone in the barn aisle, trying to remember what that felt like.

I tighten the girth strap and lead the colt out to the round pen. He follows easy, trusting. I clip the lunge line and send him forward, watching his movement. He's good. Better than good. Ready for tomorrow. My eyes slide to the rail anyway—to the empty space where Eli should be.

Footsteps sound behind me. I turn, something lifting in my chest despite myself.

Addie. Helmet tucked under her arm, coffee thermos in hand. She pauses when she sees me, something careful in her expression.

"Morning," I say, my voice rougher than I intend.

"Morning." She sets her thermos down, eyes tracking the colt as he moves. "How's he feeling?"

"Good. Ready."

She nods, jaw tight. The silence stretches, filled with all the questions she's not asking. Finally she says, "Fall Classic is tomorrow."

"I know. I feel really good about it"

She looks at me then, really looks at me. Takes in whatever's written on my face. "You okay?"

"Fine." The lie tastes bitter. "Let's just focus on the ride."

"Okay." She reaches for her helmet, fingers fumbling slightly with the chin strap. "Let's make sure we're ready then."

We work in silence after that. I call out adjustments, she corrects without argument. The colt performs beautifully—every transition clean, every cue answered. It should feel like victory. Instead it feels like evidence of everything I'm about to lose.

By the time Addie leaves with a wave that's too cheerful, the sun has burned off the morning chill. I head to the tack room because my hands need something to do. There's always work, always something that needs attention.

I reach for a bridle hanging on the rack, start checking the stitching automatically. My hands are shaking badly enough that I have to set it down. I pick up another piece of tack. Set it down. Can't focus long enough to actually accomplish anything.

I end up just standing there, staring at the wall of leather and metal, not really seeing any of it.

That's how Mae finds me—motionless in the middle of the tack room, a bridle clutched uselessly in my hands.

"When's the last time you ate?" Mae's voice cuts through the quiet, gentle but firm.

I look up. She's in the doorway, arms crossed, worry lines deepening around her eyes. "I had breakfast."

"That was yesterday." She steps inside. "You came straight to the barn this morning."

She pulls a wrapped sandwich from her jacket pocket and holds it out. I take it automatically, the wax paper crinkling in my shaking hands.

Her gaze drops to my hands—the tremor I can't control, the raw red spot where the lead rope rubbed wrong, the dried sweat at my wrists. "You've said 'I'm fine' every day this week."

"I'm just busy." I pick at the edges of the sandwich without really seeing it. "Fall Classic is tomorrow. Addie needs—"

"Fall Classic isn't why you're in here staring at walls." Mae's voice stays soft but steel edges underneath. "And we both know it."

I look up. She's watching me steadily, face serious.

"I'm trying," I say, and my voice cracks on the words.

"I know you are, honey." She settles beside me on the hay bale. "But you're trying the way your daddy used to try when he didn't want to stop long enough to feel something."

The sandwich goes still in my hands, forgotten.

"Stop," I say, sharper than I mean to. "I'm handling it."

Mae's face shifts—not hurt, just careful. "I'm not saying you're not. I'm saying you're handling it the way your daddy did. Like if you just don't stop moving, you won't have to feel it."

My throat closes. I want to argue, want to tell her she's wrong. But the words stick because maybe she's not.

The silence stretches between us. Mae doesn't push, doesn't fill it. Just lets her observation sit there.

"I don't know how else to do it," I finally admit, so quietly I'm not sure she hears.

Mae nods once, understanding in her expression. "I know, honey. But you're gonna have to figure that out today." She stands, brushing off her jeans. "You let me know when you're ready to talk about what you actually want instead of what you're afraid of."

She leaves, and I'm alone with the truth of her words.

I force myself to unwrap the sandwich, take a bite. Then another. It tastes like nothing but I keep going because Mae's right and I need to stop pretending she's not.

She's right. I have been running myself ragged to avoid feeling any of this.

She leaves, and I'm left staring at the sandwich in my hands.

Three bites in, and my stomach turns. I set it down and walk outside, needing air.

I've thought about driving to his place a hundred times this week. Picked up my keys. Started the truck once. But I always stop before I get there because what would I even say? *I haven't decided yet* is the truth, but it's also the problem. The exact thing that made him draw his line in the first place.

I lean against the barn wall now, staring at the horizon where his land meets ours. Somewhere over there, he's going about his day. Existing without me.

He meant it. The line he drew. *I won't do this again.*

And I've spent four days proving him right.

I see his truck then—just for a second, a flash of dark paint moving along the far fence line on Dawson property. Too far to make out details. Close enough that my chest aches.

He's there. Right there.

And he might as well be in another state.

***

Shae doesn't knock. Just walks in through Mae's front door late that afternoon, boots loud against the hardwood.

I'm at the kitchen table, staring at my laptop without seeing it.

She sits down across from me, no preamble. "So you're just gonna let the deadline pass?"

My jaw tightens. "I'm thinking."

"You've been thinking for four days." Her voice isn't mean, just direct. "At some point thinking becomes stalling."

I close the laptop. "It's not that simple."

"It is, actually." She leans forward. "You want to stay or you want to go. Pick one."

"I haven't—"

"Decided yet. I know." She cuts me off. "That's what you told Eli too, right? And now he's not here."

The words hit harder than I expect. My throat tightens.

"I saw him yesterday," Shae says, quieter now. "At the feed store. He looked..." She pauses, searching for the word. "Sad, Hazel. Really sad. Not angry. Just... sad."

My chest aches.

"You did this five years ago," she continues. "Couldn't decide, so you just left. Didn't even tell him you were going." She holds my gaze. "You gonna do that to him again?"

"That's not fair—"

"Isn't it?" She stands, pushing back from the table. "Fall Classic is tomorrow. Your deadline is today. At some point you have to stop waiting for the perfect answer and just choose."

She heads for the door, then stops. "He's not chasing you this time. He told you what he needs. Now you decide if you can give it to him."

The door closes behind her.

I sit there in the silence, her words echoing.

At some point you have to stop waiting for the perfect answer and just choose.

She's right.

I've been waiting for certainty that's never going to come. Waiting to feel ready. Waiting for someone else to make this easier.

But no one's coming to save me from this choice.

***

Three o'clock comes too fast.

I'm in the barn, leaning against the tack trunk, arms crossed tight. One hour. That's all I have left. This morning it was nine hours. Then seven. Then five. Now it's one.

Footsteps echo. Mae sits down beside me without a word, settling into the quiet.

Finally, she speaks. "What do you want, Hazel?"

Not what I should want. Not what makes sense. What do I want.

My throat closes. "There's too much at stake."

"There always is," Mae replies. Gentle but firm. "But you still have to choose. What do you want Hazel?"

I shake my head. "There's Fall Classic tomorrow, and work is calling, and Eli—" His name catches. "I don't know if he'll even—"

"I didn't ask about any of that." Mae turns to face me. "I asked what YOU want. Not what everyone else needs. What do you want?"

The answer is right there. Burning.

I try to shape it smaller. "I don't want to make the wrong choice."

"That's not an answer."

My hands curl into fists.

"I'm scared," I admit quietly. "Of choosing something and realizing I can't carry it."

Mae nods. "I know you are."

She doesn't tell me not to be. Just sits with it.

"Your daddy loved this ranch so much it scared him sometimes," Mae says after a moment. "Scared him that something that good could be taken away. So he worked himself into the ground trying to prove he deserved it. Trying to earn what was already his."

My breath catches.

"I watched him do that for years. Watched him run himself ragged because he couldn't just accept that this life was his to have." She looks at me. "Don't do that. Don't spend your life trying to earn something you already have permission to want."

The words settle into my chest, heavy and true.

"I want to stay," I whisper.

Mae doesn't smile. Just nods like she already knew.

"I want him," I continue. "I want this. The ranch. The mornings and the work and all of it. I want this life."

There it is. Clean. Undeniable.

Relief hits hard. Then fear, just as fast.

Mae takes my hand. Squeezes. "Then stop being so damn scared of having it."

"What if it's too late?"

"That's not your choice to make," Mae interrupts gently. "Your choice is what you want. His choice is what he does with that."

She stands, brushing off her jeans. "But wanting it isn't enough. You have to choose it. Out loud. To yourself first, then to everyone else."

She heads toward the doors, stopping at the threshold. "Fall Classic is tomorrow. But right now, you make your own choice. Not for anyone else. For you."

Then she's gone.

I don't make the call right away. I stay in the barn a few more minutes, letting Mae's words settle.

I dial before I can talk myself out of it.

Lauren answers on the second ring. "Hazel. I was starting to think I wouldn't hear from you."

"I'm not going to accept the offer." The words come out steady. "I'm actually resigning."

Silence stretches. Then: "Hazel. This is a significant decision. You've worked hard to get here. Are you certain?"

My stomach twists. "I'm certain."

"We can extend the timeline if you need more time—"

"I don't need more time. I've made my decision."

Another pause. "I have to be honest, I'm surprised. This was a huge opportunity. VP track within two years. You're throwing away a very promising career."

"I know what I'm giving up."

"Do you? Because this won't be waiting if you change your mind. We're moving to our second candidate tonight."

"I understand."

"Hazel—" She stops, regroups. "You're talented. Don't let fear make you walk away from something you've earned."

The words land hard. Because she's not wrong about the fear. She's just wrong about what I'm afraid of.

"Lauren, I'm grateful. I really am. But I'm done. I'll send the formal resignation tonight and help with the transition however you need."

A long exhale. "Alright. I respect your decision. HR will be in touch."

We exchange a few more logistics. Nothing personal. When we hang up, the call ends cleanly.

I lower the phone and stare at the dark screen.

For a moment, nothing happens.

Then everything does.

My stomach drops. What have I just done? I just walked away from everything I spent five years building. Panic flares sharp and immediate.

And then—relief. Deep and undeniable. Like I can finally breathe.

Both feelings at once, tangled and overwhelming.

I sit down hard on a hay bale, pressing my palm to my sternum. This isn't about Eli. Not really. This is about not running again. About choosing a life that feels grounded instead of safe.

About finally admitting that this place—this ranch, this land my father loved enough to die working—is home. Not a obligation I inherited or a burden I'm supposed to carry. Home.

And maybe that's enough. Maybe choosing to stay and build something here, to carry forward what he started, maybe that's its own kind of hope. Its own kind of legacy.

Eli is part of the life I want. But he isn't the reason.

I stay there a while, letting the reality settle. There's no undoing this.

When I finally stand, my legs feel steadier.

Fall Classic is tomorrow. The thought settles differently now—heavier but clearer.

I don't reach for my phone to text Eli. Not because I'm scared. Because this isn't the moment. I could drive to his cabin right now, but what if I'm too late?

I can't face that answer tonight. Not when Addie needs me focused.

I'll tell him after. When I can handle whatever his answer is.

Tomorrow matters. Addie matters. The work matters. They deserve better than me showing up desperate the night before the biggest competition.

So I'll wait. I'll get through Fall Classic. Then I'll tell him I'm staying—that I chose this, that I chose him.

And hope to god I'm not too late.

The sun dips below the horizon, painting the sky orange and purple. I watch it for a moment, breathing in dust and hay and evening air.

I look out at the ranch—the barn weathered and familiar, the pastures stretching toward the mountains, the fence line where our land meets Dawson property. All of it bathed in twilight.

For the first time in five years, I feel lighter.

The grief that drove me away—the weight of my father's death, the suffocating pressure of this place—it's softer now. Not gone. Just... manageable. Like I can finally breathe around it instead of drowning in it.

I don't know if Eli will forgive me. Don't know if I've already lost him.

But I know I'm home. Really home. Not visiting, not hiding, not proving anything.

Just home.

And that has to be enough for tonight.

I head inside to write the resignation letter. For the first time in four days, my hands are steady.

Chapter Thirty-Six

Hazel

The barn is quiet in that pre-dawn way that feels intentional. Like the world is holding its breath.

I move through the aisle alone, lights low, boots soft against packed dirt. The colt lifts his head the second he hears me, nickers once, then settles. Familiar. Steady. I press my forehead briefly to the stall door before I go in.

This part I know how to do.

Brush in hand, I work down his neck in long, even strokes. Check his legs. Pick each hoof. Adjust the blanket. Everything is slow. Methodical. Routine as armor.

On the surface, I'm calm.

Underneath, terror hums sharp and constant.

I chose to stay. The truth of it sits solid in my chest now, undeniable and heavy. But I haven't told him yet. Haven't said the words that matter most.

And today, there's nowhere to hide.

I tighten the girth, double-check the stitching on the saddle, run my fingers along the reins like they might steady me too. The colt shifts, patient, trusting, ready.

I breathe with him. In. Out.

This is the work. This is what grounds me.

In a few hours, I'll have to face Eli.

And everything I've chosen will finally be standing in front of me.

Addie shows up ten minutes later, energy already buzzing off her like static.

She's dressed and ready, helmet under her arm, braid tighter than usual. She stops short when she sees me in the aisle and grins, too wide, too bright.

"Morning," she says. "Or... whatever this counts as."

"Morning," I reply, brushing down the colt's shoulder. "You sleep at all?"

"Barely." She bounces once on her heels, then catches herself and forces stillness. "Big day."

"Yeah," I say evenly. "Big day."

She paces the length of the aisle, then stops near the tack rack, eyes flicking around like she's checking boxes only she can see.

"So Chace is hauling us, right?" she asks. Casual. Almost.

"Yeah," I say. "He'll be here any minute."

She nods, relief flashing across her face before she reins it in. "Okay. Good. I just wanted to make sure."

She doesn't say Eli's name.

Neither do I.

The absence hangs there anyway, obvious as an empty stall. Addie glances toward the far end of the barn once, then squares her shoulders and looks back at the colt.

"He feels good," she says. "I mean—really good."

"He is," I tell her. "You've done the work. He's ready."

She exhales, slow and deliberate. "You sure I am?"

I turn to face her fully. "You're ready. He's ready. Don't get inside your head today."

She nods, taking it in like instruction instead of reassurance. "Okay."

Headlights cut across the barn doors a moment later.

Chace pulls in with the hauling rig like it's any other morning. Efficient. Unhurried. He hops out, already focused on straps and angles and the practical work of getting us where we need to go.

"Morning," he says.

"Morning," I reply.

We load the colt smoothly, practiced movements falling into place without conversation. Chace checks the ramp, secures the latch, gives the divider a final tug. The colt steps in easy, calm as if he knows exactly where he's headed.

Mae appears at the edge of the barn as we finish, cardigan pulled tight against the chill, a travel mug in her hands.

She presses it into mine without a word.

Her eyes meet mine, steady and knowing. "You got this," she says quietly.

It's not about the competition.

I nod. "Thanks."

The drive to the arena is quiet.

Addie stares out the window, jaw set, replaying patterns in her head. Chace keeps his eyes on the road, radio low. I watch the landscape roll past, fences and fields slipping by in the growing light.

Every mile tightens the knot in my chest.

We're moving now.

Toward the arena. Toward the crowd. Toward my future.

And there's no turning back.

***

The arena parking lot is already chaos when we pull in.

Trailers lined up at odd angles. Horses nickering, pawing, calling to one another. People moving with purpose, voices raised over engines and slamming doors. The air smells like dust and coffee and anticipation.

I jump down from the truck and move automatically, hands busy, mind quiet in that narrow way it gets when I focus on logistics. Unlatch. Check straps. Walk the colt back a step so Chace can drop the ramp.

I don't mean to look for him.

I just... do.

My gaze sweeps the lot without conscious thought, skimming familiar trucks and faces, cataloging movement the way I always have. And then—

There.

His truck is parked on the far side of the lot, angled toward the arena. He's leaning against it, arms crossed, weight settled into one hip like he's been standing there a while.

He isn't watching the arena.

He's watching our trailer.

Our eyes meet across the distance.

Everything stops.

He doesn't wave. Doesn't smile. His shoulders tense, barely visible from here, but I see it. His weight shifts forward half an inch, like his body wants to move before his brain can stop it.

My hand lifts without permission. Just a fraction.

For three seconds, we're frozen there. Pulled toward each other by something neither of us is willing to name.

Then his expression shutters.

He looks away, pushes off the truck with deliberate force, and walks toward the registration building like he just passed a stranger.

My stomach drops so hard I have to grip the trailer rail to stay standing.

Addie's voice cuts in beside me. "Is Eli here?"

I can't look away from where he disappeared. "Yeah," I manage. "Just saw him walking in."

We move fast after that, momentum carrying us forward whether I'm ready or not. Through the gate. Toward the barns. Toward the warm-up ring.

I help Addie tack up in silence, hands working from muscle memory while my pulse hammers. Saddle pad straight. Girth snug. Bridle adjusted just so. My fingers tremble slightly when I tighten the last strap, and I curl them into the leather until they steady.

The colt stands perfectly still, ears flicking back toward my voice when I murmur to him. Calm. Ready. Everything we hoped for.

Addie swings into the saddle and heads toward the warm-up ring.

Eli takes his place at the rail, eyes tracking the colt's movement with practiced focus.

I stop ten feet away on the opposite side of the ring.

I keep my eyes on Addie, on the colt, on anything but him. But after a minute I can't help it—I glance over.

He's watching the horse, arms crossed, jaw tight. But his body is angled just slightly toward me. Not enough to be obvious. Just enough that I notice.

Then he looks at me.

We both freeze.

For three seconds, everything else disappears. Just him and me and ten feet that might as well be miles.

Then he snaps his attention back to Addie so fast it might as well be a wall slamming between us.

My chest aches.

Addie circles past on the colt, oblivious, calling out, "How's he look?"

"Perfect," Eli and I say at the exact same time.

Our voices overlap, tangle, fall apart.

We still don't look at each other.

The announcer's voice crackles over the loudspeaker. "Rider thirty-two, fifteen minutes out."

Addie rides toward the gate for her final check-in, leaving me standing alone at the rail.

The announcer calls Addie's number, and the world narrows to the gate.

She rides in like she belongs there.

Helmet steady. Shoulders relaxed. Hands quiet on the reins. The colt steps into the arena with his ears forward, body loose and focused, like he knows exactly what's being asked of him.

My hands tighten on the rail.

Mae is beside me, close enough that our shoulders brush. Chace stands on my other side, jaw set, eyes tracking every step.

Eli is... somewhere.

I don't look for him. I don't have to. I can feel him the way you feel a storm before it breaks.

But I catch sight of him anyway when Addie clears the second obstacle.

He's standing behind a small group of spectators, jaw set. His eyes never leave the arena. Never leave her.

But his hand—his right hand—is curled into a fist at his side, knuckles white.

Not angry. Tense.

Like he's fighting to stay exactly where he is instead of moving closer. To me. To the rail. To this thing we built together.

He looks like he's barely holding himself in place.

Then he looks away, jaw working, and I understand—he's been tracking my presence the whole time, even while watching her ride.

The buzzer sounds.

Addie moves the colt forward, confident but controlled. No rush. No hesitation.

The colt lifts his feet like he's been doing this his whole life, stride even, balance perfect. Addie guides him through without a single correction, posture calm, eyes already on the next mark.

I exhale without realizing I'd been holding my breath.

Second obstacle—better.

A smooth transition into the turn, tight and precise without losing momentum. The colt listens, adjusts, responds instantly. Addie's hands barely move, trust flowing clean between them.

Mae murmurs something under her breath. A prayer. Or pride. Or both.

My chest aches.

This is what we built at four in the morning when no one was watching. What we worked for through heat and exhaustion and doubt. This moment, right here.

The third obstacle looms—the tricky one.

A tight gate with an awkward approach, the kind that trips up even seasoned riders if they come in wrong. I feel my pulse spike, fear clawing up sharp and sudden.

Addie shortens the reins just a fraction. The colt gathers himself, shifts weight back without losing rhythm.

For one second, everything stops.

Then he does it.

Clean. Fluid. Like the obstacle never existed at all.

A laugh breaks out of me before I can stop it, breathless and sharp with relief. Mae grabs my arm, fingers digging in.

"That's it," she whispers. "That's it."

Addie's face changes then—concentration cracking just enough to let joy flicker through. She reins it in immediately, refocuses, drives toward the final obstacle.

The last stretch is a blur of motion and sound. The colt moves like he's floating now, energy coiled but controlled, Addie guiding him with absolute trust.

Final obstacle—perfect.

They cross the line clean, no hesitation, no faults.

For a heartbeat, the arena is silent.

Then it erupts.

Applause crashes in. Cheers erupt. Addie throws one hand into the air before she can stop herself, grin splitting her face wide open.

I feel it then—this overwhelming swell in my chest that has nothing to do with fear and everything to do with pride.

This is ours.

This moment. This horse. This win, whatever place it earns. We built this.

As Addie rides out of the arena, still grinning, still buzzing, my hands finally loosen on the rail. My breath comes shaky, my eyes burning just a little.

I should be thinking about what happens next.

About Eli. About what I still haven't said.

Instead, all I can think is this:

No matter what comes after—

This was real.

***

Addie dismounts the moment she clears the gate, breathless and glowing, helmet already coming off as she jogs over.

"That felt perfect," she says, eyes bright, hands shaking just a little. "Did it look perfect?"

I don't hesitate. "It was perfect."

The colt nudges her shoulder like he knows exactly what she's talking about, breath warm against her arm. She laughs and wraps both arms around his neck, pressing her face into his mane.

"You did it," she murmurs. "We did it."

People gather around them in quick bursts—congratulations, pats on the shoulder, quiet murmurs of approval. The energy in the warm-up area shifts, anticipation buzzing sharp and electric.

We wait.

Competitors finish their rounds one by one, each name called over the loudspeaker tightening the coil in my chest a little more. Addie paces. Sits. Stands again. The colt stands calmly at her side, unbothered, like he's already decided how this ends.

I tell myself not to look for him.

I do anyway.

Across the arena, near the scoreboard, Eli stands with his hands in his pockets, posture relaxed in that way that means nothing about him is casual. His gaze is fixed on the numbers as they update, face unreadable, jaw set.

He doesn't look at me.

Not once.

The announcer's voice cuts through the noise, and the crowd quiets in a rush.

"And in first place—"

Everything stops.

"Addie Dawson."

The arena explodes.

Mae's arms are around me before I even process the words, crushing me into a hug that knocks the breath from my lungs. Chace lets out a shout so loud it echoes off the rafters. People clap and cheer and surge toward us in a wave of celebration.

Addie stares at the scoreboard like she doesn't quite believe it, then breaks, laughing and crying at the same time as she buries her face in the colt's neck.

"I can't believe it," she keeps saying. "I can't believe it."

Hands reach in from everywhere—patting the colt, clapping Addie on the back, voices layering over each other with congratulations and disbelief.

People surge toward us—not just friends, but other ranchers too. Faces I recognize from the circuit, competitors, trainers. A woman I don't know shakes Mae's hand, her expression warm.

"Heard you were shutting down," she says. "Glad to see that wasn't true. You taking on any more boarders?"

Mae's eyes light up. "We might have room for the right horse."

"I'll call you next week."

Another man approaches, older, weathered. "That's some quality training. You do outside clients?"

"We do now," Mae says, and I hear the satisfaction in her voice.

This is what winning does. Not just proves the colt is good—proves Clark Ranch is back.

I catch snippets of conversation around me—people asking about Mae's training methods, about boarding rates, about whether we're taking new clients for spring. The win isn't just Addie's. It's advertising. Proof of concept. Validation that the business model works.

This is it—proof the ranch works. Proof the training works. Proof that everything we poured into this mattered.

I should be flying.

I am—almost.

But even as the celebration swirls around me, my eyes keep scanning the crowd, searching instinctively.

Looking for him.

Because none of this means what it should until I know he's still there.

The celebration continues around me—Addie accepting congratulations, Mae beaming with pride, people already talking about next season. I'm scanning the crowd for Eli when I notice Mae step away from the group, moving toward the rail with that deliberate walk that means she's handling something.

I follow her gaze.

Cole Maddox.

He's approaching from the parking area, dressed too nice for the venue—pressed shirt, expensive boots that have never seen real work. That opportunistic smile firmly in place.

I start moving toward them, but Mae's already turning to face him. Her posture shifts—shoulders back, chin up. Ready.

"Ms. Clark." Cole stops a respectful distance away, gesturing toward where Addie stands with the colt. "Impressive showing today. That colt of yours just proved what I've been saying—you've got real potential here."

Mae doesn't respond. Just waits.

"With the right financial backing," Cole continues, voice smooth, "you could build on this. Expand the operation. I'm prepared to make a very generous offer—"

"Ranch isn't for sale," Mae interrupts. Her voice is pleasant. Dangerous. "Never was. Never will be."

Cole's smile tightens but holds. "I understand you're protective of your family's legacy. But Ms. Clark, one good ride doesn't guarantee the future. Winter's coming. The bank still holds your note. I'm simply offering security. Stability."

"We're doing just fine without you," Mae says quietly.

He shifts tactics, leaning in slightly. "I admire your determination. Truly. But sentiment doesn't pay bills. Let me help you—"

"And whatever happened with those fence lines a few weeks back?" Mae's voice stays level, but steel runs underneath now.

Cole goes very still. His expression flickers—surprise, then calculation, then that careful neutral mask sliding back into place.

"I have no idea what you're talking about," he says.

"Good." Mae holds his gaze. "Because we can't prove it. Yet. But we're watching, Mr. Maddox. Very carefully. You understand me?"

The air between them goes taut.

Cole's jaw tightens. He glances around—at the celebration, at the people watching, at Addie still glowing with her win. When he looks back at Mae, the friendly mask is gone.

"I was trying to help," he says, voice colder now.

"We don't need your kind of help." Mae takes a small step forward. Not aggressive. Final. "You're not welcome here. And you're not welcome on my property. Ever. Are we clear?"

For a long moment, Cole doesn't move. Then he nods once, sharp and controlled.

"Crystal clear."

He turns and walks away, back stiff, hands in his pockets. Mae watches him go all the way to his truck, doesn't move until his taillights disappear from the lot.

I reach her side. "Mae?"

She turns to me, something satisfied in her expression. "Just making sure certain people understand where things stand."

I follow her gaze, understanding settling. This wasn't just about shutting down another offer. It was about showing Cole Maddox that Clark Ranch isn't dying. That we're not prey anymore.

"Think he'll try again?" I ask quietly.

Mae considers. "Eventually. Men like that don't give up easy. But he won't be coming around here anytime soon."

She squeezes my arm once, then heads back toward the celebration, leaving me standing there with the knowledge that we just closed one threat.

Even if others are waiting.

I turn back to the celebration, heart still racing from the confrontation. But the moment of satisfaction fades when I scan the crowd again.

Looking for him.

The crowd parts for a moment, bodies shifting, and suddenly there's a clear line between us.

Eli stands at the edge, hands in his pockets, watching the celebration with an expression I can't read from here.

For a second—one suspended second—we just look at each other.

The noise fades. The movement blurs.

His hands come out of his pockets. Not reaching. Just… uncurling. Like maybe he's about to step forward. Like maybe this changes something. Like maybe—

Someone bumps into him from behind, breaking the spell.

His face shutters.

His hands come together in that slow, deliberate clap. Once. Twice. Measured. Respectful.

Not celebration. Acknowledgment.

The difference guts me.

The sound barely reaches me over the noise, but I see it clearly. The way his shoulders lift with each clap. The way his jaw tightens like he's holding something in place.

Our eyes meet.

For one heartbeat, the world narrows again. The cheers fade. The movement blurs. It's just him and me across the space between us.

For a heartbeat, I think he might come over.

Think he might close the distance the way I've been too afraid to all day. Think that maybe this changes something. That this—this win, this proof, this moment—matters enough to pull him back toward me.

Then he drops his hands.

Turns.

And walks away.

Not rushed. Not angry. Just deliberate.

He doesn't hesitate. Doesn't glance back. Doesn't pause to see if I'll follow.

He threads through the edge of the crowd with the same steady purpose he brings to everything, and I watch him go because I can't do anything else.

Ten feet. Twenty. Fifty.

He reaches his truck.

I'm still standing there, frozen in the middle of the celebration, people laughing and talking all around me while my heart cracks open in a way that has nothing to do with joy.

The engine turns over.

Mae's hand settles on my shoulder. "Go," she says. Firmer this time.

"He just left," I whisper. "During the win. He just—"

"So go after him," Mae interrupts.

Something in me finally gives.

I turn and run for the truck.

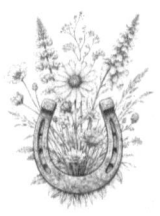

Chapter Thirty-Seven

Hazel

The truck hums beneath me, steady and familiar, like it doesn't know my entire body is vibrating apart.

My hands are white-knuckled on the wheel. I keep loosening my grip, then tightening it again without realizing. My palms are slick. My shoulders ache from holding themselves too high. There's a dull, hollow feeling behind my ribs, like the crash after adrenaline, but the fear is still sharp enough to sting.

I practice the words anyway.

I quit my job. I'm staying. I chose this.

They sound different every time I say them in my head. Sometimes confident. Sometimes fragile. Sometimes like they might dissolve the second I open my mouth. I rearrange them, discard them, try again. None of them feel strong enough to carry what I'm about to do.

The road stretches out ahead of me, a ribbon of dark asphalt cutting through land I know by heart. Every curve, every fence line, every dip where the shadows gather. I've driven this route a thousand times. It feels different tonight. Charged. Like it's watching me, waiting to see if I'll follow through.

I chose, I remind myself. Now I have to tell him. And hope it's not too late.

His truck is already there when I turn onto his drive.

The sight of it hits me straight in the chest. Relief and terror crash together so hard I have to pull over before I overshoot the parking spot. My foot stays pressed to the brake long after the engine idles down. I just sit there, counting my breaths, staring through the windshield like I might find courage etched into the glass.

Twice, my hand drifts toward the door handle, then pulls back. My chest feels too tight. My fingers tremble when I finally force them to move. If I don't get out now, I won't.

The air outside is cool and sharp. It hits my face and wakes me up just enough to stand. My legs feel unsteady as I start toward the cabin. Every step feels deliberate, heavy with the weight of what I'm about to undo or remake.

I stop at the door. Lift my fist.

And freeze.

My heart is hammering so hard I swear he can hear it through the wood. This is the moment. The point of no return.

No more running.

I knock.

The door opens before my knuckles ever make contact.

Eli stands there barefoot, jeans worn soft at the knees, an old t-shirt hanging loose over his shoulders. No boots. No armor. Just him, caught off-guard in a way that makes my chest tighten.

We stare at each other. One second. Two. Three.

His hand tightens on the door handle. For a heartbeat I think he might close it.

Then something in his expression shifts — not softening, just resignation. Like he already decided how this ends and made peace with it.

I swallow. "Can I come in?"

The pause stretches long enough that my stomach drops. Long enough that I'm sure this is where he says no.

Then he steps back. Doesn't say yes. Doesn't look at me when he does it. He just makes space.

I take it.

The door closes behind me with a quiet finality that echoes through my ribs. The cabin smells the same — wood and soap and something faintly him. Familiar in a way that makes my chest ache, and foreign in the way anything does after you've stayed away too long.

We end up standing six feet apart in the living room. The distance feels intentional. Measured.

He crosses his arms, leaning back slightly like he's bracing himself. He doesn't offer me a seat. Doesn't ask why I'm here. Doesn't soften the moment in any way.

He just waits.

Every version of what I practiced on the drive evaporates. The careful phrasing. The soft edges. None of it survives the way he's looking at me.

He's not going to help me. He's not going to meet me halfway or make this easier. If I'm here, I have to own it. All of it.

My hands are shaking. I curl my fingers into my palms, grounding myself in the sting.

I lift my eyes to his, take a breath that scrapes my lungs on the way in.

"I quit my job."

The words come out flat. No buildup. No cushioning. Just the truth, dropped between us like it can stand on its own.

Eli doesn't react. Not a flicker. Not a blink. His face stays exactly the same, guarded and still, like he's already decided this isn't real.

"Yesterday," I add. "I called Lauren and quit."

That gets something. Not surprise. Not relief.

"Why?"

It's not why did you quit. It's why are you standing here telling me this.

"Because I'm staying."

The words settle heavy in my chest. Solid.

"For how long?"

"Permanently."

His jaw tightens. "Until you change your mind."

"I'm not going to change my mind."

"You don't know that."

"I do." My voice is steadier than I feel. Stronger. Certain in a way I haven't been before.

"So you're staying for me."

"No."

He goes still. "No?"

"I'm staying for me. Because this is the life I want." I take a step closer. "You're part of that life. But you're not the reason."

"What's the difference?"

"If I stayed for you, I'd resent you eventually. Feel trapped. Like I gave something up and blamed you for it." I don't look away. "I'm not giving anything up. I'm choosing what I want."

His jaw works. "And what if what you want changes?"

"Then I'll deal with it. But I won't run from it."

He studies me like he's looking for the exit sign I used last time. "Why should I believe you?"

The answer comes from somewhere deeper than rehearsed words.

"Because I'm terrified right now." My voice breaks despite my effort to hold it. "And I'm still here. Standing in front of you, shaking, scared you're going to tell me I'm too late. That you're done. That I already lost you."

I swipe at my face, uselessly.

"And I'm still here," I whisper. "That has to count for something."

For a long moment, he says nothing.

Then, quietly: "Five years ago, I told you I loved you."

"I know."

"And you left before I woke up."

The words sit between us, old and sharp and still bleeding around the edges.

"I panicked," I say. It sounds small. It feels small.

"I waited for you." His voice strips down to nothing but truth. "Kept telling myself you just needed time." He pauses. "I went to Denver."

The words stop me cold. "What?"

"Six weeks after you left. I drove out there. Found your apartment." His eyes drop to the floor. "I saw you coming out of your building one morning. You were laughing at something on your phone. You looked lighter. Like a weight had been lifted."

"Eli—"

"I couldn't do it." His voice cracks. "Couldn't knock on your door and ask you to come back when you finally looked happy. So I got back in my truck and drove home."

The weight of that crashes into me. He was there. He saw me. And he left to protect me.

"I wasn't happy," I whisper. "I was surviving. There's a difference."

His eyes meet mine. "I didn't know that. All I saw was that leaving made you lighter. And I spent five years thinking I wasn't enough. That if I'd been different, or better, or more — you would've stayed."

"That's not true."

"I know that now." His jaw tightens. "But that's what it felt like."

"I'm sorry I hurt you," I say, the words tumbling out. "I'm sorry I ran. I'm sorry I made you feel like you weren't enough when you were always more than enough."

He scrubs a hand over his face. When he looks back at me, his eyes are dark and tired and painfully clear.

"I can't do that again," he says.

"I know. I won't ask you to."

He exhales slowly. "So what does this look like?"

"I don't know yet," I say. "I just know I'm here."

He studies me. Not skeptical. Careful.

"You have a plan?"

"Work the ranch. Build the boarding business. Take on more clients. Maybe freelance consulting if we need the income." I take a breath. "Figure it out as I go."

"With me?"

"If you'll have me." I hold his gaze even though every instinct tells me to look away. "I'm staying, Eli. Whatever that looks like. However hard it gets. I'm not running again."

His jaw tightens.

"I can't promise I'll be perfect at—"

"I don't need perfect." His voice cracks. "I never needed perfect."

"Then what do you need?"

His gaze locks onto mine. "I need you to stay when it gets hard. When you get scared and it feels easier to leave — I need you to stay anyway. I need you to fight for this instead of running from it."

"I can do that."

"Can you?"

I step closer, close enough to feel the heat radiating off him. "I'm not asking you to trust that I'll never panic. I'm asking you to trust that I'll stay anyway."

Something finally breaks in his expression.

He reaches for me — then stops, hand hovering between us like he's afraid to touch what he might lose.

"Eli."

"If I let you in again—"

"I'm not going anywhere."

He closes his eyes. Opens them. "Promise me."

"I promise."

That's all it takes.

He closes the distance in two strides and pulls me against his chest, arms wrapping around me hard, like he's afraid I might slip through if he loosens his grip. I press my face into his shirt, breathing him in, anchoring myself there.

He's shaking.

Or maybe that's me.

We stand there, holding on, the past and the future suspended in the same fragile moment.

"I missed you," I whisper into his chest.

His arms tighten. He doesn't say anything. He doesn't have to.

He pulls back just enough to see my face. Both hands cup my jaw, thumbs brushing my cheekbones, studying me like he's memorizing every detail — the freckles across my nose, the way my breath hitches, the tears still wet on my face.

Then he kisses me.

This is different from every time before. This is claiming. This is choosing. No uncertainty about tomorrow, no question of whether I'll still be here when he wakes up. Just five years of want and loss and longing finally allowed to exist without apology.

His hands slide into my hair and I press closer, needing to eliminate every inch of space between us. We stumble toward the bedroom, mouths never breaking apart, hands pulling at clothes with desperate urgency. We don't make it far before my back hits the hallway wall.

"I need you," he says against my mouth.

"Then take me."

We make it to his bedroom somehow. Moonlight streams through the window, casting everything in silver. Once we're there, beside his bed, everything slows.

He reaches for the hem of my shirt, pulls it off deliberately. His eyes never leave mine as he removes each piece until I'm standing bare in front of him. Vulnerable in a way I haven't let myself be in years.

I reach for his shirt. He lets me pull it over his head, lets my hands map his chest, his shoulders. His belt. His jeans. Until we're both standing there with nothing between us.

"I love you."

The words fall between us and everything stops.

He goes completely still, hands frozen on my hips. His eyes search mine like he's afraid to believe it.

It's the first time I've said it out loud. The first time I've let myself.

"I should have said it five years ago," I whisper, voice breaking. "I should have said it instead of running. I should have—"

"Say it again." His voice is wrecked.

"I love you, Eli."

His eyes close. When they open again, they're wet.

His hands cup my face. "Again."

"I love you."

He presses his forehead to mine, breathing unsteady, and for a moment neither of us moves. Just standing there in the moonlight with five years of unsaid things finally out in the open.

"I've loved you since we were kids," he says quietly. "Even when I was trying not to. Even when it hurt." His thumbs brush my cheekbones. "I drove to Denver and watched you walk out of your building and told myself you were happy. That you'd made the right call. I got back in my truck and spent five years trying to believe that." His voice cracks. "You were never supposed to come back. And you did. And you're still here, standing in front of me scared half to death, and you stayed anyway." He pulls back just enough to look at me, eyes raw and certain. "That's everything, Hazel. That's the whole thing."

I can't speak. My throat is too tight. I pull him back to me instead.

He kisses me like I'm something precious. Something he's afraid might disappear. His hands map my body like he's re-learning every curve, every place that makes me shiver.

His mouth finds my neck, my collarbone, the hollow of my throat. Taking his time. But I can feel the urgency underneath. The restraint he's barely holding onto.

My hands tangle in his hair, pulling him back up to me. "Tell me what you need."

"You." His voice is rough, wrecked. "Just you."

The reverence tips into fire.

His mouth crashes into mine, harder this time. Claiming. His hands grip my hips, thumbs pressing into the hollow just above my hip bones. I arch against him, needing more, needing everything.

He walks me backward until my knees hit the bed and we go down together, a tangle of hands and breath and five years of wanting finally given permission. When he pulls back to look at me — really look, chest heaving, eyes dark — something in his expression makes me go still.

He's not rushing. Not anymore.

He takes his time. One hand smoothing up my side. His mouth finding mine again, slower now. Like he's reminding both of us that we have time. That I'm not going anywhere.

When he finally enters me, we both stop.

Foreheads pressed together. Breathing the same air. The sensation is overwhelming — too much and not enough all at once.

"Mine," he says, voice rough.

"Yours." I move against him, pulling him deeper. "I'm yours."

He starts to move and I meet him stroke for stroke. The rhythm builds slow at first, deliberate, like he's savoring every second. But it doesn't stay slow.

His hands grip tighter. My nails drag down his back. His mouth finds my neck, my shoulder, teeth grazing skin.

"Don't stop," I gasp.

He shifts his weight, catching both my wrists in one hand and pinning them above my head. His other hand cups my jaw, tilting my face up.

"Look at me."

I open my eyes. Meet his. The intensity there steals my breath.

"I need you to see me," he says, voice strained. "Need you to know who you're with."

"I know." My voice breaks. "I know exactly who you are."

The rhythm builds faster. Harder. My wrists flex against his grip but he holds firm, keeping me present, keeping me here with him.

"I love you," I gasp between breaths.

"I love you too."

The pleasure coils tighter until I can't hold it anymore. I break apart beneath him, his name tearing from my throat. He releases my wrists and I wrap my arms around him, pulling him closer as the waves crash through me.

He follows seconds later, my name breaking from him like a prayer. His whole body shakes with it. Both of us holding tight, neither willing to let go.

Afterward, we don't let go. Stay tangled together, breathing hard, hearts beating against each other.

I rest my head on his chest. His fingers trace lazy patterns on my shoulder. The quiet settles around us, comfortable and warm.

After a while he says, "Stay here. Move in with me."

I lift my head to look at him. "What?"

"We've waited our whole lives." No hesitation. Like it's already decided. "I'm not waiting anymore."

A smile tugs at my mouth. "Okay."

"Yeah?"

"Yeah. Okay."

His arms tighten around me. His lips brush my temple.

Outside, the ranch is dark and quiet. Inside, we're building something new. The moonlight stretches silver across the bed, the floor, the future neither of us is running from anymore.

I press closer and close my eyes.

Finally home.

Epilogue - Eli

I wake to cold November air seeping through the window and Hazel's weight pressed against my side.

It's 4:30 in the morning. Early enough that the world outside is still dark, still quiet. The kind of cold that makes you want to stay in bed until spring. But I've got horses to feed and she's already stirring, trying to slip out without waking me.

I tighten my arm around her waist. "Where you going?"

She freezes. "Barn. Go back to sleep."

"I'm up."

She turns to look at me, hair messy, eyes still heavy. "You don't have to—"

"I'm up," I repeat.

She smiles, small and soft, then presses a kiss to my shoulder before sliding out of bed. I watch her pull on jeans and one of my flannels, the fabric hanging loose on her frame. Six weeks and she still steals my clothes more often than she wears her own.

I don't mind.

By the time I make it to the kitchen, she's already started the coffee. Her mug sits on the counter next to mine—hers chipped at the rim, mine with the ranch logo fading from too many washes. Small things. Domestic details that six weeks ago felt fragile, temporary. Like if I acknowledged them too hard, she'd spook.

Now they just exist.

Her jacket hangs by the door next to mine. Her books are stacked on the side table. Her toothbrush sits in the holder in the bathroom. Evidence of her everywhere, woven into the fabric of this place so completely I can't remember what it looked like without her.

She leans against the counter, staring out the window at the dark, lost in thought.

"You good?" I ask.

She turns, smiles. "Yeah. Just thinking."

"About?"

"How easy this is."

I cross to her, drop a kiss on her temple, and reach for my coffee. We stand there together in comfortable silence, watching the sun start to break over the mountains.

She's right. It is easy. Easier than it should be after five years apart. Easier than I let myself hope it could be.

"Ready?" I ask after a while.

"Yeah. Let's go."

At the barn, we fall into the rhythm we've built over the past six weeks.

I handle feed while she checks water buckets. She grabs the training schedule off the board—her handwriting mapping out the week, my notes scribbled in the margins about which horses need extra attention. We move around each other without talking, no wasted motion, no need to coordinate.

Three new boarders since Fall Classic. Two more inquiries came in this week.

The business is working.

Red Fern's horses are still here, thriving in the far paddock. Renee Whitman's two are in their usual stalls. The new gelding from a family in town occupies the stall near the tack room—young, green, but willing. Two mares from a competitor who saw Addie's win are settling in nicely.

We're starting to build a waiting list.

The financial pressure that was crushing Mae when Hazel first came back has eased. Not gone—it never really goes away on a ranch—but manageable. Sustainable.

I lean against the fence, watching Hazel work with the new gelding in the round pen. The horse is nervous, flighty, not trusting the bit yet. But she's patient. Knows when to push and when to ease off.

After a few minutes, I call out, "Try softening your inside hand."

She adjusts without hesitation. The horse responds immediately, dropping his head, relaxing into the circle.

She grins at me across the pen. "Show off."

"That's why you keep me around."

"One of many reasons."

The easy affection between us still catches me off-guard sometimes. How simple this is. How she can tease me without second-guessing herself. How I can touch her without worrying she'll pull away.

Mae's truck pulls up around eight. She climbs out carrying a bakery bag and thermos, because apparently the coffee we make isn't good enough.

"Morning," she calls, heading into the barn.

We find her in the main aisle, spreading pastries on a hay bale like she's setting a table.

"You two look tired," she says, eyeing us both with that knowing look.

"Early start," I say.

Mae gives me a look that says she's not buying it. "I'm sure."

Hazel's face goes red. Mae laughs, the sound echoing off the rafters.

Six weeks ago, this would've made Hazel defensive. Skittish. Now she just rolls her eyes and reaches for a pastry. The family dynamic has shifted, settled into something that includes both of us.

We're halfway through the pastries when Addie's truck appears.

She hops out with more energy than anyone should have at this hour, still riding high from Fall Classic. She's got two more competitions lined up and can't stop talking about them.

"I need to adjust the colt's schedule," she says, pulling out her phone. "Can we add an extra session on Thursdays?"

"Yeah," Hazel says, already mentally rearranging the board. "We can make that work."

"Perfect." Addie grins at both of us. "You guys are good together."

She's not talking about training. We all know it.

My hand finds the small of Hazel's back automatically. She leans into me slightly.

We don't deny it.

The colt is still boarding here, thriving. Addie rides him three times a week. He's the proof of concept we needed—the success story that convinced the other boarders to come.

After Addie leaves and Mae heads back to the main house, Hazel and I take our lunch break in the barn. Sandwiches Mae packed this morning. We sit on hay bales, shoulders touching, comfortable in the silence.

My hand finds hers automatically.

"You happy?" I ask.

She looks at me. "Yeah. You?"

"Yeah."

Simple. True.

We sit there for a while, eating and watching dust motes drift through the shafts of sunlight. Then she remembers something.

"I talked to a potential client yesterday," she says. "Wants to board four horses."

"We have room."

We. Us. Ours.

The language of partnership.

Six weeks ago, those words felt dangerous. Like saying them out loud might scare her off. Now they're the easiest words I know.

Today we're just this—sitting in the barn eating sandwiches, making plans for paddocks and training schedules and all the ordinary things that make up a life together.

And that's enough.

***

By six that night, the work is done and we're sitting on the porch with whiskey for me and wine for her, watching the sun drop behind the mountains.

The temperature's dropped with the daylight. Cold enough that she pulls her jacket tighter, but neither of us suggests going inside. We just sit, watching the ranch settle into evening.

Clark Ranch spreads out in the distance. I can see the lights coming on in Mae's barn, her moving through her own evening routine. The horses are in their paddocks, content and settled. Closer, Dawson Ranch—my property, our property now—stretches out with fencelines that nearly touch Clark land.

The land we both love. The life we've built.

"Six weeks ago," she says after a while, "I was standing in that barn trying to decide if I was brave enough for this."

I turn to look at her. "And now?"

"Now I can't imagine being anywhere else."

"No regrets?"

"Not one."

I study her for a moment, making sure she means it. Then I nod and turn back to the view.

We sit in comfortable silence as the sky shifts from orange to pink to deep purple. Six weeks ago, silence like this would've felt loaded. Heavy with all the things she was too afraid to say. Now it just feels peaceful.

"I used to think staying meant giving something up," she says quietly. "Like I'd have to make myself smaller to fit here."

"And now?"

"Now I know I was wrong." She leans into me. "I'm more myself here than I ever was in Denver."

My arm comes around her, pulling her closer against the cold. "Good."

That's all I say. But I mean everything underneath it. The relief. The certainty. The permanence.

We've both stopped waiting for the other shoe to drop.

"I've been thinking," I say after the sun fully sets.

"About?"

"Expanding the barn. Adding six more stalls."

She takes a sip of wine. "That's a lot of work."

"Worth it if the business keeps growing like this."

"It will."

I glance at her. "Confident."

"I've seen the numbers. We're good."

We are good. Better than good. The boarding business has exceeded every projection she made when she first quit her job. The ranch is thriving in a way it hasn't in years.

"Been thinking about other things too," I say, more carefully now.

"Like what?"

"Like what comes next."

"Next?"

"For us."

She sets her wine glass down on the porch railing. "What are you thinking?"

I turn to face her fully. I've been thinking about this for weeks now. The ring I haven't bought yet. The question I haven't asked. The future I can see so clearly it feels like it's already happened.

But not today.

Today I just need her to know.

"That I want everything with you."

The words hang in the cold air between us.

I don't pull out a ring. Don't get on one knee. Just look at her with the certainty that's been there since the night she showed up at my door six weeks ago and promised she wasn't going anywhere.

"I'm not in a rush," I continue. "But I want you to know. This is it for me. You're it."

Her throat works. For a second, she doesn't speak.

"I spent five years trying to want a different life," she says quietly. "Turns out I just wanted this one."

"You're it for me too," she finally manages.

"Good."

That's all. Just good. Like we've settled something important but there's no need to make a production of it.

For now, it's enough.

We sit there as dark fully settles over the ranch. Stars come out one by one overhead. The temperature keeps dropping, cold enough now that I can see our breath, but neither of us moves to go inside.

My arm stays around her. Her head rests on my shoulder.

I'll ask her someday. Put a ring on her finger. Give her my last name if she wants it. Build cribs in the spare room and teach our kids to ride before they can walk.

But not today.

Today we're just this—two people who found their way back to each other, sitting on a porch in the cold, watching stars appear over the ranch we're building together.

And that's everything.

Enjoyed Legacy & Lace?

If you loved Hazel & Eli's story, leaving a review helps more than you know.

Thank you for supporting indie authors.

Ashford Ridge Book Two

"Oh my God, you're incorrigible."

I say it slowly, because if I don't, something sharper might slip out instead.

Chace's smile is lazy. Practiced. The kind men wear when they think annoyance is an invitation instead of a warning.

"You keep saying that," he says. "Makes me think you like it."

I step closer, close enough that he finally has to pay attention.

"Or," I say, "it means you should stop."

His mouth opens like he's about to make it worse.

I don't wait.

I lift my hand, flip him the bird, and turn on my heel. "I don't have time for your bullshit today, Chace."

Behind me, I can feel his grin like a presence. Feel him watching.

Chace Walker is my brother's best friend. Has been forever. Tall, broad-shouldered, with that cocky cowboy swagger that makes buckle bunnies stupid. Which means he's been in my orbit my entire life—loud, smug, and way too convinced the world enjoys him as much as he enjoys himself.

Two years ago, a shoulder injury ended his riding career when he was on track for a championship. Now he does ranch work and shows up at events like this one, apparently just to get under my skin.

I don't have the energy for his ego today.

I've got more important things on my mind than Chace Walker and whatever reaction he was hoping to get out of me.

The fairgrounds are already buzzing when I head down the drive, trailers lining up, dust hanging low in the morning air. Today isn't just another event—it's a qualifier. A real one. The kind that decides whether you're spending the season chasing weekends or standing still, watching everyone else move forward.

This Qualifier matters.

And I'm not letting Chace Walker—or anyone—get in the way of it.

Also by Rebecka Cole

Ashford Ridge Series
Legacy & Lace
Standalone Novels
Winterberry Inn

Not ready to leave Ashford Ridge yet?

Join Rebecka's Readers for:

    Bonus scenes

    Sneak peeks

    Early access to new releases

    Exclusive content

visit www.rebeckacoleauthor.com or scan the QR Code to join!

Acknowledgments

They say writing a book is a solitary process, but this story would not exist without the people who stood beside me along the way.

To my husband — thank you for your patience, your unwavering support, and your belief in this dream. Thank you for every late night, every pep talk, and every moment you reminded me to keep going when doubt crept in. None of this would be possible without you. I am endlessly grateful for your love, your steadiness, and the life we are building together. I will never stop thanking you, my love.

To my children — you are the heart of everything I do. Thank you for sharing your time, your laughter, and your endless understanding while I chased this dream. Your love, your joy, and your belief in me mean more than you will ever know. I hope one day you see these pages and understand how deeply you inspire me.

To my parents — thank you for your encouragement, your support, and for always believing in me, even long before I believed in myself. Thank you for the foundation you gave me, for the lessons, the strength, and the constant reminders that dreams are worth pursuing.

To my beta readers and ARC team — thank you for your time, your enthusiasm, and your thoughtful feedback. Sharing this story with you early has been such a gift, and your support has meant more than I can say.

And to every reader — thank you for being here and for giving this story a place in your heart. It is truly an honor to share these stories with you.

About the author

Rebecka Cole is a writer of intimate, emotional fiction with a focus on love, identity, and the quiet turning points that shape who we become. Born and raised in rural coastal Maine, Rebecka grew up surrounded by family and small-town living. That upbringing instilled in her a love for quiet moments and emotional depth, elements that thread through all her stories.

A devoted wife and mother of five boys, Rebecka writes in the in-between spaces: early mornings, late nights, and stolen hours when the house finally settles. An introvert at heart, she is drawn to stories that linger, characters who feel real, and love that stays.

She lives with her family and is currently working on multiple future novel ideas.

You can find Rebecka on **instagram @rebeckacole.author**

www.ingramcontent.com/pod-product-compliance
Lightning Source LLC
LaVergne TN
LVHW091654070526
838199LV00050B/2173